ORDINARY
SOIL

A NOVEL

ALEX WOODARD
Afterword by ZACH BUSH, MD

GREENLEAF
BOOK GROUP PRESS

This book is a work of fiction. Names, characters, businesses, organizations, places, events, and incidents are either a product of the author's imagination or are used fictitiously. Any resemblance to actual persons, living or dead, events, or locales is entirely coincidental.

Published by Greenleaf Book Group Press
Austin, Texas
www.gbgpress.com

Distributed by Greenleaf Book Group

For ordering information or special discounts for bulk purchases, please contact Greenleaf Book Group at PO Box 91869, Austin, TX 78709, 512.891.6100.

Design and composition by Greenleaf Book Group
Cover design by Greenleaf Book Group
Cover Images: Vaceslav Romanov/stock.adobe.com; JT Jeeraphun/ stock.adobe.com; kinwun/stock.adobe.com.

Publisher's Cataloging-in-Publication data is available.

Print ISBN: 979-8-88645-104-7

eBook ISBN: 979-8-88645-105-4

To offset the number of trees consumed in the printing of our books, Greenleaf donates a portion of the proceeds from each printing to the Arbor Day Foundation. Greenleaf Book Group has replaced over 50,000 trees since 2007.

Printed in the United States of America on acid-free paper

23 24 25 26 27 28 29 30   10 9 8 7 6 5 4 3 2 1

First Edition

The soil you see is not ordinary soil—it is the dust of the blood, the flesh, and the bones of our ancestors . . . You will have to dig down through the surface before you find nature's earth.

—ASHISHISHE, Crow Nation Warrior

For Ariel, who gave me a beautiful,
ancient connection to the land.

And for Armando, who tended this soil
with love long before I was here.

о–●–о–●

This symbol, drawn by several indigenous nations to indicate the passage of time, is used in this story for the same purpose.

CONTENTS

FEBRUARY

A frigid wind howled through the frayed weather stripping of the truck, rattling the windows in concert with his vibrating phone.

Jessica.

He wasn't going to answer, not now.

Not anymore.

His focus shifted from the full-moon midnight abyss of the pig-weed-infested wheat field to the fine layer of dust coating the idling truck's windshield. The cracked glass morphed into an unwelcome mirror, where a stranger, lit by the harsh, artificial glow of the phone screen, stared back at him.

Two chins too many. Lifeless eyes, weighted by sandbags filled with worry. Pale, loose cheeks, hollowed by pills and creased by bourbon.

A ghost of himself at thirty-two.

He'd touched his nose to the cheek of his sleeping wife a moment longer tonight, as he tucked the top sheet around her shoulders and whispered a hopeful goodbye.

The money would help her, more than he ever could.

He'd made sure of that, forgoing farm maintenance these last few months to pay the life insurance premiums. The policy was tucked into the laundry pile, along with a letter to her and the wheat subsidy claim.

A light flickered a few hundred yards to the west in the old bunk-house, where he'd moved his parents last year when the tremor in his dad's hands didn't go away. His mom could still handle the cooking and cleaning. For now, anyway. About six months ago, sometime in August, she'd started flipping the light switches on and off in the bunkhouse every night, in a search only she understood and rarely remembered. And since then, the widening gaps in her memory were just being filled by more and more confusion.

When it rains on the plains, it pours.

Jake's gaze turned back to his reflection in the windshield, the barely recognizable face mercifully reduced to a shadow in the darkness of the now dormant phone. He slouched into the bench seat until the moon pierced the dim outline of his forehead, like the all-knowing third eye on the cover of the hippie book Jessica had bought him when he stopped going to church. Only good use for that self-help bullshit was to help hold down his nightstand. He hadn't been back to church since last fall, when he'd confronted the pastor in the receiving line after the service.

"Tell me, Reverend. What kind of God would punish an innocent child? Hailey, our little girl? Remember her?"

The canned "Trust in Him" response—one he'd expected—had opened a line of questioning he'd been rehearsing for months. "You mean trust the Him who blessed our girl with leukemia, and then—"

Jessica had dug her fingernails into his forearm and dragged him away, but he'd kept calling over his shoulder. "Or trust that devil you're always railing against? Which one of those fellas kills little—"

She'd stopped in the grass bordering the church parking lot and covered his mouth with her other hand. "Jake. Enough."

He remembered the drive home, how that same hand had stead-ied his shaking leg.

How he'd been staring vacantly into his reflection in the passenger-side window, much like he was doing now, and shut his eyes tight against the tears starting to leak out.

How her gentle fingers moved to and through his hair, as she spoke calmly, always the deep, quiet ocean to his raging storm on the surface. "Everything'll be okay, baby."

How he wanted to believe her.

How that was then.

And this is now.

A shotgun would be too obvious. So would a rope or a belt or a handful of the Oxys hidden in the glove compartment. This had to look like an accident . . . his old F-150 with the sticky clutch, wrapped around the elm by the dry creek bed, during a late-evening check on the wheat.

He took a long pull from the bottle of bourbon stashed under the seat, to both steel his resolve and sell the story. Bitterness lingered from the pill he'd chewed on the way out here—he'd heard doing that could speed the opioid release, and he was out of time—so he hit the bottle one more time to kill the aftertaste, before shoving a cassette into the ancient tape deck. He cranked the radio volume all the way to the right and waited for the first tentacles of numbness to creep behind his eyes, and within a few labored breaths, scenes started playing on the movie screen draped over his brain.

Hailey, chasing a butterfly through the wheat, bathed in late-afternoon light.

Foot slipping off the brake, truck rolling in neutral.

Jessica, tears dancing with the early spring rain on her cheeks, the morning he proposed.

Dropping into first, hitting the gas, turning away from the house, lurching toward the creek bank.

Grinding the gears into second, then third, and then the old elm taking over the frame.

In the final, blissful detachment of no past and no future, a muted present-tense washes over him. His spine turns to rubber as his head nods to the right, and there, in the half-breath before the truck hits the tree, he sees what has truly driven him to this opiate-addled madness.

The figure with the braids, in a fringed leather shirt, with deerskin breechcloth and leggings, raising a translucent hand, reaching to the passenger window . . .

Windshield shattering, engine pushing into the cab, gravity escaping the creek bank against a grinding orchestra of metal and glass.

And, as suddenly as it was stolen, the quiet peace of the open sky returns, save for the warbled playback from the thin reel of the cassette tape, echoing through the dead night of the prairie.

> *See this hole, I dug her deep*
> *With these two hands*
> *Black as coal like forever sleep*
> *I hope you understand*
> *I'm a working man tired of fighting the land*
> *Gonna let these bones turn to oil*
> *In this ordinary soil*

GHOST DANCER

—1898—

The American Indian is of the soil, whether it be the forests, plains, pueblos, or mesas. He fits into the landscape, for the hand that fashioned the continent also fashioned the man for his surroundings. He once grew as naturally as the wild sunflowers: he belongs, just as the buffalo belongs.

—LUTHER STANDING BEAR, Sioux Chief

He climbed the creek bank, holding the elm sapling for balance as he ground his bare foot deep into the soft earth.

No fish today, but he had much to be thankful for. The spring rains had come early, not too strong, and the growing season for the three sisters of corn, beans, and squash would be good.

His father had told him the story of the three sisters, how they lived in peace and loved one another with all their hearts, protecting and helping each other grow strong. And yet, they were all so different from one another . . . the smallest, youngest sister, crawling in a vibrant green dress . . . the middle, dressed in yellow, as she wandered through the field . . . and the oldest in a pale green shawl, standing tall, yet bent to the wind, long yellow hair falling from her body.

His gaze traveled across the field. The squash leaves were beginning to weave their protective blanket over the ground, and soon, the cornstalks would rise high enough to support the sprouted beans.

He followed the shoots of green to the horizon, where man-made warriors stood ready, trained for combat against the soil, their metal talons poised to dig deep into the earth's skin. He knew she would not like this penetration, hard and unwanted, an undesired aggressor forcing himself into his virgin bride.

How many more growing seasons would there be, with his fingers dug into the earth, the mother blackening his palms?

The big machines had already come for the land, as the government had for his son.

The man in the suit had been impatient, standing in the strong sun of last harvest season and speaking fast words, as he wiped his wet brow with a white handkerchief.

I don't know when he'll be back. But the boarding school at Chilocco's for his own good. And compulsory. Means you ain't got no choice. The Indian Wars are over, and your people lost. Boy, you don't need no Indian clothes where you're going. Leave that sack there.

He had never known helplessness, and still did not know the word, but a foreign energy brought his heart into his throat when he watched the government man dig his fleshy fingers into the boy's small left forearm and pull him from the porch.

He paused now in the small field by the creek and closed his eyes, trying to see his son in short hair and a stiff shirt, like the horse trader in town. But his *shilombish,* his spirit, would not allow the vision, only the image of his boy looking back, dark eyes wide and confused, his soil-smudged cheek disappearing in the dust of the buckboard wagon.

His eyelids fluttered in deeper meditation, as he touched the fringes of the leather shirt he'd worn every day since his son had been taken. Rhythmic words rose against his breath, a spoken song learned from the Lakota Sioux who had given him the shirt in gratitude for making camp by the creek.

Wear this Ghost Shirt
Dance this Ghost Dance
Loved ones will reunite
White man will retreat
Old ways will return

He stood unmoving, creek water pooling at his feet, earth ground into the fabric of his skin, yet separate from his loved ones, in the eclipse of the white man's machines and laws.

Here.

Indian Territory.

Where the Trail of Tears had come to an end for his Choctaw.

Where his father and mother settled on this unclaimed land and taught him the old ways.

Where he lost his wife to smallpox and his son to the government.

Where he began to move in the slow circle of the Ghost Dance, fringes of leather swaying in rhythm, late afternoon sun making shadow shapes behind his eyes.

MARCH

A sharp, searing pain in his left forearm rocketed Jake awake. "Goddamnit!"

A nurse hustled into the room, frowning as she reinserted the needle in Jake's arm. "Third time you've pulled this thing out. First time you've noticed."

He blinked against the fluorescent light. "How long have I been here?"

"Couple of weeks . . . only started to come out of your coma about an hour ago. Looks like you're completely out now, though. I'll get the doctor and let your wife know."

She left the room and Jake craned his neck to get a glimpse out the window. Bright white lines on new asphalt, parking attendant checking his phone in a dilapidated booth, no trees in sight.

I've been here before. Oklahoma City. U of O Medical Center.

Hailey had spent a couple of months in this place's pediatric cancer facility, and Jessica had brought him to the emergency room here last year, when she'd found him doubled up in the fetal position, wedged between the toilet and the tub in their bathroom. He hated doctors, so he'd been burying his excruciating stomach pain with Advil, leftovers from the liquor cabinet, and everything on offer from the Sonic in

Guymon. The ER resident had said he had severe advanced diverticulitis and ulcerative colitis, and probably leaky gut . . . words that didn't register, and he promptly forgot them as soon as she sent him home with a list of dietary changes and a bottle of pain pills.

Could use a few of those right now.

Everything hurt.

Everything.

Jake rang the nurse call button, in search of something stronger than saline solution, or whatever was in the IV drip. "Me again, sorry. Can I get something to take the edge off? Hurts to even blink."

"No can do. Doctor's orders. You had enough Oxy running through you to take down a horse when they brought you in here. And your wife let us know you've developed quite an affinity for opioids."

Thanks, Jessica.

"She wasn't ratting you out." This nurse must've studied to be a mind reader as well as a medical professional. "You were in bad shape, and she was trying to help."

He clenched his fist in frustration, immediately relaxing his fingers when another surge of agony ran from his wrist all the way up to his shoulder. A guttural expletive, indecipherable even to him, caught in his throat as he watched the door close behind the nurse. He recognized the familiar chart taped a few inches under the coat hook . . . a laminated piece of paper with a line of happy to angry cartoon faces numbered 1 to 10. The ER resident had shown him that same scale last year and asked him where his pain landed before writing him that prescription for the pills.

Jessica was probably at least three hours away, and apparently the only way out of this place was to escape being awake. He closed his eyes and tried to paint pictures behind his eyes, doubting his body would let him sleep on command. Sometimes imagining scenes of mountains or the ocean or other places he'd never been sent him into dreamland, but the only image he could see now was a man with braids standing in the wheat, the reason he . . .

He woke to soft fingers combing his matted, thinning hair, his blurred vision coming into focus on a tanned, lean forearm. His gaze shifted to the familiar feminine jawline, then moved to his wife's corn-flower blue eyes.

"Hey, Jake."

"Hey."

"Took you long enough to wake up."

He breathed shallowly, trying to find pockets in his lungs that didn't hurt. "That wasn't part of the plan. Which you know by now."

"Pretty bad plan, huh?"

"You think talking about this right now is a good idea?"

"You think killing yourself is?"

Jake stared past her, at the television mounted in the upper corner of the room. *America's Most Wanted* at work, catching those bad guys. "I'm sorry."

"What?"

He brought his eyes back to her. "I said I'm sorry."

"You're sorry? That's all you can come up with?" Her fingers raked his scalp as she pulled them away, sending stinging strikes of light-ning into his skull. "How could you *ever* think we'd be better off without you?"

Jake waited for the flashes to die behind his eyes before answering. "I thought the money would help."

"Really? The money? What the fuck . . . am I supposed to buy a new dad for Hailey? Or a son for your parents?"

"Please . . . don't bring the Hailey thing into this. And I guess I didn't think about my parents."

"You didn't think at all."

Jessica leaned into the vinyl chair by the window. Her tired eyes reflecting in the glass took on a warped sadness, as she stared at the shimmering waves of heat rising from the hospital parking lot. "And the Hailey *thing* isn't a thing. She's our daughter."

"She's not—"

Jessica raised her hand in warning, forcing Jake to search for another response in the calloused crease of her soil-stained palm.

"Everything just got so tangled up, Jess."

She turned from the window. "Better start untangling."

———

Two floors up, a lab coat pocket rattled with electromagnetic radiation.

Damn phone.

He knew the paralegal he'd met last night had only taken his number to be polite, so the only person likely to be calling him was his mom. His thirties had disappeared into a black hole of long nights at this chemo lab, punctuated by the occasional nervous dinner with a lovely match from the online dating service he'd reluctantly joined. The women had always been more kind, intelligent, and attractive than he thought he deserved, which stymied most decent conversation, as well any hope for finding *the one.*

And so, here he was, another night at work, trying to distract himself from these things that mattered—these moving goalposts thrust into an impossible sky of dreams, forged from meaningful work and a life partner, wedged into the dirt of where he thought he'd be by now.

He'd come up with that metaphor on the elevator ride up this morning. His time spent sitting alone in the bleachers, under the Friday night lights of high school football, was finally paying off in useless verbiage.

His pocket vibrated again.

Yep. The woman in his life.

"Hey, Mom."

"Mark, you better come home."

He knew what those five words meant, and watched them fall through the phone, cleaving the night into everything that was before, and all that would come after.

He wasn't sure when he'd be back, so he grabbed the cardboard file box filled with his research and raced to his apartment, where he threw some clothes in a bag and made coffee for the drive. The city skyline was soon in his rearview mirror, buildings melting into double-wides into the occasional lonesome shed, until the pale night clawed at the dawn and livestock silhouettes cut across the horizon to the north of the highway. A few stray shadows loitered near the roadside, and he rolled down the window to let in the lowing of the cows. Maybe they had some self-help mantras he could cop, a quick fix for a cracked soul.

The answer was indeed there, in their instinctual acknowledgment of the new day, but Mark only heard the baritone rumble of cattle and shuddered against the frigid night, turning over and over what his first words to his father might be. But he knew no matter how much he might rehearse, all bets were off when he actually walked into his parents' house.

He scrolled through his phone for an artist that a colleague had told him about, hoping to replace his mental chatter with a better soundtrack.

Started with a *B*, right?

Right.

He hit *Play*, left the window down, cranked both the heat and the radio, and settled a little deeper in the seat. The songs were good, every-man stories sung by a road-weary voice that carried Mark through that hour before dawn that is not only the darkest, but also the coldest.

At first light, he passed the field where the high school kids used to circle up their trucks, headlights illuminating whatever their corn-field whiskey bonfires couldn't. He'd only been invited to one of those parties, but he still sometimes wistfully replayed the scenes of tilted red Solo cups and Daisy Dukes dancing under the dripping summer sky.

Was that single July night, when he skirted the edge of popularity, actually a coming-of-age highlight?

And maybe the starkness of the frigid gray light was lending a depressive bend to the landscape, or maybe he was overtired, but that field looked bleak now, bordering on barren.

Not quite apocalyptic, but no Garden of Eden, either.

The sun was barely cresting the roof when he pulled into his parents' driveway, dropped his chin to his chest, and sobbed for the first half of Bruce Springsteen's "The Rising" until the clutching of drapes in the living room window caught his attention.

His mom, silhouetted in the glass, waved him in. He made his way out of the car, stepped onto the porch, and pushed through the front door to see a withered figure crumpled into the living room couch.

His father waited until he was sitting next to him to pivot his head in acknowledgment. "Hey, kid."

Mark's unease with confrontation, rooted in this place, in this man, rose from his childhood up to his chest, where nerves fought the first few words for air. "Oh, you taped the Thunder game last night? I haven't watched the NBA in a long time. How are they doing?"

"Better than me, I guess. Which is the only reason you're here."

"Come on, I—"

His father pushed himself up against the cushions. "Just saying you haven't seen fit to find another reason."

Mark bristled at the passive-aggressive bend. His old man had never asked him to come visit. Ever. "So, now this is my fault? What about you? Why did you . . ."

"Why did I what? Wait? I knew what was coming. Didn't want to worry your mother."

"But we could've done something. I mean, this is what I do for a living. What we took loans out to pay for . . . for Christ's sake, I'm an oncologist."

His father waved a dismissive hand at the air of separation that would always linger between them. "You work in a lab."

"I'm still an MD. I work on the cure."

"You don't cure anything, son. You figure out ways to kill one demon at a time, and there's a million of 'em."

"Where are you getting this bullshit from? *Coast to Coast AM*?"

His father angled his torso and leaned in toward Mark, as if he was about to share a deep secret. "This cancer didn't just show up out of thin air for Sunday dinner."

"No one really knows where non-Hodgkin's lymphoma comes from."

"Well, the enemy came from somewhere. Seek and destroy that target, and you'll really be onto something."

"This is medicine, not the Marines."

"Semper Fi, baby."

"Alright, then. Nice work using military lingo to solve medicine's greatest mystery, all while making your son feel like shit for being a doctor. I'm going upstairs to check on Mom, and then we're going to not talk about this ever again."

Mark left his father to stew in sickness on the couch and headed upstairs to find his mom. She'd been full of life when she was younger, according to his aunt. Big smile, big laugh, big dreams of being a dancer. But almost fifty years of living with his old man had shrunk her somehow . . . she talked less and laughed quieter these days, if at all. One of two things was probably going to happen when his father passed: Either she was going to retreat and get even smaller, or she was going to allow herself to be who she was supposed to be, at least for the last few laps of her life.

He was hoping for the latter.

For both of them.

———

Jessica handed her ticket to the parking lot attendant, who looked up from his phone just long enough to take her two dollars. She pointed the Toyota Tercel toward Highway 412, thankful for the little car she'd bought from another sales associate at the Walmart in Guymon.

She'd picked up shifts there to help soften the monthly gut-punch of bills. Decent employee discount, too, but probably not what her daddy had in mind for his baby girl. Stocking shelves and driving a '95 Tercel hadn't been in her plan, either. But they needed a car. And the money.

And an addicted, suicidal husband? Also not part of the plan.

She turned onto 412 and shifted gears as quickly as the tiny four-cylinder engine would allow, finally getting ahead of the momentum-laden semi in her rearview mirror. The metaphor for her life wasn't lost on her, but outrunning her kind of trouble took more than a Tercel. A few days after Jake's accident, his doctor had told her he'd eventually come out of his coma, with a long road back to any kind of normal. But he'd live.

After the wave of relief had washed over her, the tide of anger filled in. She'd walked around the house for the first few hours, turning the suicide note over and over in her hands, trying to shake the sense of betrayal. Screaming at the walls. Crying in the mirror. Whispering to Hailey.

Reeling, for two weeks.

And now, she was so tired of thinking. Feeling. Everything, really.

She looked at Hailey, smiling from the rearview mirror.

Didn't plan for her, either.

But the Lord works in mysterious ways, right?

At least according to the only Oklahoma City station that the radio could pick up at the moment, courtesy of the broken tuner.

The Lord is coming.

Any day now.

Tick, tick, tock.

Talk, talk, talk.

Some of these preachers made the worst salesmen. Politicians, too. Never a real conversation, just one insecure guy trying to be louder than the guy next to him, looking for ways to crawl into this car radio and her computer and television . . . and especially the goddamn smartphone sitting on the passenger seat.

Only way not to drown in all this noise was to turn everything off, which she couldn't do. Especially now, with a husband teetering on the edge of suicide.

And not with a sick daughter, although Hailey was always with her now.

Still, there was Jake. She needed to be available if he got into trouble. Had to be a better way, though. Growing up in a family of five, she'd survived with the simplicity of a landline. Sure, as a teenager she'd had to convince her dad to buy an extra-long phone cord, so she could talk to boys in the privacy of her room. And a flip phone had admittedly come in handy here and there in college, but she'd resisted these smartphones until Jake got her one last Christmas.

Wait.

That's it.

She could answer calls on an old-school flip phone just as easily as a smartphone.

And those fat media bastards would have a way harder time crawling into a flip phone.

The evangelist's screams through the tiny Tercel speakers distorted into warbles, as he reached the only kind of climax he'd probably ever have. Jessica cranked down the car window and turned the radio volume knob all the way to the left, until she heard nothing but the elm branches rustling in the late spring air. She caught and held a piece of the prairie wind deep in her chest, let the breath slowly escape, and felt her cheeks rise against an unexpected smile.

Poor guy.

She pulled into the driveway and took the dog-eared photo of Hailey from the rearview mirror. The heat exposure from the direct sun already was starting to fade the image, so she tucked the picture into her jeans pocket and brought Hailey straight from the Tercel to her garden, craving the dirt therapy that had helped her cope over the last year.

And especially the last two months.

She picked up right where she left off this morning, when she got the call from the hospital that Jake was out of his coma. Digging her fingers deep, she pulled out a handful of soil, dropped in a few squash seeds, refilled the hole, and moved down the row. Her garden was cranking all around her with winter vegetables finally ready to be harvested, and she'd saved this section in the middle for spring seeding. Young plants would still get plenty of sun but wouldn't get hammered by the midday heat.

That was her theory, at least. She'd started winging this gardening thing last summer, with the help of a few books and the occasional YouTube rabbit hole, and wasn't far from putting together a meal almost entirely from the garden. Not bad for a novice.

Jake wasn't on board with just spinach and beans for dinner, of course. But she couldn't force him. Can't force anybody to do anything and expect it to stick.

Hailey was here, dancing through the green rows like she always did. Jessica watched her disappear behind the small stand of corn, just now tall enough to hide her.

"So that's how you want to play, huh? Ready or not, here I come!"

She dove into the corn, grabbing for air where she thought Hailey had been crouched.

The kid was good at this.

Even when the leukemia sapped her strength, she was good.

Jessica pulled herself up and out of the corn, knowing Hailey was still around somewhere. She went back to planting the squash seeds, one small hole at a time, waiting for her daughter to materialize again.

And until then, she had a garden to grow.

WARRIOR

1908–1936

Dust coming over the horizon
Papa can't you see
There's a dark cloud coverin' the high sun
And you and me
Papa says breathe
If you close your eyes
There will be green fields as you can see
Rivers running strong and free
As far as you can see

—BISON BRIDGE

He fingered the drawstring of the knapsack, the worn canvas bag nearly weightless with all he didn't want to bring home from this place.

Home.

After ten years.

Long time gone.

Gone, torn away from a simple life with his father and mother, much of which he couldn't remember, except for sporadic flashes of images attached to Choctaw words . . . lean, strong *Aki* pulling corn from their stalks, gentle *Hashki* mashing the kernels into meal, his own toes tracing patterns in the dirt floor around the hearth.

This way of living that he didn't even know was simple until it, like him, was gone.

He'd lived with white families every summer and had learned to look forward to the reprieve from this school, where he'd been forced to allow every small piece of himself to be cut away by the sharp blade of what they called "rules," as well as their vengeful, threatening God. No gratitude to Mother Earth, no speaking in native tongue, no talk of the old ways, no visits from family, only these "yes sir, no ma'am" rules made by a brigadier general in the East.

And a brigadier general must be someone who turns ancestors into demons and Choctaws into dogs. Just took a few lashings from the headmaster and a handful of work punishment days in the school's quarry to figure that out. And he'd submitted, to make survival a less painful proposition. But only on the surface.

Underneath the compliance, he was so much stronger than they thought, holding power that had been contained, not drained . . . power that he was waiting to unleash when he was released. Or, in their terms, when he "graduated."

But graduating, and the waiting, were no more. Not after he walked into the bathroom last week to find a group of his classmates huddled in a circle, and his suppressed will to fight finally exploded.

"What's going on in here?"

The circle had parted as the biggest kid stepped forward, exposing blood splattered across the concrete floor. "New kid. Different tribe. And none of your business."

He looked past the school uniforms to see a small boy, not much older than he'd been when he arrived, bleeding from his temple and ear.

Tears streaked his dirt-smudged cheeks, and in the reflection of a single salty drop falling to the floor, he saw himself when he first set foot in this place as a child, late in the school year: bullied, beaten, bruised.

"The hell it's not."

He dropped the ringleader with one punch, watched his head hit the sink, and left him crumpled against the exposed plumbing. The other kids scattered immediately, leaving only the three of them in the bathroom.

He stepped over the ringleader, pulled a coarse paper towel from the dispenser, and knelt next to the trembling, wide-eyed boy. "Hold that against your ear and go to the nurse, understand?"

The boy looked at him with confusion, so he tried a few words in Choctaw, which elicited a nod. He waited for the swinging bathroom door to quiet before considering the unconscious heap under the sink. Should he kick him, maybe just once, for good measure? Get help? Get out of here and let someone find him?

He hadn't yet decided when the headmaster burst through the door, the nurse on his heels. And this was why he was being sent away the week before graduation. They didn't care where he went, they just wanted him gone.

He'd refused the short ride to the train station from his farming teacher, the one person who'd taken a real interest in him. An escort to the school gates was compulsory, though, so the rugged, hatless man, whose sun-beat wrinkles belied his youth, met him outside the dormitory. "I know they aren't letting you graduate, but I got you a graduation present."

He accepted the package but didn't look up from the small pockets of dust billowing under his footsteps as they walked. "Thank you, sir. I'm going to remember what you taught me."

"Good. And listen, we're not all this way."

"We?"

"Yeah. White people. Only reason I'm here is to offer a counterbalance to some of what I see happening, almost every day. Injustices, big and small. We all see 'em. Good people do, anyway."

"I know. I lived with nice families during the summers. But—"

The teacher held up his hand, and then offered it. "Say no more. I know. You better get hustling if you want to catch that train."

He shook the teacher's hand before shoving the brown bag–wrapped gift into the knapsack, alongside the bundled paper remnants he'd used as a journal over the last few years. Learning to write had been a revelation, the weaving together of words a release, the occasionally pilfered blank scrap a friend.

And the only piece of this place he wanted to keep.

With a last nod to the teacher, he headed down the mile-long dirt road toward the Chilocco depot. The headmaster's passing Model T engulfed him with choking clouds of fine dust as he approached the station, and by the time the dust settled, the train to Kildare was starting to pull away.

He ran the remaining few hundred feet, until he was almost even with the conductor standing at the open railcar door. The fleshy folds of skin draped over the uniform's starched collar sent stabs of panic into his gut, momentarily paralyzing him. Was this the government man who'd taken him away, now ready to deny his homecoming?

But the conductor only smiled and urgently waved him on the train, before asking for his ticket and motioning toward the second-class compartment.

He headed to an open seat by the window, where he pulled another small piece of paper from his pocket, written in the same kind hand that had graded his farming tests.

Get off at Kildare, take the Santa Fe headed west to Guymon, Oklahoma.

Home was called Oklahoma now, a new state named with the same Choctaw words he wasn't allowed to utter in school.

Okla, "people," and *humma,* "red."

He waited until he'd successfully navigated the transfer to unwrap the present: a framed speech from Thomas Jefferson to his own nation, the Choctaw. The unjust irony intensified to anger as he read the speech, over and over, his rage building until the train shuddered to a halt at Guymon.

> I rejoice, brothers, to hear you propose to become cultivators of the earth for the maintenance of your families. Be assured you will support them better, and with less labor, by raising stock and bread, and by spinning and weaving clothes, than by hunting. A little land cultivated, and a little labor, will procure more provisions than the most successful hunt; and a woman will clothe more by spinning and weaving, than a man by hunting. Compared with you, we are but as of yesterday in this land. Yet see how much more we have multiplied by industry, and the exercise of that reason which you possess in common with us. Follow then our example, brethren, and we will aid you with great pleasure . . .

He threw the white man's words against the seat, shattering the glass frame as he rose into the aisle. Knapsack in hand, he kept his head down as he threaded through passengers until he reached the platform, where he searched the crowd for his father.

The small, stooped Choctaw waiting off to the side of the platform wasn't him. Couldn't be.

The son turned away to find the father he remembered.

Aki.

But the wet eyes of the old man told him the truth. And in the next breath, familiar fingers came to rest on his shoulder, as a single word spoken in his native tongue drifted past his ear.

"Son."

His father had ponied a mare for him, knowing the way of the horse was in the son's blood. They rode side by side from the train station, with the silence of a lost decade between them. There was no space for words, as cacophony reigned all around them. He stared in disbelief at the busyness of so many people, rollicking through a town that didn't even exist when he'd been taken away. Herds of the headmaster's automobiles fought horses in the dirt street, top hats battling wider straw brims. Chaos spilled from a crowded doorway, assaulting him with the unfamiliar syncopated piano of ragtime and drunken laughter. A boy screamed the news of the day, trying to sell the stack of pulped dead trees at his feet.

The noise and confusion infected his being instantly, quickening his breath and speeding the blood through his body. Jumbling his thoughts. Rattling his skull.

His horse sensed his anxiety and tightened her back in anticipation of the need to flee, away, away, away from this unnatural world, already divorced from its source.

The horse knew.

He looked to his left, where his father rode calmly through the eye of the mayhem. Did he possess such inner peace that his spirit was not swayed by the commotion? Had he become accustomed to the noise?

Or was his father already somewhere else?

But he didn't ask such questions. Shouting to be heard would only put the horse on even higher alert, and by the time the town mayhem had faded into the prairie cicada calls, his father's eyes were already half-closed.

His body swaying, in rhythm with the animal beneath him.

And the earth beneath her.

The next morning, he woke to a low hum before dawn, and he quietly moved through the two-room clapboard house to find his father sitting on the slanting porch, singing an ancient song.

"Of what do you sing, Father?"

The answer remained hidden behind creased eyelids, fluttering against the rising sun. He wondered if his father was trying to unsee the hills rising to the horizon in the distance, land they would have ridden through yesterday if yesterday had been many moons ago.

But that way home had been cut off by a wire fence, the scrub oak he'd played in as a child ripped out of the plowed soil. They had ridden the network of roads that divided the land, holding their breath against more headmaster's automobiles. And because their horses were unable to do the same, they let them stand still to find cleaner air for many breaths.

Still, no words between them.

The three sisters waited in their field next to the house and had welcomed him home as he pulled his mare to rest and dismounted. Corn, beans, and squash, growing together, their green shoots of promise rising in the early summer sun . . . he inhaled the living earth and exhaled relief that they were still here.

But so much else was gone.

Maybe this is why his father sang now, as the first rays of filtered sun touched his deeply creased forehead.

And so, he softly stepped down the single porch stair and headed toward the creek to see if the young elm was still there, the tree that had been his friend, giving him branches to fashion make-believe spears and leaves to float as tiny canoes.

That evening, they sat on the horses on the far hill and watched the invisible hand paint the sky in lilac. The old man spoke in their native tongue, knowing his son would remember. "I sense your anger."

"I am angry for many reasons."

His father raised a single finger. "Only one. The white man."

"The white man is making war on our way of life."

The old man moved his hand up the horse's neck so the reins would drop far enough for the mare to graze. "Fight if you must, but remember, the way of your most respected ancestor warriors was not to kill."

"How did they defeat their enemy if they did not kill?"

"By counting coup, a greater dishonor to the enemy than killing."

"You never spoke of counting coup."

He watched his father stroke the mare's neck, breathing in the musk of the mane before finding his words. "Many moons ago, before the Trail of Tears, the best fighter would intimidate his enemy with such bravery and skill that killing was not necessary. His adversary's pride would be wounded in a disgrace more dishonorable than death when the warrior touched him with his coup stick and forced him to admit defeat."

"But the books in school showed that the white man knows little about honor, especially in battle. They kill from far away with their guns, using no bravery, only good aim." He'd borrowed that observation from the farming teacher, and offered him a subtle smile in gratitude.

His father's eyes danced with a whisper of humor. "Yes, the white man may try to kill you from afar also. If not with guns, then with laws. I only ask that you follow the way of your warrior ancestors. Show honor, and count coup."

"How?"

"That is your answer to find."

The son studied his hands, skin dry and cracked from the last week spent in the school quarry as punishment for the bathroom incident. If he looked long enough, he would find the answer there, but the dusk turning dark made the calloused lines hard to follow.

Pieces of light pierced the sky before his father spoke again. "You ask about my song. I sing of sorrow. People are forgetting the old ways, and I am sad."

"The white man calls these machines and new techniques 'progress.' They believe this is the way forward."

"The earth gives to us what she offers—we cannot take more from her. My shilombish has shown me a grave future."

"Shilombish?"

"My spirit. While I slept, it traveled to another place and saw what is coming."

"What is coming?"

"Sick people. A sick earth. This is why I am sad. Sad, and tired."

"Rest. I will tend to the land and the herd."

The old man leaned toward his horse's head, caressing the neck again as his deerskin leggings held the bareback mare. "No, I am tired in my bones and my heart. You must prepare for my death. My shilombish will leave this body and stay for a moon, resting for the journey to the Land of Ghosts. Bury me under the new elm and keep a fire burning by my body for four days so my shilombish has comfort."

He fingered the reins in his hands, not allowing the tears to come. His father had waited for him. "I will."

"Every man also has a *shilup*, a shadow. My shilup may haunt this land for many moons, in warning of what is to come."

A sliver of moon crested the ridge, the pale light threatening to expose the doubt written in his eyes. He did not believe in such spirits, not anymore. But he would do his father's final bidding, whatever that may be. "How can I honor your shilup?"

"Honor the earth, and my shilup will have peace and retreat."

At dawn, he heard no soft song drifting from the front porch. He found his father when the sun was highest in the sky, lying on boughs by the creek bank, long, graying braids draped over his shoulders.

He walked back to the shed for a shovel and matches, started a fire at his father's feet, and dug beneath the elm until sundown. The moonless night fell black as he sat next to the body, tending the low flame. He closed his eyes, searching for a few moments of rest, but a quiet rage did not allow him to sleep, growing loud against the silence of this first solitude since he was a boy. Now, he was truly alone, his father killed by sadness, and his mother killed by the white man's disease.

He watched the embers push against their charcoaled boundaries and let himself drift into an afternoon in the headmaster's office, toward the end of his assimilation at Chilocco.

"You love your mama, son?"

"Yes."

"Yes what?"

"Yes, sir."

"Well, she's almost dead. You want to say goodbye?"

He'd begun trembling uncontrollably—even worse than he usually did against the cold north wind that impaled the school grounds every morning.

"Stop shaking and stand straight, son!"

The headmaster came around the desk and slammed an open hand across his face. "Stop shaking!"

A light sob escaped.

"And don't cry, goddamnit!"

Another slap. "Maybe I'll let you say goodbye if you remember our motto."

He choked on the words, regurgitated from the depths of his belly. "Kill the Indian, save the man."

Another slap. "What?"

"Kill the Indian, save the man, sir."

"Tell you what. I'll let you go."

"Thank you, sir."

"If you can pay your own way."

The headmaster knew he had no money for the train to take him across Indian Territory. He could hear the smirking, sneering chuckle behind him as he left the office, and waited until he'd turned the corner down the hall before he sank to the floor with his head in his hands. But even then, he had kept a shield around his core, so he wouldn't explode with anger.

He fanned the coals until they ignited again, finally allowing the headmaster's abject cruelty to infect every cell of his being, like the small-pox that took his mother away.

And now, he knew what he must do.

He let the shovel rest in the fire until the metal glowed with searing heat, then sliced each of his wrists with the edge of the blade. He coaxed viscous blood from the cuts and rubbed his wrists together, bowing his head into the reek of burning flesh.

A brand, and a blood vow with himself.

He would be the fiercest of warriors and honor his father's request never to kill, but he would intimidate the enemy with such bravery and skill that killing would not be necessary. His adversary's pride would be wounded in a disgrace more dishonorable than death.

That was what the headmaster had tried to do—intimidate him with power, and wound his pride in disgrace, by using his poverty against him.

Money *was* power.

And this is how he would count coup.

He would make more money than even the headmaster and become more powerful than the stiff suit with the sagging neck who took him away from his family.

The white man had made a mistake, arming him with the new rules of progress. When he wasn't grinding limestone at the Chilocco Indian Agricultural School quarry, he'd been taught to farm the most profitable crop, so he could toil efficiently for another white man when he was released.

But he wasn't going to toil for another white man.

This land was his now, the 160-acre homestead granted to his father in exchange for abandoning his tribal affiliation. Only in word, not in deed, because his father had also learned what the white man's word was worth. Treaties signed and broken, land promised and stolen.

These fields would be the battleground, and he would go to war with what he could plant now, this autumn. The soil would give him a new weapon.

Wheat.

The first wisps of gray light were cutting the sky as he planned his initial attack. For this land to help him fight, the old ways must be left in the past. Including the horses. He knew now that a tractor could do the work of many horses, faster, and only needed to be fed while working. These fields had been wasted on stock feed for too long.

At daybreak, he lowered his father's body into the deep grave and spread the first layer of dirt across the deerskin leggings and thin, threadbare leather shirt with fringed sleeves. He climbed out of the hole and finished the burial, before stomping out the fire. His father had told him to keep the fire burning for four days, but there were more important things to do now, things that would honor his father in a much greater way.

He stood with the small herd in the split-rail field bordering the three sisters, guessing what they might sell for in town. His next inhale caught in his throat as the image of the small, bloody boy in the school bathroom flashed across his mind.

That boy was him. And these horses were pieces of his father, remnants of his past that had been stolen from him at school.

His fingers grazed the mane of the mare his father had chosen to bring him home.

She would stay.

And his father's horse.

He found the rope halters draped over a fence rail, caught the two mares, and opened the makeshift rope gate to let the other horses wander into open space. While they looked for traces of grass on the dry plain, he took the halter off his mare, looped the lead over the neck of his father's mare, and swung up onto her bare back. He asked his father's mare to back up, slowly, keeping the other horse in the small fenced field until he could close the gate. Pushing into the older horse's flank, he clicked his tongue to the herd, knowing they'd follow.

Which they did.

All the way into town, where shopkeepers stared through their windows at the Indian boy riding with no saddle down Main Street, leading horses free to run but choosing to follow. He stopped in front of the saloon, tied his father's mare so the others would stay close, and walked inside to ask where the horse trader did his business.

The barkeeper pointed the boy to a table by the window, where the horse trader offered him too little for a herd so docile. He started to rise from his seat, but the trader grabbed his forearm, his grimy nails digging into his flesh. He felt the blood course faster through his veins and readied for a fight, pulling his free hand into a fist.

But the trader only motioned for him to sit back down.

"How is your father?"

"Dead. Why?"

"I see. Well, he bought two of those horses from me."

He searched the trader's eyes for a trace of honesty. "That means you know what they're worth. And you know they're better horses now, standing out there like that."

More bills than he'd ever seen moved from the trader's billfold to the table. "Happy now?"

"Lead mare isn't for sale."

The trader peered through the window at the horse tied to the post.

"That was your father's, I'm guessing."

"Mine now."

"Alright. Take the money. Do me a favor and leave them in the roundpen behind the feed store."

The son untied the mare and led the herd into the roundpen, where he closed the gate and draped the mare's lead rope over the rail. He headed into the feed store and waited for the clerk to finish every small task that didn't seem to need doing, before finally asking him for a Fordson Model F tractor order form.

"You need real money for that deposit, son. We don't take beads."

He slammed the bills on the counter, in his first act of war.

"These aren't beads. And I'm not your son."

O●O●

The metal blades of the iron plow sliced the top layer of dirt, leaving only a surface wound. He needed a deeper cut, like the brand he wore on his wrists, so he climbed off the tractor and reset the level, unsure whether the Model F could generate enough horsepower to pull the lowered drag. He remounted, hit the hand lever, and turned his head to watch the gouge trailing the machine.

Success.

His father's small field of corn, beans, and squash were first to fall, the dried stalks and vines turning over until they were dead soldiers strewn across the battlefield. He moved on to digging a furrow through the relatively untouched land, across which he'd run as a child, hiding from imagined foes in the scrub oak.

But his enemy was no longer make-believe.

He plowed a single row all the way to the creek, quitting when the darkness afforded him only black earth against black sky. Needing some semblance of light to maintain parallel furrows, he left the Model F by the young elm and walked back to the clapboard house, where he ate beans from a tin and stared into the flames dancing in the hearth.

Work, eat, repeat.

Ritual.

O●O●

The rusting Fordson Model F sat orphaned against the shed, the false poetic warmth of a dying day betraying the cold, jagged steel of the old tractor. He'd abandoned the workhorse a few summers ago, when he bought this 1929 John Deere GP with a flathead.

He killed the big machine's engine and listened to the last cough of her two cylinders echoing across the field. Shifting his gaze from the Model F to the near-perfect rows of soil to his right, he raised a hand to his father, who watched from under the elm.

Aki, I am not killing anyone. You will see, and I will make you proud.

His adamant denial of the spiritual world had changed since he'd come home from Chilocco . . . not enough that he accepted his dying father's claims about a shilombish and a shilup, but he'd begun thinking that maybe people left an imprint when they died. Almost like a footprint in memory, if nowhere else.

The brakes on the John Deere were already shot, but he hadn't bothered replacing them. He didn't have much need to stop, or even slow, his attack on the soil. The plow was heavy and dug deep, its forked metal rage grating against the buried torso-sized rocks he didn't try to avoid. He'd even named a few of them, after the government man, the headmaster, and the teacher who'd given him the graduation gift. Each stabbing pass with the plow was another stake in their hearts.

The winter wheat had been filling the Mason jars hidden on the top shelf of the pantry with enough cash for the deposit on a combine . . . probably after next summer's harvest. The Fordson had been a bow and arrow in his war, this John Deere a rifle, but a combine would be a howitzer. Keeping almost 160 acres in wheat was a lot of work for one man, even with this newer tractor, and especially without children to help.

He'd been working dawn to dusk most of the last five years. When he wasn't in the field, he was repairing machinery, or covering the house's dirt floor with the pine planks milled in the shed he'd built, or digging another well, or adding another room in anticipation of more mouths to feed.

No time to find a woman, and no place to find a woman, either. Only possibility was at the Masonic lodge in town, where they held a dance every other Friday night in the summer.

He didn't dance.

And the last one of the season was tonight, but he still had a lot of work to do if he wanted to have all 160 acres of seed in the ground before the rains came.

Couldn't plow at night, though.

He washed up in the stock tank behind the house, dressed, and rode his father's mare into town, where the Masonic lodge was full of farm boys, a handful of women, and a few natives clustered in corners.

And the most beautiful living thing he'd ever seen.

Long blonde hair, with the brown eyes of a doe. She wasn't from here. Maybe Cimarron County, but not Texas County . . . he would have noticed her a long time ago.

She was white, and he didn't have the courage to approach her, so he got lost in her from afar. He caught her eye by mistake, looked away quickly, and a few minutes later, four farm boys surrounded him. The ringleader stepped into the circle.

"Lady says you're giving her a problem."

His clenched fist wavered at his side. He was dressed in stiff town clothes, bought with his first good harvest, and he couldn't fight all of them. Head held high and staring straight ahead, he pushed through the crowd and walked to his horse, expecting to hear the farm boys following. Footsteps did shuffle in the dust behind him as he swung up on the mare, but the grip of his heels on her flank sent the horse out of their reach. He looked back as he coaxed the mare back down into a trot, but there was no group of men in sight.

Just a woman.

Her.

The tension between flight and fight released in relief, and the relaxation eased the sensitive mare into a walk. He turned the horse and stopped to face the woman, who had already closed the gap separating them to spitting distance. Her slender fingers settled on her hips. "So you were looking at me, huh?"

He dropped his stare to his hands, again looking for answers in the creased trails. "I suppose I was. Haven't seen you in town."

"I ain't been in town. We just moved here. Daddy's trying to work some land his brother left him. Why don't you come down here and talk to me?"

He dismounted and faced her, still too nervous to make eye contact. He'd never talked to a girl, not like this. She smiled and lifted his chin with her index finger.

"Come on now. I won't bite. How about I walk back to the dance and tell the girls to cover for me, and meet you behind the building. You can throw me on the back of that mare and take me home."

His eyes widened, and she laughed. "No, silly. Not like that. You'll be my ride back, and you can tell me all about this godforsaken town I just moved to. Or not."

They rode under moonlight bright as day, toward her daddy's house and then nowhere in particular. Their stories gained strength as the land passed beneath them, until no sacred stone remained unturned and the first wisps of dawn were teasing the horizon. She asked him to stop just out of sight of the house, swung her legs off the mare, and stroked his calf twice, sending a pulse of desire raging up his leg. He watched her float over the dirt road and shimmy up the post supporting the porch to an open bedroom window, and he knew she was the one.

They found each other in secret spaces for those first few months, hidden away from judgment and immediate consequence. Her swollen belly became impossible to disguise by the time winter wheat was pushing through the soil, and the night of reckoning arrived on an early December evening at the farm. He'd figured they might as well start seeing each other there, since she'd be living with him soon enough. He hadn't made enough money yet for real furniture, so like most nights, they lay next to each other on his bedroll in the living room, quiet, content.

Their peace was pierced by firelight dancing against the pane glass, and they rose in tandem to see her father and two other men storming toward the house, makeshift torches in hand. He allowed a buffer of a few hundred feet before he went for the shotgun in the corner.

She pulled him back. "Stay by the window. You're already fighting them in your own way. Let me fight them in mine."

She threw open the front door and stood her ground on the porch as they approached the stairs. With one hand on her swollen belly, she raised a single finger in warning. "Don't you get close to this baby. You're going to have to go through me to get to him, and if this little one's born not right, you'll have blood on your hands. Mine."

Her father raised his hand, stopping the two behind him short of the porch.

"A hardworking man, owning 160 acres outright, is rare in Texas County, white or not. You should know. Get on back to where you came from. Especially you, Daddy. I'm telling you, there will be my blood on your hands. Put the fires out. Now."

She waited until the torches fell from their burning salutes and touched the dust before turning back into the house and softly closing the front door.

He traced the branded scar on his wrist as he touched his nose to the living room windowpane, watching the pack of coyotes retreat into the star-soaked spring night, tails between their legs.

Another battle, won.

He steered the tractor to the left of the ranch hand, who was a couple hundred feet away, picking up the smaller rocks in the field.

"Leave the big ones in the dirt, hear me?"

That dirt had been changing over the last couple of seasons. They'd been getting decent rain, up until this year, so he wasn't sure why the soil felt so light. He knew his fight on this land bore no resemblance to his dad's love affair with the three sisters, but there was no money in the small yields of corn, beans, and squash.

And he hadn't made enough yet to count coup, but he was getting closer, and his enemy now had a face in the same county: the leader of the coyote pack that his woman had run off his land, before their daughter was born.

His father-in-law had side-eyed him the last time they saw each other in town, muttering something about a bastard half-blood under his breath. If he'd had a couple whiskeys in him, there's no telling what he would've done. But he only traced the branded scar on his wrist and closed his eyes, like he was doing right now, to see his father-in-law pleading on his knees, jealous of his daughter's fine linens and curtains and furniture, despondent that his own farm had failed, and begging him for a job.

The truest disgrace and dishonor.

He dropped the tractor into gear and yelled at the ranch hand through the cigarette sagging from his cracked lips. "You want to get turned over too?"

"I'm over here, boss. Headed home. See you tomorrow."

The kid was already almost to the county road, but whoever was in front of him hadn't moved.

Probably a drifter, looking for a handout.

A lot of those around these days, after that stock market crash back in '29 turned cities into ghost towns and sent men scattering around the country. That's what the feed store owner said was happening, anyway. All he knew for sure was that folks were getting worried about prices for this season's harvest, and he didn't need to be giving away money that he didn't have yet.

"Hey . . . get the hell out of the way!"

Thirty yards away.

Dark silhouette against the wheat.

"You better move!"

Twenty yards away.

"Move, goddamnit!"

Braids, a fringed leather shirt, with deerskin breechcloth and leggings, raising a translucent hand.

Ten.

Mouth widening into a gaping abyss.

"Hey!"

Five.

Hair burning to ash, skin dripping off bone, eyes disintegrating into hollow sockets.

Gone.

"Pa, stop. *Pa!*"

He could hear his son's horrified pleas, but he couldn't stop. No reins to hold, no way to slow the runaway horse of his mind, a bro-ken-free stallion bucking and kicking at the injustice of confinement and control.

Broken free by the brown water in his bottomless glass, spilled by the careless boy playing with that damn dog—some stray his son had found abandoned in town and brought home. When he was done beating respect into the boy, he'd take care of the dog.

He threw the boy against the wall and watched him crumple to the floor, before charging toward his wife in the back bedroom. His rebuffed kicks to the locked door told him that she'd pushed the new dresser across the threshold, but that was no match for the hatchet by the fireplace.

He made quick work of splintering the thin pine barrier, despite the blur of colors flashing across his eyes. Climbing through the jagged hole and over the expensive dresser, he spilled onto the bedroom floor, where he heard an unfamiliar snap and immediately recoiled against the pain searing through his left forearm.

"Goddamnit!"

The agony flushed his veins with temporary sobriety, and after breathing through the initial shock of the pain, he slowly pushed up to his knees, expecting his wife to have the shotgun trained on him.

But the air was quiet. Peaceful, even, like the gentle breeze lifting the linen curtains and drifting through the open window. She and the daughter must have escaped that way and run to the neighbors.

One foot on the floor, then the other, until he swayed in front of the open window, in awkward rhythm with the linen curtains lilting in the night air. He stared into the field where he'd weaved through the wheat after dinner, bottle in hand, as if whiskey-infused guttural threats would keep the demon away.

He turned to the bedroom door, moved the dresser, and opened the hacked door. His son was still in a quivering pile on the floor.

"Get up, boy."

His son rose like a timid field mouse, probably waiting for his open hand to land on the back of his neck. But he walked past the boy and into the small pantry, where the worn leather journal was hidden on the top shelf behind the money jar.

Where he turned when he had nowhere else to go.

Where he'd found an unexpected friend at the white man's school, waiting under paper cover in the blank pages.

Where a lover listened, in the drying ink.

Where he wrote his uneven, half-drunken truth, curled fingers numbing from his broken wrist.

Bad one today.

Saw it again, same place.

Not sure why, looked more real when I'm on the tractor. Face stayed with me, just needed a drink. Helped. Forgot.

Hit the boy again, hard this time. He is still here, wife and daughter gone again, this time she said for good. I don't blame her. Blame me. I don't want to be like this anymore. Got no choice. Got no choice. Got no . . .

And he sank into the hard, straight-backed wooden chair, pencil in hand, eyes closed, labored breath escaping in fitful snores from the bellows of his chest.

O-O-O-O

"Is that a thunderstorm, Pa?"

"No. Wrong direction. That's not water."

The curtain of black billowed toward them, galloping across the plain faster than any horse.

"Leave the machine and run. Go down to the root cellar. Now!"

He followed his son, flinging open the door into the house just as the first wave of dust hit. He'd never felt such violence in the wind, the abrasive air digging into the back of his neck before creeping between his lips and turning his throat to sandpaper, all in the course of a single breath.

He closed the windows and ran back outside, collecting whatever tools he found scattered on the ground as he fought his way to the root cellar. With one arm guarded against the dust, he pulled the door open, threw the tools into the darkness, and leapt in.

His son was crouched in the corner with an unlit lantern.

"Just breathe, boy. Close your eyes. And breathe."

"What is happening, Pa?"

"I don't know. Feels like a reckoning."

"Reckoning?"

"Your grandpa knew. Nothing we can do now."

"Grandpa knew what?"

But he'd already closed his mouth against the grit falling through the cellar door, these small pieces of what used to be his battleground, now lifted into the sky and taken away.

○●○●

"Give us a minute. You stay, son."

The doctor closed his medical kit and left the room, as the boy shuffled to the side of the bed. Not a boy anymore, but *his* boy, a nineteen-year-old, damn-near man, thrown into running the farm these last few months.

There wasn't much of a farm to run, not since last year—Black Sunday, 1935, spent in the cellar while his land blew away. This Oklahoma panhandle had been hit the worst by the massive dust storm, and almost everybody had already packed whatever they could carry and headed west. Anywhere was better than here, where the land had turned to dust and blown into his lungs.

The doctor had said something about dust pneumonia, even offered to find his wife and let her know. But he hadn't seen his wife in months, and doubted she'd care. He'd heard that she and the daughter were hitching a ride to California. Maybe already had. The boy was probably thinking about leaving too.

He waited to speak until the doctor shut the bedroom door. "I'm tired, son."

"I know, Pa. You've worked harder for longer than anyone out here."

"No, different kind of tired. Tired of the fight. Been angry most of my life. But you know that."

"Nothing was easy, especially after Ma left."

He hacked in agreement. "Reckon that's why I wasn't the best father. Mad and drunk and no woman around. But I was no good when she was here, either."

"It's alright."

"No, it's not alright. I knew what I was doing, just didn't choose to be better than that. And you were always trying to make peace and dance with this devil in me, but you won't have to dance much longer. Doctor said I'm about finished."

"Maybe tomorrow will—"

"Tomorrow may not come. And I know I ain't in much of a position to ask a favor, but I need one."

"Whatever you need."

"Don't leave."

"I ain't leaving you, Pa, not when you're like this."

He waved weakly toward the window. "No, I mean don't leave the farm."

"But there's been no crop for two seasons. This dust—"

"The land will come back. There's enough food in the cellar to last until the rains come and you can get another garden planted. And you know we canned everything we got our hands on."

"How do you know the rains will come again?"

"Earth ain't going to stay dry forever. Until then, the well by the house has enough water to get you through. Just don't try to irrigate."

"I don't know, Pa. They're calling this the Great Depression. Even if the land comes back, the price of wheat might not. We're barely feeding ourselves with the garden."

He raised a shaking index finger and pointed toward the boy's heart. "You're a peacekeeper, son. Mend this land. Repair the damage I caused and live with her in harmony. She'll take care of you."

"But how do you know?"

"Took me this long to realize that I used Mother Earth to fight. Made her a warrior in a losing battle, and she became even angrier than I was. Doesn't have to be that way."

He could tell that his son was wringing his hands behind his back, like he always did when he was nervous. But he also knew the boy wanted to leave his father proud.

"Okay, Pa."

"There's something else."

"Yeah?"

"I was no good at talking, about anything. But up by the money jar, on the top shelf in the pantry, are some leather books with my writing in them."

"You want me to bury you with them?"

He clutched his son's left forearm in a final act of futile violence, his unkempt nails digging into the skin. "No. I want you to read everything."

The boy recoiled but couldn't pull himself away from the locked fingers. "You know I can't read that good. Tell me what you want me to know."

"No time, boy. No time. Your grandfather gave me wisdom that I didn't listen to, but I should have, about living with the land, in the old ways. I wrote down his words. He saw Black Sunday coming."

"How could he have seen—"

"And something happened out in the field when you were still in your ma's belly. I wrote about what I saw, but I ain't ever told anybody. You need to know, in case someday . . ."

He released his grip on his son's forearm.

"Someday *what*? Pa? Pa?"

He heard his son calling to him as his eyes fixated on the pine ceiling above the bed, now dissolving into green fields as far as he could see, rivers running to the sea, as far as he could see.

And there.

Aki.

Waiting.

APRIL

Jake howled as Jessica stood in front of him holding his wrist, trying to force his arm from stomach to chest level. "Jesus, Jess. Ease up."

She pushed even further. "This is what those hospital hand-outs told us to do for your range of motion exercises. Extended arm, shoulder high."

"Yeah, well, you don't have to take it out on me."

"What's that supposed to mean? Take *what* out on you?"

These small, passive-aggressive digs had become his feel-good default response to the more vulnerable moments he couldn't control. Like this one. "I'm the patient you never got to have, since you didn't finish school and get to be a nurse. Frustration's turning you into Nurse Ratched."

Jessica let his arm drop to his side. "You don't want my help? Fine."

She might as well have taken a sledgehammer to his shoulder. "Was that fucking necessary?"

But Jessica was already out the front door, probably sulking in that stupid garden.

Just as well. She could apologize when she came back inside.

Jake grabbed hold of his walker and stood up from the living room couch. He shuffled toward the kitchen and opened the refrigerator, hoping a beer might magically have appeared since he last checked.

Nope.

He balanced the club soda on the handle of the walker and shut the refrigerator, watching the wallpaper of Hailey's drawings swing back to stand guard over the linoleum.

Was there such a thing as too many stick figures?

He made his way back to the living room, past the crayons on the table, and flopped down on the couch next to a couple of her stuffed animals. Even some of Hailey's pajamas were still on the floor in their bedroom.

If he could, he'd clean this stuff up.

Why wouldn't Jessica?

He sank as low as he could into the cushions, searching the stuffed polyester for any support for his back. Plywood would be more comfortable than the bed in the downstairs guest room, which is where he'd been relegated until he could climb stairs. He'd probably be there for a whole lot longer than that, the way things were going with Jessica. He knew he wasn't the easiest person to deal with right now, but she'd been no cakewalk, either.

Especially since last summer.

He probably shouldn't have brought up that thing about her not finishing school, though. And she wasn't really a Nurse Ratched, either. He downed the rest of the club soda, reached for his phone resting on the arm of the couch, and scrolled to their text thread.

Hey, sorry.

Jake knew she had read-receipts turned on, because she didn't know how to turn them off, so he watched for the indication that she'd seen the message. More than likely, she had her phone turned off. She'd been doing that lately, which frustrated him, because that's how he communicated most of the time. Even if they were in the same house, sometimes texting was easier than talking.

He checked his phone one more time before pushing up from the couch and embarking on the journey to the bathroom. These small trips had become odysseys, where a whole day's worth of thoughts could unfold as he lurched down the hallway. So, he'd learned to get ahead of having to pee.

He made his way around the couch and out of the living room, then looked for Jessica through the dining room window, expecting to see her in the garden.

She was on her knees in the dirt, talking to someone.

Who was here?

He turned his head toward the living room window, but no one was parked in the driveway.

He left the walker and lumbered around the dining room table, using the chairs for support, until he could see the full width of the garden. Jessica had twirled vines around her forearms and was waving them like some kind of plant monster, laughing as she pretended to attack someone.

Someone who, best as Jake could tell, wasn't there.

———

On her way back into the house to get some water, Jessica saw Jake standing without his walker by the dining room window. She wasn't ready to make up, but she didn't want to have to peel him off the floor if he fell, so she pushed the walker within his arms' reach and headed into the kitchen.

She filled a glass and walked into the screened-in back porch, which served as their graveyard of records and receipts. The paper tombstones were scattered through the file boxes stacked on the counter above the washer and dryer, in a proprietary organizational system that only she understood.

She'd had a thought while she was playing with Hailey in the garden . . . more of a nagging, really, that there was something more she could do, and with one hand gripping her water glass, she dug through the cardboard casket that read *Hailey* for her medical records.

She found the file and started flipping through the papers for anything she might have missed, as far as treatment recommendations. They'd thrown the kitchen sink at Hailey's leukemia, but she was still desperate to find a better answer. So many advances in medicine, so many miracles, every day.

Why not her little girl?

Leukemia was so rare in kids, and the survival rate was getting better and better, which made the Hailey situation all the more frustrating . . . not responding to chemo as well as they'd hoped, bad days broken up by good ones, no real remission.

Had to be something she missed.

But nothing here.

Jessica closed the file and stuffed the folder back into the drawer. At least she felt like she'd been coming to terms with life post-diagnosis. She'd found a smile here and there, gotten a lot of healing from that garden, and focused more on her own health. And Hailey was still here, whenever Jessica wanted to color with her or play hide-and-seek. Letting Hailey go completely would ruin her, but there was no need for that.

Thank God.

Jessica returned to the kitchen to see Jake barely managing to ease down into a chair at the table. She watched him struggle to sit comfortably, and his failure to hide his pain hit a sympathetic nerve. "Can I get you anything?"

"No, I'm alright. The more I eat and drink, the more's gotta come out. Listen, about that Nurse Ratched thing—"

"Forget about it. We're both running on empty."

She watched Jake turn one of the crayons on the kitchen table with his index finger, familiar with this variation on spin-the-bottle. He'd do the same thing with the remote control on the coffee table and his phone on the kitchen counter, whenever he was hesitant to talk.

True to form, he waited until the tip pointed at him to speak. "You think we should leave these crayons out like this?"

Jessica turned to the sink and refilled her water glass. "I like having them there. Makes the place feel lived in."

"I was just thinking, we could put some of this stuff in her room, and—"

She pivoted toward him, digging her hands into her hips. "Since when have you been concerned about clutter? I'm thinking an early dinner tonight, as soon as you're back from your doctor's appointment. I'll make your favorite . . . chicken-fried steak. Rules are meant to be broken every once in a while."

Jessica glided to the fridge, opened the freezer, and pulled out a lean slab of beef. "That steer from next door is lasting a long time, huh? Another plus to eating less meat. I'll come back in to start fixing dinner when I'm done with the squash."

And she skipped out the back door to the garden, leaving her husband to his spinning crayons.

———

Jake sighed and stared at the army of stick figures still stuck with Scotch tape to the refrigerator door, before holding his walker for support and pulling himself up from his seat at the kitchen table.

No use talking to Jessica. They'd been on different planets since last summer, revolving around the same sun that was Hailey. He had no idea how to fix something that seemed to be so broken. . . . The occasional tractor repair was no problem, but metal and grease didn't have revolving emotions. Just gears.

He dragged himself back to the living room and craned his neck toward the warped front window put in by his great-grandfather. His dad had told him to keep the drafty glass panels in place, just like his dad before him had, and Jake was happy to oblige. One less thing to deal with.

He looked past the driveway and out to the patches of winter wheat bordered by their dead brethren, stems that for some reason had stalled on their journey from the dirt. Weeds crept through the bare patches of ground where the seed hadn't taken, leaving a tangled mess where there should be even rows.

Bound to happen, the guy at the feed store had said. *Considerin' how much everybody's sprayin'. Nature's gonna find a way to survive and fight.*

Jake watched the stands of sparse wheat bristle against the stiffening afternoon wind. Survive and fight. His waning will to do either right now looked nothing like the stuff of Hollywood underdog heroics. Hell, his motivation revolved around managing what he drank so he wouldn't have to shit as often.

Speaking of.

Just as he averted his gaze from the window, he saw a rustle run counter to the wind in the wheat. He squinted to make out the movement, and maybe there was nothing really going against the grain, more through it. Jessica went on her morning walks every day out there, but she'd already done that today.

He was in no position to defend himself, let alone the house. His gun was unloaded and locked in the safe with a combination known only to Jessica, per the dark deal he'd made with himself—and her—not to have an easy way out.

The chime of the old clock on the mantle startled him, and he glanced at the time.

3:00 p.m.

He looked back outside in time to see the silhouette of a man against the late afternoon sun, standing just inside the first curtain of struggling wheat. Long braids hung down his shoulders, intertwined with shirt fringes that refused to be influenced by the wind.

This was no man.

He turned toward the back door and yelled for his wife. "Jessica! Get inside!"

When his head ricocheted back to the window, the figure was pushed up against the glass, mouth widening into a gaping abyss.

Hair burning to ash.

Skin dripping off bone.

Eyes disintegrating into hollow sockets.

His heart started to pound in his chest. "Jessica!"

The back door slammed. "Jake, are you alright? Jake?"

He reflexively turned his head toward her hurried steps thumping from the kitchen, and pointed through the warped glass of the living room window.

Where now nothing but his own field stood under the cobalt-sky promise of spring, in the kind of America that the folks in Nashville wrote songs about.

———

Mark stood in the waiting room, looking over the chart for his last patient of the day. He'd taken a few shifts at this little clinic in town to cover for the slowly retiring doctor, who'd had a hard time letting go of his patients. The old-timer had actually been his pediatrician when he was a kid, and he had helped just about every family in the county one way or another.

He'd also needed to get out of the house, but still be close enough to keep an eye on his mother. His father hadn't lasted long . . . his rugged skin had quickly started to hang even further from the once-sturdy frame, angular bones rising to the surface like tipis pushing to the sky. Mark had been delivering his old man's breakfast toward the end of his second week back when he thought he saw a shadow drifting down the hall and into his dad's bedroom. By the time he'd dropped the oatmeal on the floor and rushed to his bedside, the enemy had already identified the target and taken the kill-shot.

His mother had taken his father's death quietly, like she took most things, and Mark didn't feel right leaving her to head back to the city. Not yet. She wasn't eating much, talking even less, and he knew she'd never accept paid help coming to the house.

And so, here he was.

Mark brought himself back to the chart in front of him, belonging to a guy who'd wrapped his truck around a tree last month and was coming in this afternoon for a follow-up. Finally, a patient not presenting the usual characters of COPD, obesity, type 2 diabetes, Crohn's, ulcerative co—

Sudden movement to his right drew his attention outside the clinic window, where a cat darted down the empty main drag, chasing a windblown Sonic paper bag. The familiar pang of altruistic hubris, which had convinced him he could save the world by resolving the pesky nuisance of cancer, bit at his gut.

I should be in the lab, not begging patients to stop digging their own graves with chili cheese fries.

He hated himself immediately for the thought. Being back home had blown the dust off an unfamiliar negative streak, and the cynicism ran counter to his being. He'd pursued medicine to help people and had sunk a lot of his time, and his parents' credit, into his education, residency, and research.

The bell hanging from the clinic door jangled against the glass, offering Mark an opportunity to actually help somebody in person. He knew he should be embracing the change, since what he'd been doing in medicine hadn't seemed to be filling whatever hole he needed filled. "Hang on, be right with you."

He hurried into the exam room, threw the patient's chart on the folding chair by the sink, and quickly washed his hands. Inherited crystal blue eyes studied him from the mirror, delivering his father's cancer origin story. *The enemy came from somewhere.*

"Okay, old man. I hear you. Haven't forgotten. Seek and destroy, wherever it comes from."

A confused voice punctured Mark's conversation with his reflection. "Huh? Hello?"

Mark turned off the water and straightened at the waist. He checked the chart sitting open on the counter next to the sink and dried his hands on a paper towel as he walked out of the exam room. "You must be Jake." He offered his right hand. "I'm Mark."

PEACEKEEPER

1942–1976

Be selective in your battles, sometimes peace is better than being right.

—CHIEF SHENANDOAH

Waves of pain came and went and came again in the early days of his convalescence, the temporary retreat of morphine blurring reality and nightmare, light and dark. The white elm framed by the window was his only measure of time, her shadow moving across the courtyard of the converted country estate from dawn to dusk to now . . . another night of oblivion, if he was lucky.

He stared out the warped glass at the full moon . . . the same moon that would be over the family farm in Oklahoma in a matter of hours. Hard to believe such different worlds existed under the same sky. He shouldn't even be here—the only reason he was lying in this makeshift military hospital was the draft. His father had been the fighter, fancying himself a warrior, first against the white man and then his own family. But not him. Enough beatings from Pa had taught him to avoid conflict whenever possible, but the government had forced him into this one.

A sudden shift from familiar to foreign shattered his brooding meditation.

An intruder.

There, under the tree.

"Nurse, there's somebody out there. Nurse?"

The room was quiet, save for the snores and grunts of other wounded, lonesome men. He scanned the light under the closed door for shadows.

As a boy, sometimes he would sense someone watching him as he slept, and wake to Pa swaying in the doorway, staring at him. He had the same sense now, and he kept his head turned toward the door, fearing what he might find at the foot of his bed if he shifted his eyes.

A force outside his own will torqued his neck violently, as if Pa himself was in the room. But this wasn't Pa, this was braids falling on broad shoulders, fringed leather shirt, deerskin breechcloth and leggings, raising a translucent hand.

His cracked and creased body cemented deeper into the mattress, pushed down with the same power that had made him look. There was no escape, only surrender to this faceless shadow. "What . . . what do you want?"

The door to the infirmary swung open and light flooded the room, bringing immediate normalcy.

"*Quel est le problème?*"

"Nothing, nurse. Sorry. Just a dream."

"*Mon ami, tu trembles. Qu'est-ce qui te fait peur?*"

"I don't know what scared me."

"*Je vais chercher de l'eau.*"

She left to get him some water, and he breathed as deeply as his collapsed lung would allow.

He didn't know what had scared him, but he had an idea as to why. The same knife edge of anxiety that had carved a thousand tiny cuts into his everyday life since Pa had died was slicing even deeper now, in the first breaths since seeing that . . . thing. Retribution, he was sure of it. . . . Constant punishment had taught him that consequence would find him, one way or another.

Especially for a transgression like breaking a sacred promise to his father.

He'd severed his tie to his ancestral land. And the reckoning had finally come, delivered by an apparition, perhaps more visible through the window opened by medication and sleep deprivation, but no less real.

And now he knew. His ultimate punishment was to die here, in this bed, and be buried among countless military graves in an improvised cemetery, rather than under the elm next to Pa and Grandfather.

Because there was nobody to notify at home. No next of kin. No one would even know he was gone. Ma was already somewhere in the vast unknown of the West, having left for California long before he'd been drafted. She'd half-heartedly suggested he join her when she came by the farm to watch him bury Pa. "You can go too, you know. Disappear into whatever is out West. Make a new life."

He hadn't stopped shoveling the unearthed soil, hadn't turned to look her in the eye. He couldn't. "I told him I'd stay."

"You worried about keeping a promise to that man? I should've known—you were always afraid of upsetting your father, always trying to keep the peace. You could have left with us the first time, when he still could hurt you, and you won't even leave him now that he can't. Suit yerself. But no woman's gonna want a boy who can't—"

The soothing voice of the nurse interrupted his mother's warning. "*Voici de l'eau. Maintenant, essayez de dormir un peu.*"

"Thank you . . . and yes, I'll try to get some sleep."

But no woman's gonna want a boy who can't be his own man.

Her last words to him.

He drifted into a convulsive sleep, flashes of the final air attack puncturing the film screen behind his eyes. Bombs gashing the earth from the back of his B-29, eyes closed and screams stabbing his organs with silent knives to kill the good in his heart, so he might survive this violence and all that is foreign to his being, then a sudden drop, another sudden drop, and now he is falling, falling, falling, here, into this bed, with a fractured leg, a broken soul, and a different dream of a ghost that did not seem to want to hurt him after all, but was only asking him to come home.

He stood on the sagging front porch of the farmhouse for the first time since he had left to work for the WPA, before the war. Back then, Ma's last words to him had been a constant soundtrack of fingernails on the town schoolhouse chalkboard, driving him away from the canned beets and potatoes in the cellar, away from the dust and wind and rain and floods that followed, away from the promise.

But he didn't hear her now.

He pulled open the tattered screen door, the only barrier standing between the front room and the prairie. The furniture Pa had been so proud to buy from the Sears Roebuck catalog was still in place, waiting under shrouds of dust for an ancient family to come in from the fields.

He surveyed the room in disbelief.

Nobody had touched anything.

But somebody had been there, judging by the footprints in the grit covering the pine planks. Squatters, maybe. But they'd left everything, even the single piece of linoleum by the kitchen sink that Pa had bought for Ma as a promise of more wealth to come.

First the furniture, then this whole kitchen will have that fancy lino-
leum you want. We'll see what your daddy has to say then.

His knapsack bit deep into his shoulders, weighted by the thick stack of letters from a woman in Tulsa who'd been assigned as his wartime pen pal. He set the bag on the dining room table, the physical relief of such a simple act unleashing a torrent of unexpected emotion, so overwhelming that he couldn't tell if he was happy or sad or angry.

The rush of unburdening brought him to his knees, head in his hands, until the floor turned to small puddles of mud and his eyes held nothing but the moonlight falling through the kitchen window.

The next morning, he pushed himself up from the bedroll in the back bedroom and shuffled into the kitchen, where he put on the water for coffee and absently flipped through the newspaper he'd picked up in town. His bleary eyes landed on an advertisement for ammonia fertilizer pellets, made from the nitrogen that infused the bombs he'd dropped all over Germany.

Probably using the same factories, now that the war's over.

He looked out the living room window, still caked with the dust that had buried the house almost a decade ago. He could barely make out Pa's Fordson Model F, fighting gravity by the storage shed. Stilted stop-action photographs ran through his mind, and he let them, hoping they would pass into a forgotten ether—the axe in his father's hand, the gritty Black Sunday air of the root cellar, the dirty nails dug into his forearm the afternoon Pa passed.

The last request.

He rose from the table and walked to the pantry to see if the worn leather volumes were still tucked behind the empty money jar, waiting to be read.

They were.

Maybe someday. But for now, he had work to do.

Halfway on his walk into town, he hitched a ride with a man from Oklahoma City, heading into Guymon to collect payment on ammonia pellet orders. "Faster than waiting on the mail, if you know what I mean."

He thought of his backpack full of letters, still sitting on the kitchen table. "I do, sir."

"Say, what are you doing way out here without a truck? Or even a horse?"

"Just got back from the war. Going to see about getting my family's farm up and running again. Saved the fifty bucks a month they paid us privates, and they sent me home with a little more for getting hurt. Not sure what that'll get me, but I need to start somewhere. Actually saw something about your ammonia pellets in the paper this morning."

The man didn't take his eyes off the road. "Tell you what. There's a card in the glove box with my number on it. You give me a call if you want to try out that fertilizer, and I'll make sure the first load is free."

"Don't have a phone, sir."

"Then write your name down on the back of that card, tell the feed store in town where your farm is, and I'll get you taken care of. As a thank-you for your service."

"Much obliged, sir."

He bought an older mare in town, thanked the trader for throwing in a small cart she could pull, and loaded it with a bale of hay and a few supplies to mend the fences around the small field where he'd keep her. He spent the rest of the summer repairing holes in the roof and replacing floorboards, siding, and glass, except for the living room window. At least once every day, he wanted to look through that reminder of wrath and fragility . . . the warped relic that Pa had worked so hard to afford, which had already withstood storms of dust, water, and wind.

And he wanted to honor his promise to his father to repair the land, but he knew that getting these cracked fields to produce would be like pulling blood from the bones buried under the elm.

Maybe there was something to that fertilizer.

Couldn't hurt to try.

○●○●

His fingers nervously gripped the flowers hidden behind his back as he waited for the train to pull into the station. The girl from Tulsa, whom he'd only seen in the photographs she'd sent him during the war, was coming here.

To Guymon.

What if he wasn't what she expected? What if she didn't like the farmhouse?

And the most worrisome question . . .

What if she stayed?

Worrisome, only because he was scared that, given enough time, he'd be found out, his true vulnerability exposed and abused, like the father who beat him into compliance and the mother who'd left him, twice, because she saw his sensitivity as weakness.

He'd been working the land this last year since he'd been home, rebuffing repeated requests from the young woman to visit, because he wanted everything to be as perfect as possible when she saw the farm. To his surprise and relief, the old John Deere had started with little trouble, and he'd learned how to use the ammonia fertilizer after a fair amount of trial and error. The fields had produced the first season, and this new winter wheat crop was going to be even stronger.

He couldn't keep her away any longer.

She stepped off the train, a light from the sky attached only to her, and their eyes found each other immediately. He waited until she was within arm's distance to offer the shaking bouquet, but she dropped her suitcase and threw her arms around his neck, launching her lightly perfumed blouse into his chest. Instinct pushed his hands to the small of her back, lifting and spinning her around and around until the fear drained from his heart, replaced by a deep knowing that this girl with the fair skin and blonde hair would never, ever leave.

❍❶❍❶

Their daughter tossed her auburn hair and offered her signature doe-eyed plea. "Can I go, please, Daddy, please?"

"You think I'm going to let you drive six hours to see a rock 'n' roll program?"

"Buddy Holly's never going to be closer than that—not with Jerry Lee Lewis. And Chuck Berry!"

"It's a school night."

"But it's a straight shot! Highway 64 all the way. And we can stay with Betty's aunt in Bartlesville after the show at the Civic Center. Come on, please? It's 1958, not the Stone Age, Daddy! Please?"

Those big brown eyes got him every time. "Get the aunt on the phone and we'll see."

But he already knew he was going to let her go.

Always keeping the peace.

He sank back into the new La-Z-Boy and looked out the same living room window he'd vowed never to replace when he returned from the war. Not quite the same as the brand blood vow Pa had made with himself, but at least he'd made good on his promise to never leave.

Well, the second time.

The farm was doing alright. He'd been able to finance another tractor and combine this past year, and even help a cash-poor friend by buying his adjacent parcel. This season's wheat had seen a few invaders—brown mites and aphids—but he'd paid the neighbor to crop dust those buggers with carbaryl, which did the trick. Anything to keep that wheat happy.

Speaking of, he'd tried to get in touch with the man who'd given him that ride into town and arranged for more ammonia pellets than he'd needed for two seasons to be delivered to the farm. But the guy didn't work for the fertilizer company anymore and didn't leave a forwarding number . . . just an angel who'd disappeared into the ether, to whom he owed almost everything.

But most important, fifteen years gone, and the girl from Tulsa was still here, despite the kids.

He allowed himself a small smile. The kids were fine. Everything was, really. The fifties had been a joyful relief from the war, the Dust Bowl, and the Depression of the decades before. Buddy Holly was a far cry from Woody Guthrie, that was for sure.

He was lost in gratitude, watching another thunderstorm build in the darkening skies, when a rustle in the wheat caught his eye. His son was standing in the middle of the field closest to the house, hands at his side.

He pushed up from the La-Z-Boy, opened the screen door, and stepped out onto the porch. "Get in here, boy! Lightning don't care that you're young."

His boy didn't move, only stood still as a statue, facing away, the first heavy drops of rain falling off his bare shoulders.

"And why don't you have a shirt on?"

He took the steps from the porch with a worried hurry, wondering if his son had gotten into the liquor cabinet again and drank himself catatonic. Somehow this preferred view from the bottom of a bottle had skipped a generation. Both he and his granddad had avoided becoming raging alcoholics. His own Pa, not so much.

"Son?"

His boy was motionless, rigid under the intensifying downpour.

"Son, what are you doing?"

"He called me here."

"Who?"

"The man."

"What man?"

"The man in the wheat. He has braids and a fringed leather shirt."

"Where is he? Wheat ain't tall enough to hide anyone yet."

"There."

The boy raised his hand slowly, a single shaking finger pointed straight in front of him, as a clap of thunder boomed close by.

Too close.

"Come on, son. We have to get inside."

"He says we're forgetting."

"Forgetting what?"

"The old ways."

"That's it. Come on."

He grabbed his son by the left forearm and dragged him toward the house, the boy's limp body lurching forward, head turned back toward the field, unwilling and unable to look away.

He had no problem looking away, though, because he'd been looking away for years, usually about a month before harvest season.

Right around now.

Better to just keep the peace.

He called to his son, who was watching the 1976 Super Bowl with his wife and toddler in the living room, and spun his wheelchair to face the open bedroom door.

"What's up, Pops? Need something?"

"Come on in. Close the door."

"But the game . . . ?"

"I'm taping the game on the VCR. We'll see if the fancy technology works. This'll only take a minute."

His son pointed to the worn leather books spread across the bed. "What's all this?"

"These are your grandfather's journals. I called him Pa, remember?

He started keeping them while he was at boarding school, sometime in the early 1900s."

"Wow." He tucked his shaggy hair behind his ears and flipped through a few pages, his clear blue eyes skimming the handwritten scrawl. "Incredible."

"Listen, I need you to do something for me."

"Sure, whatever you need."

"Read them."

"Now? What's the rush?"

"Well, Pa asked me to do the same thing when he was getting close to dying. Like I am. And I never—"

"Come on. You—"

"No, son. You and I both know what pancreatic cancer does, and how fast it does it. I made the choice to stay here and not spend the rest of my days in a hospital, filling this old body with toxins and prolonging the inevitable. I'm alright with it. And the train is leaving the station soon. I can tell."

"Well, looks like the train is still here. So, let's—"

"I got a couple more things to say. Three, actually. Sit for a minute."

His son eased down on the bed next to the journals. "I'm listening."

"First, keep this place in wheat, alright? That USDA secretary's still bullying everybody to get into corn and paying 'em to farm every inch of space. You know his favorite saying: *Get big or get out.* And I don't think it's right."

"How come?"

He shrugged his shoulders and shifted his seat in the wheelchair. "Maybe he's crooked. In bed with agribusiness. . . . Could be he's wanting to increase corn supply to push prices down and drive family farmers like us out of business, so his fast-food, commercial farming, and feed-lot buddies make out. Sounds crazy. I don't know. But I'm telling you, everything we eat is going to have some by-product of corn in it soon. Meat, bread, everything. Food's gonna be cheap, but bad for you. And I don't want this place to be a part of it."

"But if it's the only way to survive as a family farm—"

"You'll figure it out. Just keep the wheat."

His son held up both of his hands, in mock surrender. "Okay, okay. I'll figure it out."

"Second thing is, I never told you how proud I was when you came back from Vietnam. Not just going over there to fight, but what you've done here since then. Pouring yourself into this place, talking about starting a family someday. You could've gone a lot of different ways. But I'm proud of you."

His son studied his socked feet. "Nobody seemed too proud of us when we came back."

"I know, I know. I'm ashamed of how the country handled that. And war is already worse than hell. I've been there."

"Yes, you have."

"And that's the other thing I wanted to talk to you about."

"You've told me a lot of stories about the war, Pops."

He shook his head. "I never told you about this. Never told anybody, not even your mother. When I was recovering in the hospital, I saw something."

"Saw something?"

"Yeah, at the foot of my bed."

"And?"

"I think I saw what you saw when you were a kid."

"Huh?"

"The man in the wheat."

His son pushed up from the bed and stared straight ahead, too hurt to look at him. "What? You acted like I was making that up. Told me I was seeing things."

"I guess I wanted to pretend like you'd never seen it, because I wanted to pretend like I never had either."

"What did it say to you?"

His gaze shifted to the bedroom window, which framed the two of them in a single pane. "Didn't say anything, but it had braids and a fringed leather shirt, like you said."

His son turned to him. "I can't believe—"

Still looking at the reflection, he offered his hands, cradling an explanatory plea. "Avoidance was how I made my peace with it. I'm sorry, but it is what it is."

"Anything else you've been holding back?"

He turned his head back toward his son, but was still unable to make direct eye contact. "I might've seen it more recently, over the last few years. I mostly talked myself into believing it was just a shadow. And I have a feeling your grandfather might have seen it too. That's why he told me about the journals, right before he died. I think he wrote about it."

"Wouldn't you know, since you read them?"

"Never did."

"Why not?"

He looked away again, only now realizing that a character trait he'd relied on so heavily might also have been a flaw. "Avoidance again, I guess. Learned to do that as a kid, served me pretty well. Your grandfather was a difficult man to live with, and I didn't want to go back there. Just wanted to get along with what I'd been given, which meant loving your mom and raising you and your sister. And finding some harmony with the land here. Not ghost hunting."

His son's glare softened. "Always the peacekeeper, right?"

"I suppose. And before you ask, I don't need to read them now. Ignorance is bliss for a dying man."

"So why should I, then?"

He breathed as deep as his failing lungs would allow. "You might find some answers, or guidance, that I couldn't give you. Maybe something about what we both saw."

"You got it, Pops. I'll get to them. And don't worry about not talking to me about what we saw or didn't see. I don't know if I would've been able to have a conversation about it, anyway. Part of me still thinks that maybe . . . it was a dream."

"Me too. Another reason I didn't put much stock into it. I didn't even know if it was real. But now, as I'm getting ready to go—"

His son stepped behind the wheelchair. "Hey. Only place you're going is in front of the TV. Second half of the Super Bowl has probably started by now, and our Cowboys are giving the Steelers a hell of a game. And the wife's almost got supper ready."

"Well then, push your old man in there."

His son guided him to his favorite spot in the living room, where they ate meatloaf and mashed potatoes from TV tray tables and watched in agony as the Steelers' Steel Curtain helped beat their Cowboys, 21–17, the loss sealed by a final Roger Staubach interception in the end zone.

He offered a small smile to the hallway mirror on the way back to his room, where he eased out of his wheelchair and into the cotton layers of his winter bed. A few breaths later he'd already drifted off to sleep, having finally made his peace with the only name left unchecked on his mental list. And the unkept leather-bound promise between son and father traded generations, when the train came to get him on the second Sunday of spring. . . a morning as bright and crisp as the after-church crowd waiting on Frank's fried chicken could remember.

MAY

Jake shuffled across the sidewalk in front of the clinic, late again. This time he had an excuse, though. More like an explanation, which Jessica had told him didn't *excuse* anything, but counted as a step forward from the lies he used when he was drunk or high.

He'd had to wait for her to get home from work, since all they had now was the Tercel. Not only that, but he was moving so slowly, one lumbering step at a time. First the wheelchair, then the walker, then the cane. And now, nothing but his own power to support him. The rehabilitation process seemed to be working, in spite of his bitching and moaning.

The doctor held the door open for him as he moved into the waiting room. He still couldn't remember the guy's name, even after four visits.

"Looks like somebody's been putting in PT overtime."

"Yeah, the wife pushes me pretty hard."

"You're lucky to have her."

"I suppose." Jake followed the doctor into the exam room, each excruciating step a flashback to the brutal physical therapy sessions Jessica had been putting him through. The wheelchair work of flexibility and arm-strengthening exercises had seemed tough, but they turned out to be a seated cakewalk compared to what had come next.

The minutiae of relearning something like walking, which he couldn't remember learning in the first place, had amounted to a tedious hammering of a million small nails into his legs.

Just to move a few feet across the living room floor.

His frustration had blinded him to any sense of progress, besides the ability to walk like a dying T-Rex, so he was a little surprised when the doctor looked up from his clipboard twenty minutes later. "Nice work, Jake. Everything looks pretty good. You're way ahead of schedule. Don't forget about the dietary changes—more whole foods, less packaged and processed."

Jake heaved a sigh of relief. He knew he'd gotten a second chance that he didn't deserve, and he found himself holding his breath every time there was a chance of bad news.

"Thanks, Doctor . . . what was your last name, again? I know you've told me before, but I keep forgetting."

"Mark. Just call me Mark. And you probably have post-traumatic amnesia from your brain injury. Short-term memory can be affected for several weeks or months. Very normal to experience that."

"Okay, thanks, Mark. See you in a couple of weeks."

———

Mark held the clinic door open again for Jake and watched him maneuver to a beat-up Toyota Tercel, moving like a man fifty years his senior, but moving. He'd lost weight since the accident. A lot, according to his chart. An IV diet, then hospital food, followed by a determined wife cooking healthier meals and making him do PT, had helped knock his obesity down a couple rungs. Even his blood pressure looked better.

He exhaled as Jake eased himself into the driver's seat. Every week since he'd been here, he'd been diagnosing versions of the same story. Obesity? Check. Type 2 diabetes? Yep. High blood pressure?

Of course. Depression? Likely, given his addiction. Not to mention the diverticulitis and ulcerative colitis that had put Jake in the hospital the first time.

Jake had mentioned in passing that his father was battling Parkinson's, and the dated patient notes left behind by the outgoing doctor had mentioned early indications of leukemia in Jake's daughter.

And on top of all this, the accident.

Bad luck?

Maybe. But he knew Jake had been raised on that farm, just like Jake's father, and his father before him, so he had to know every landmark like the back of his hand. Especially an old elm, which he'd told Mark he'd crashed into while checking his wheat.

After midnight, with a shit-ton of booze and Oxy running through him?

Something besides bad luck was going on.

In Jake, in Jake's family, in this town. That enemy he'd seen take out his old man seemed to be taking over the community.

Why? And why now?

Mark watched the Tercel pull away and stop at the intersection, one taillight oblivious of the need to cooperate with the other. He turned from the plate-glass clinic door and headed back to his office, eyeing the box of chemo research gathering dust in the corner next to the file cabinet.

He hadn't looked at that stuff since he left Oklahoma City. Maybe next weekend.

He shoved a blue Mead notebook, which he'd been using as a journal in between patients, into his briefcase and hit the office lights. His father's truck was waiting a block away, in an attempt to leave a makeshift designated parking space in front of the clinic for the folks who had a harder time getting around.

Like Jake.

Mark frowned as he pulled the door handle and climbed into the massive cavern that was the cab of his father's Duramax. Horse to water, right? He could tell his patients to eat better and exercise, but he couldn't make them. Only thing really in his power was prescribing pharmaceuticals, and he was so tired of using chemical Band-Aids to cover gaping internal wounds.

What bothered him more was the possibility that he could be doing the same thing with his chemo research. All this time, he'd thought cancer was the disease. But something had to be causing the cancer he'd been trying to cure, right?

That's the enemy his old man had been talking about.

Cancer doesn't just rise up out of nowhere.

He wasn't going to be seeking and destroying anything from the driver's side of this Duramax, so listening to music would have to do for now. He searched for the artist he'd first heard on the way home, when his father was dying.

Bison something . . .

Bridge.

Bison Bridge.

He found the album, plugged his phone into the truck stereo, and pulled onto North Main Street, ready to not think about the potential futility of his career.

He passed the Dollar Store, then McDonald's, Mr. Burger, and finally Walmart, where Main became Mile 30. Somewhere around Little Goff Creek, he let go of the day and drifted into the music.

My brother Tom fought your holy war
Came back different than he was before
He got the flower in his vein
He got the nightmare in his brain

So tell me your Jesus turned water into wine
And tell me he healed a beggar man born blind
Then why is he leaving my brother behind

Well, that was a fair enough question. Mark could understand where this guy was coming from. Absolutes like religion and medicine didn't seem quite as . . . absolute anymore.

Don't send your son
Don't send anyone
Walk these streets with me
And tell me what you see
If you ain't surprised
Then your eyes just ain't the seeing kind
If I had your strength
I'd fix what I find

Probably bordering on blasphemy in some Sunday circles, especially out here.

Mark turned the volume up.

Maybe I can't deal in water or in wine
Maybe I can't heal a beggar man born blind
But I ain't gonna leave my brother behind
My eyes are the seeing kind
And there ain't enough love out here sometimes

Not enough love? Probably true.

But cancer, obesity, neurogenerative disease?

Nobody was going to solve those kinds of problems with love.

Somebody willing to do God's dirty work would have to handle that.

———

Jessica watched the Tercel roll to a stop behind the wrecked F-150, which was still waiting for a visit from the insurance adjuster.

She met Jake on the front porch, kissed him on the cheek, and held the screen door open as he shuffled into the house. She really was trying to do right by him . . . feeding him out of the garden, dialing back the meat, practically forcing him to do his PT, and dodging his complaints as they ricocheted between the farmhouse walls.

All this, while struggling to keep herself from asking whether he really wanted to be here anymore. Whether he might try again. Whether he was sneaking booze or pills. Whether he actually gave a shit.

She doubted these were questions she should be asking a suicidal addict, so she had to come up with others. "How'd the doctor's appointment go? Almost done with those, right?"

"Pretty good, I guess. Mark says I'm coming along."

"So now you're calling the doctor by his first name."

"I just can't remember his last."

She pointed to the couch and helped ease him down. "I guess we went to high school together, but I can't place his family farm."

"They're on the other side of town, way, way out. His dad was huge . . . hands like dinner plates. Overheard somebody at the feed store talking about how he just died."

"Like you almost did."

"Yeah, almost, I guess."

Jessica headed to the kitchen, where she saw Hailey buckled into her chair by the table, making paste with Cheerios and milk, head flung back in joy.

God, she loved that kid. Almost too much, if that was even possible.

She turned to the pantry, scrolling her phone for a recipe she'd used back in college, and within a couple of minutes was smashing black beans against the side of a bowl with a fork. She added an egg from one of their hens, some breadcrumbs, and leftover cooked quinoa, and was spooning the patties onto the griddle when Jake shuffled in.

"Burgers!"

"Kind of."

"Kind of?"

She waved at the ingredients on the counter. "There's no meat in them."

"That looks a lot like what you made on one of our first dates."

"That's right."

"What the hell kind of a burger is that?"

Jessica nudged him with an elbow. "Why don't you make yourself useful and set the table."

"Hey, I'm glad I didn't, you know?"

"Didn't what?"

"Die. I mean, I know that whole thing was over three months ago now, but—"

"I know, Jake. I know."

RAINMAKER

1976–2002

Before our white brothers arrived to make us civilized men, we didn't know any kind of money and consequently, the value of a human being was not determined by his wealth.

—LAME DEER, Lakota Holy Man

He drove Highway 412 out of Guymon, on the endless stretch of asphalt cutting through the maze of expanding corn fields.

Hard to blame a guy for wanting to make a buck on corn these days. *And if you can't beat 'em, join 'em.*

His pops was probably turning over in his grave under the elm, and not only because he'd joined the rest of Oklahoma in double-cropping with corn. He'd also just bought the neighbor's parcel to the west. The paperwork on the passenger seat sealed the deal, with a massive loan tied to the farm.

He didn't want to miss out on the land grab, so he'd jumped on the debt bandwagon with everybody else. Nobody was worried, though. The money had been so good these past few years. International demand for both corn and wheat had doubled, sometimes tripled, how much profit they could turn.

And he had to play the game to make this kind of rain.

He limped toward the house, his right foot dragging against the porch stairs. The shrapnel from Da Nang, buried deep in his hip, had decided to be more of a bitch today than usual. Nothing to complain about, compared to what some of his buddies brought home. That kill-yourself kind of crazy had skipped over him.

He threw the newly recorded deed on the dining room table, next to the October issue of *Rolling Stone*. Elton John was on the cover, but he'd hadn't bought the magazine at the mini-mart in Guymon because he wanted to know more about that fruit-ball. *Rolling Stone* was the only publication willing to print whatever the U.S. Secretary of Agriculture had said to get himself kicked out of the government. The daily newspaper wouldn't even disclose the exact words.

He understood why, after he leaned over the table and flipped through the magazine to the comment Earl Butz had made.

"I'll tell you what the coloreds want. It's three things: first, a tight pussy; second, loose shoes; and third, a warm place to shit. That's all!"

His eyes widened. Maybe his pops had been right about that guy.

The loudest, most important government voice in agriculture, telling everybody what to do with their farms—"Get big or get out" . . . "take on more debt" . . . "pack in more industrial corn to feed cows and corn syrup"—had also said *that*?

He closed the magazine and headed to the fridge to get a beer, a twinge of apprehension starting to surface.

That racist fuck better not have been wrong about the rest.

O●O●

The deputy's hand bumped the paunch lumped over his belt as he pulled the holster snap on his service revolver. He'd never had a distress call like this, with someone he knew from childhood. "Come on, man. Just put the gun down. Your being gone isn't going to help anything."

The shell of the man cowering in the corner of the barn kept the shotgun barrel wedged under his own neck. "The hell it's not. My life insurance policy is worth more than this land is now."

"They don't pay on suicide."

He lifted his chin toward the deputy. "Well, you kill me then."

"I'm not going to kill you." A single trail of sweat trickled from his temple, diffusing into the stiff fabric of his uniform. "Just put the gun down."

"Three years I've tried to get somebody to listen."

"Put the gun down, and I'll listen." The deputy watched his friend drop the shotgun barrel to the floor, still white-knuckling the grip. He took his hand off his own firearm. "I'm listening."

"I did and saw things over there that no human should ever have to do or see, ever."

"I know. I was in Vietnam too."

"I drink more than my granddad ever did, just trying to make some of the pictures in my head go away. But nobody cares. Government doesn't care. They made their decisions behind their big desks that sent me to kill the yellow man, blamed me when I came home, and then they take all of this away. After what I gave to them."

The deputy took a cautious step forward. "Is that really what this is about? Vietnam?"

"I tried to do the right thing. Started a family. Worked hard. Buried my pops out there under the elm by the creek, with his dad and Choctaw granddad. I made that coffin myself, right here in this barn. Shoveled that dirt with my own hands. We've been on this land longer than Oklahoma has been a state. They're telling me I have to auction it off."

"You're not alone. Grain embargo hit everybody around here hard."

"Maybe. But I'm going to die before they take this land from my family. At least my wife and kid will have something to survive on."

The deputy took another step toward him, holding out his hand. "I told you, they don't pay on suicides. How about you give me the gun?"

The shotgun's tremble slowed to a soft tremor, his friend's fingers loosening just a little around the grip. "How did you find me?"

He dropped his hand to his side. More conversation, less pressure. "Your wife's been worried. She's called us a few times, asking what to do when your mood started getting darker. And when you didn't show up in Guymon this afternoon for—"

"Guymon?"

"Yeah, you were supposed to meet her there for a meeting with the bank."

"I told her I wasn't going to meet somebody so they could tell me what a failure I was."

"Well, she thought you'd be there. And when you didn't show up, she called us from the bank. I came straight here." The deputy again offered the hand that wasn't on the holster. "You know, the government approved a lot of money to help guys like you last week. I'm surprised you didn't hear about that."

"I stopped watching the news a long time ago."

"Maybe that's what your meeting was about."

"Maybe."

"Will you give me the gun?"

"Will you give it back?"

"One step at a time."

The deputy noticed his friend's quaking shoulders settle slightly as the shotgun traded hands. "And listen, man, for what it's worth, you can get out of this and make something else happen. I'm not sure what, but you've always been able to pull things off."

"I don't need a self-help seminar right now."

"I'm just saying, I saw it in you when we were growing up. You could get yourself out of trouble when the rest of us would be grounded for weeks. And remember when we wanted to go see The Who in Oklahoma

City? We didn't have a car, let alone money, or tickets, or permission. You made it all happen. You were always making things happen."

"This isn't the same."

"The hell it's not. You're a rainmaker."

He looked around the main hall of the Masonic lodge, recognizing a few of the other area farmers who'd survived the 1980s downturn. They probably hadn't all tried to kill themselves, but they must've gotten the same invitation he did.

A company man had pulled into his farm last week, claiming to be some kind of scientist. An agronomist, which was something he'd never heard of. "Hey, friend. I was driving by and noticed some pigweed in your field. I think I can help you with that. Don't mind this fancy word on my business card. . . . I'm just an expert in soil management and crop production."

He'd been using atrazine and 2,4-D as herbicides, but the company man thought he could do better. And he was more than a little concerned about weeds growing into his long-awaited profit, finally realized with a little help from Mother Nature, a few chemicals, and Uncle Sam. The right balance between carbaryl and fertilizer made damn near anything grow, including pigweed, so he'd accepted the offer to learn more about this weedkiller during a free dinner at the Masonic lodge.

And now that he was here, he had to admit that the evening was starting out particularly well. His older son had just won an album in the raffle, his wife was getting a free night out with the wives' club, and best of all, tenderloin kept appearing on his plate.

The company man squeezed his shoulder as he passed by, working the room. "Did I mention, all you can eat?"

Before dessert, he showed some slides with graphs and tables, and said his company's weedkiller was not only safe, but did the best job out there. "Couldn't put this in the presentation, but what I will say is that we know what we're doing. We made Agent Orange to take down the commies' vegetation in Vietnam, and everyone knows how good that worked."

He'd been there. He knew.

"Any vets here?"

Almost all the adult males in the room raised their hands.

"Well, thank you for your service. I'm sure you know that 2,4-D was one of two active chemicals in Agent Orange, and I'm here to tell you, you can stop using that on your fields, because what we're offering is much, much safer."

The slide of dead pigweed on the screen dissolved into the young child with chemical burns staring at the end of his M16, just before he took the shrapnel hit.

Didn't take much to send him back to Da Nang.

He excused himself and limped away, hoping that if he escaped the room, he could somehow erase the scene. The men's room was thankfully empty, and he splashed water from the sink faucet on his face before taking stock in the mirror. He was still hiding plenty of scars under these Carhartts, and not just from the shrapnel. But he hadn't seen a shrink, like he'd promised he would after he almost blew his own head off. He'd convinced his wife he didn't need therapy now that things were turning around. And he didn't—he took pride in manning up and pulling through.

What his cop friend had said about being a rainmaker had spoken to his ego enough to get him focused again. That kick start had been all the therapy he'd needed. And after these last few years on the farm, he did feel like a rainmaker . . . able to buy his family whatever they wanted for Christmases and birthdays, adding a new combine for himself and just-because surprises for the wife and sons. Hell, just yesterday he'd bought all three of them new Apple computers.

He was making things happen.

This weedkiller might help him get even better things.

And the dark memory he'd had was just that . . . a memory.

He wiped his face with a paper towel, and before walking back into the lodge room, he took a last glance at his reflection.

I am alright.

Better than alright.

He placed an order at the feed store the next time he was in town, and the company man delivered the product two weeks later. He could smell death in the first bucket, and the rep winked at him when his older son's nose wrinkled at the stench.

"Perfectly safe, kid. See this label? EPA says so."

After a quick demonstration of how to mix the coffee-brown sludge with surfactant and water in the spray tank, the rep stepped back into his sedan with a grin. "Welcome to a new world, boys. And listen, if you really want to make your life easier and lower your costs, use it as a desiccant on that wheat before you harvest. No need to wait on Mother Nature to dry it out."

His son watched the fancy car pull away, waiting until the rep was out of earshot. "Dad, what's a desuh-can?"

"Desiccant . . . a chemical that we spray on the crop, so it all dies at the same time. Don't have to swath and dry the wheat . . . just straight cut and harvest. Saves time and money."

"So we're killing what we're harvesting? Why would—"

"Hush, boy. Apple's dead when you eat it, right? Everything dies, that's a fact. Just like the Springsteen song says."

"What Springsteen song?"

"'Atlantic City.' I clearly got a lot more important things to teach you than I thought." He climbed on the tractor and pulled the tank across the lower forty, distributing the mixture out of the boom arms.

His son was waiting for him by the drum of weedkiller when he got back, wanting to help. "I can mix the next batch, Dad. I paid attention."

He watched his son pour the sludge and surfactant into the spray tank at the right ratio, but recoiled as his kid shoved the hose into the mixture before turning the water on. "Goddamnit, Jake, the water!"

He cranked the spigot handle, thinking a small amount of the sludge and surfactant had probably already siphoned through the hose and back into the well, but he wasn't overly concerned. The well was deep, and the weedkiller was safe. After all, the EPA said so—and that company man seemed like a hell of guy. Why would he lie?

He pulled the hose from the tank and let the water run for a couple of seconds. A little foamy, but probably just air bubbles.

"Dad, I'm thirsty."

He handed the hose to his son. From the corner of his eye, he saw the Choctaw ranch hand jump the roundpen fence and run toward them, and before Jake had even taken a drink, the old Indian had ripped the hose away.

"Evil water. Stay away."

Nobody was going to tell his son what to do, especially an old Indian. "Leave the boy alone, hear? Mind your business."

He took the hose from Jake and looked down at the foamy stream, almost clear now, before turning to face the Choctaw, staring at him while he drank.

"Tastes fine."

O●-O●

He stared across the field at what would soon be golden grain, waving in the wind.

That's straight out of "America the Beautiful" right there.

His older son was silhouetted against the wheat, standing straight and still as a statue, already much taller than the crop. Which wasn't saying much, because while they were going to yield a shit-ton this year, the plants hadn't really reached their usual height.

But at least his son was growing.

Growing, like their bank account.

And this was what made America great.

Ingenuity.

Free enterprise.

Capitalism.

The company knew he needed a better weedkiller and made him one. And then, just a couple of years ago, they started fixing the corn seeds to be resistant to their product, so there was no real limit on how much he could spray.

They weren't making special wheat seeds yet, so he could still use the weedkiller as a desiccant, like he was about to do now. This strategy had been a game changer. . . . Sure, he might have to use a lot, but in two weeks, this whole spread would be evenly dried. He'd harvest soon after, then plant corn.

Double-cropping was paying off. The yield on both corn and wheat had been incredible this year, so profitable that he'd been able to pay off this combine his wife had been so worried about. She'd been concerned about buying out their neighbor to the east, too, but now they had close to sixteen hundred acres, producing all year long. Jake was going to have a hell of a Christmas, and so was she.

Rainmaker, right?

He sat in the air-conditioned cockpit and looked across the field at the old elm, wishing his great-grandfather could see what had become of the land. He didn't know much about him, other than the faint, diffused stories about how he'd been granted this homestead in the late 1800s and raised corn, squash, and beans in the old ways.

The three aunts, or sisters, or something like that.

He'd probably know more if he'd read those journals his pops had asked him to read. But what was the point? The past wasn't going to pay for the trips to the Gulf they'd started taking, or the new Escalade for the wife.

Things were good.

Don't fix what ain't broke.

He did know that his grandfather had been the first to use a tractor on this land, because he still had the Fordson and John Deere under cover in the shop. His pops had done a lot, too, doubling down on fertilizer and getting the wheat back up after the Dust Bowl years.

His daydream shifted to the real dream he was sitting in.

This new combine was a hell of a present to himself. Practically drove on its own.

He'd outfitted the rig with new spray booms, which meant his job this afternoon would mostly entail hanging out in the cockpit with George Strait, Randy Travis, and Alan Jackson. With any luck, he'd be almost done before his wife's birthday dinner tonight. And by the time his hangover cleared tomorrow, there'd be plenty of time to finish the job.

He'd have to hustle to get the corn in the ground this year, though. Plow, fertilize, plant, before the heat of summer hit.

He wished he could use the same fertilizer on his older son. Jake was pushing thirteen years old, and while he was getting pretty tall, he had yet to sprout a pubic hair. He only knew because he'd walked in on him brushing his teeth naked before bed a couple of nights ago. Bald as a cue ball, poor kid.

His wife had said they should consider themselves lucky to have a kid at all, let alone two healthy boys. The young couple they'd just bought out couldn't have kids, and neither could his sister-in-law. Which didn't make much sense. Used to be, if you wanted to get somebody pregnant, the most you'd need was the backseat of a 302 Mach 1 Mustang. In green, if possible.

Worked for him.

Jake was still standing out there in the last stretch of wheat, facing the setting sun. He'd been a peculiar boy from the start. Quiet. *Introverted*, according to his mother.

But the kid was conscientious, worked hard, and did his chores, so he'd given up trying to pull him out of his shell. Talking didn't help much in farming, and his younger brother more than made up for that. Wouldn't shut up, in fact. Wasn't much for work, either. Or school. Funny kid, though.

Jake was paying attention to the family trade. Busting his ass, actually.

And someday this would be his, if he ever came out of the field.

"Jake! Get over here!"

Probably has that damn iPod thing in his ears.

"Jake!" He climbed out of the combine and approached his son, covering the twenty yards quietly before putting his arm around him. "Let's go, son."

A humming vibration infused his fingers as he touched the boy's shoulder.

Trembling.

The kid was trembling.

"What's wrong?"

His son raised his hand slowly, a single shaking finger pointed straight ahead, just as he'd done in this same field when he was a kid. "He called me here."

"Who?"

"The man."

"What man?"

"The man in the wheat."

And he didn't ask what the man had said, didn't need to, because everything was the same, this repeated fleeting scene from a bad horror movie, the grabbing of his son by the wrist and dragging him toward the house, the boy's body lurching forward, head turned back toward the field, unwilling and unable to look away.

JUNE

—Monday—

Jessica walked along the dry creek bed, the homestretch of her daily afternoon meditation that took her around almost the entire five-mile circumference of the sixteen-hundred-acre farm. Her self-imposed rule was, by the time she got to the old elm, to say out loud something she was grateful for.

Some days were easier than others.

Today was not one of those days.

She still didn't have an acceptable expression of thanks as she approached the tree. Her fingers traced the chunks of trunk taken out by the front end of the F-150—the gouges spoke to the heavy trauma of absorbing the truck's momentum, but the old tree had held her ground. The few roots raised from the dirt almost seemed to scoff at the true impact of the steel. . . . *That all you got, Detroit? Bring it.*

Jessica looked up at the late spring flowers turning to leaves on the massive branches. She'd given plenty of thanks that her husband had lived, but should she be grateful that the tree survived? Nature had won, in a way. Survived.

She was formulating and reformulating the right way to say thank-you when she noticed a strangely shaped piece of wood wedged deep under one of the roots. She bent down to get a closer look, pulling out the splintered, decayed fragment, held together by cemented soil and the faintest remnant of a rusted nail.

What would have been buried here?

Maybe one of Jake's ancestors had buried a dog out here, or someone before their time had hidden something they didn't want found. Jessica's heart raced at the idea of the mystery, somewhere new to put her attention besides her garden. She'd grown up wishing Stephen King was her dad, with books like *It* and *Misery* her constant companions until she left for college.

But this was the real thing.

Jessica tucked the decomposed clue in her pocket and hurried back to the barn to get a shovel.

She settled for the first thing she found, a pickax leaning against one of the empty stalls, and almost bowled her husband over on her way out.

Jake staggered backward, catching himself on an old hitching post. "Where's the fire?"

"Jake, Jake, let's go!"

"Where?"

"Out to the elm!"

"What? Why—"

"I'll explain on the way." She watched him struggle to push off the post. "But it'll take you two years to walk out there. I'll go get the car. Stay here."

She skidded to a stop in front of him, trying to stay patient as he slunk into the passenger seat and shut the door. "I was on the porch and saw you running, all the way from the field. That's why I came out to the barn. What's up?"

Jessica fished a small piece of wood from her jeans pocket. "This."

"An oversized splinter?"

She cleared her throat impatiently. "No. Well, yes. But I found this under one of the elm roots. There's a little nail attached. . . . I think something's buried under that tree."

"So now we're digging for treasure?"

"You don't have to do anything but watch."

The Tercel coasted to a stop a few yards from the tree. Jessica bolted out of the car and trotted to the elm. "Come on, see what I find!"

"Nope. I'll stay right here. I don't think there's a damn thing under that tree."

She tried to use the pickax to loosen the dirt under the exposed roots, getting progressively more aggressive with her technique, until she was pile-driving the pointed edge into the ground.

She pushed a poof of air from her bottom lip, encouraging the sweaty wisps of hair to get out of her eyes. "Why isn't this working? This dirt is so effing hard."

Jake leaned his hand out the window with a dismissive wave. "Just dirt. Same here as everywhere."

Jessica pounded the pickax into the dirt a few more times, until the head snapped at the base. "Damn it."

Jake rolled up the window. "Looks like we're done here. Sun's getting low, anyway."

They drove the perimeter road back to the house in silence. He touched her shoulder. "Hey, let's go into town for dinner. No cooking tonight. I'm sure my folks wouldn't mind hanging out in the main house and watching the big TV."

Her deflated excitement took in a little more air. "That would be nice."

"I'll even take a shower. Wash all the dark parts."

"So, what I hear you saying is that I should probably eat something now, because we won't be going to dinner until close to midnight."

"Maybe. But I'll hustle. If we get home early enough, who knows what might happen."

Human touch.

What a concept.

Jessica didn't wait for Jake to pry himself out of the car and summit the porch stairs. She flew into the house, calling a hello into Hailey's room on her way to the shower and a long overdue night out, having found yet another thing to be grateful for.

———

Mark stood on his parents' front porch, watching the sun go down on another Monday away from the lab. He'd called his boss today, and after he'd explained the continuing need to be near his mother, the hesitation in the research head's voice was all he needed to hear.

So, another Monday wasn't all the sun was going down on. Understandable, given that he'd been gone almost three months and chewed up all of his accrued vacation time, sick days, and bereavement allowance.

And finally, his boss's patience.

Mark sank into the porch swing and opened the Pabst Blue Ribbon he'd brought outside. PBR had always been his old man's go-to, and he held the can to the sky in a toast.

"Hope you're doing better now, wherever you are."

The cobalt blue above dissolved into a deep purple, as the soundtrack of early-season cicadas lulled him into a slow trance.

His gaze had just settled somewhere between the horizon and the gradient of darker sky, when his focus was stolen by the red-tailed hawk arcing into the porch roofline and out of sight.

What now?

For the first time in his life, he didn't have a plan.

He was used to not having a girlfriend. Or a date. Or a family of his own. Or any of the other Instagram moments he wished he could post, so friends he didn't really have could approve of his beautiful life.

But a plan?

He'd always had one of those . . . didn't improvise, didn't take risks, didn't cross the double yellow line, didn't throw caution to the wind.

The first pinprick stars lit the steel-blue bullet points in the sky for all these things he didn't do. What kind of life is that, to be defined more by what you don't do than what you do?

Mark took a draw of the evening air and closed his eyes. One of the Bison Bridge songs he'd had on repeat on the drive from Oklahoma City creeped over the cicada rhythm, words he'd heard a thousand times, but never really heard.

If those old boots don't fit no more
Leave 'em where they are outside the door
Let me see your feet slide across the floor
Maybe those boots don't fit no more

He pushed up from the porch swing and bowed to the empty prairie, nodding his head before shuffling his socked feet back and forth, up and down the entire length of the whitewashed planks, to the melody he was now singing out loud.

Which was strange.

Because he didn't sing.

Didn't dance, either.

———

Jake rolled onto his back, matching his own breathing to Jessica's soft snores. The measured inhales and exhales left a relative calm in his already satiated being. He was grateful for this semblance of normalcy. . . . Dinner had been decent, and what came next had been even more satisfying than the porterhouse. Which was saying something.

He turned his head toward the open bedroom window and followed the cascade of stars dropping into the farm's back forty. This is what ordinary people did, right? They ate, made love, slept, worked.

Why couldn't he be ordinary?

He knew why, of course. And the reasons he'd tried to kill himself were still there, the failing farm being the most likely to induce an understanding nod from the regulars at Frank's Diner.

The biggest reason, though, nobody would believe.

Couldn't do much about that, but maybe the farm wasn't a totally lost cause. He pressed into the mattress until his back rested against the headboard. There had to be some option for field productivity that he hadn't exhausted.

Had to be.

Jake eased out of the bed as quietly as his massive frame would allow and pulled on the clothes crumpled in a pile by the bed. He headed out to the Tercel and released the emergency brake, letting the car roll out of earshot before popping the clutch and starting the engine. He rolled down the window and drove along the small access road cutting through the wheat, listening to the tires fight the dry dirt for traction and watching the dust billow in the rearview mirror.

Aphids bashed into moths in the harsh shafts of halogen light as he pulled up in front of the old elm. The small divots from Jessica's pickax were barely visible, and Jake allowed a small spark of curiosity to surface. Maybe something was buried out here, but anybody who might have known was long gone. His dad had never said anything and sure as hell hadn't buried anything under this tree. Probably never touched a shovel to this land again after he bought that huge combine.

This land.

Sixteen hundred acres, ten times what his dad had started with in the late seventies. Unreal. The farm didn't look as big from where he sat now, in the torn-up fabric seat, headlights trained on the abandoned rows dying into the old elm. His dad had grown this place into one of the bigger private pieces outside Guymon, and around the time this '95 Tercel was born, he'd started double-cropping wheat and corn, so the fields were always producing.

Rainmaker.

That's what his dad had liked to call himself. Didn't mind when other people called him that, either. He remembered helping his dad plant corn as soon as the wheat harvest was done, around this time of year—anytime from late May to early July, depending on the weather. Those childhood and adolescent memories were mostly of abundance; seemed like there were two decent crops a year, no matter what.

He'd followed the same formula as his dad, right down to the herbicide and pesticide schedule, but he hadn't seen nearly the same kind of yield over the last four or five harvests. Maybe a couple of low-water years were to blame, or bad luck with the exotic aphids and this pigweed, who knows.

Maybe he just didn't have it in him. Being fat and addicted didn't help his sense of optimism, either.

Jessica's tough-love words, not his.

He'd neglected the fields these last few months because of the wreck, and he was late to harvest. Too late, really. But he hadn't gotten out of bed tonight to take a drive and think about what he couldn't do.

If he could kill the fields quickly and evenly, they might dry in time to salvage at least some of the yield. So tomorrow, he'd desiccate what was left of the wheat with weedkiller, just like his dad did.

Then reassess.

A shadow played across the old elm, probably cast by a squirrel dancing in the headlights. A prick of illumination to the left caught his attention, and he looked toward the house to see their bedroom light on. Jessica had probably woken up to no one next to her and was worried he was doing something he shouldn't be.

He put the car in reverse, turning to the right as he backed up. The headlights swept across the wheat and landed on a man, standing fifty yards away, between two rows.

Jake rolled down the window. "Hey, you lost?"

He dropped the Tercel into first and eased toward the figure, a dark and motionless silhouette against the wheat.

"You can't hang out here."

Thirty yards away.

"You hear me? My .38'll be here way before the cops are."

Twenty yards away.

"Last warning!"

Jake reached under the seat for his dad's pistol.

Ten yards away.

Mouth widening into a dripping, gaping abyss.

Five.

Hair burning to ash, skin dripping off bone, eyes disintegrating into hollow sockets.

Gone.

—Tuesday—

Mark washed his hands in the exam room sink and studied his patient, slumped and disheveled in the mirror's reflection. "You doing alright?"

Jake sat on the edge of the examination table, his fingernails digging into the protective paper covering the vinyl. "Rough night. Had a weird dream. Kind of a nightmare, I guess."

"You want to tell me about it?"

"Since when did you become a shrink?"

"Point taken. What did you want to see me about?"

"I can't turn the chaos in my head down on my own. I'm not

sleeping, can't run a tractor for shit. Hoping you can help with the mental noise somehow."

Mark knew where this was heading but wanted to give Jake a chance to make a different choice. "Do you want me to refer you to a therapist? You've been through the wringer."

"No, I need help right now. Just to get me through. . . . I gotta take care of what wheat is left for harvest. Was hoping to start desiccating today but couldn't get out of my own way. I was thinking you could just—"

Mark held up his hand. "I can't do that. Not with your dependency issues."

"Well, what am I supposed to do, then?"

"Maybe you could start with talking about it."

Jake pushed off the table, grazing Mark as he passed. "Never mind."

The bell slammed against the doorjamb, followed by the Tercel engine sputtering to life. Mark went into the office to finish up his end-of-day paperwork—and to avoid thinking about where Jake might be headed. A soft knock sounded at the back door, but he wasn't expecting any deliveries, so he wrote it off as a mistake. He'd just sat down behind the desk when a louder, more urgent banging motivated him to get up, walk the few strides past the file cabinets and medical supplies, and open the steel door.

"Jake? Why are you back here?"

He shoved his fists into his coat pockets. "I don't know, guess I didn't want anybody to see me like this, and . . ." His eyes, already red-rimmed and bloodshot, started to well with tears.

"Hey, hey . . . it's alright. Come on in."

Mark pulled a couple of chairs together in the waiting room, dropped the shades in the front window, and locked the glass door. "What's going on?"

"I think I know why my crops are failing, why I got so sick, why my daughter got what she got, why my parents have their health issues . . . everything."

"And why is that?"

"We're damned."

Mark raised his eyebrows. "What?"

"Damned."

"How?"

"I saw something, some kind of demon-ghost, standing out in the wheat last night. Skin melted away like somebody was pouring acid on it. Pure evil."

"Jake, were you on—"

"No, I wasn't on anything. Never mind, I shouldn't have said—"

"Hang on, hang on. Relax. Just trying to see the whole picture. I believe you."

"Sounds like there's a *but* attached to that."

Mark did a quick inventory of the few psych classes he took as an undergrad, landing on a visualization lecture that he hadn't paid much attention to at the time; maybe that kind of exercise could ratchet down Jake's anxiety a couple of notches. "There's no *but*. But if you want to quiet some of the noise right now, we could try to reframe this."

"Reframe?"

"Yeah, basically that means we're going to look at what you saw through a different lens. Stand up and close your eyes."

"Mark, I—"

"Please. Humor me."

Jake pushed to his feet and let his eyelids drop.

"Imagine you're in that field, darkness everywhere. Cold, biting cold. You don't have any gloves, no coat, no way to get warm."

"Alright."

"Your fingers are freezing, you're going to lose them soon to frostbite, the house is gone, everything's gone."

"How is this supposed to help me?"

Mark rested his hands on Jake's shoulders, trying to ground him. "See the man in the wheat, smiling, with open arms."

Jake stepped back, shook his head, and opened his eyes. "No. You don't understand."

The words hit Mark harder than he expected.

Jake was right—he didn't understand.

And he had a decision to make, right now. He'd never thought much about *how* to be a doctor, probably because he'd spent most of his career in the lab. But standing here, in this little farm town clinic, he realized that he could be the doctor who believed his education made him omniscient and treated symptoms instead of humans, or he could be . . . different.

Maybe he could help Jake find his own answers to better health, which would make them more likely to stick. But that had to start with knowing him. Really knowing him.

He motioned toward Jake's chair and took a seat himself. "Tell me what's going on, Jake. What you saw . . . everything."

Late afternoon had given in to evening before Jake's voice finally ran out of story. Mark had made occasional silent connections as Jake talked. . . . When Jake spoke of the extreme stress the Hailey situation had brought to his marriage, Mark saw the hypertension, stomach pain, and drive to cope through chemicals. Jake's struggle to keep the farm going translated to severe anxiety, amplified by no sleep . . . and without any real rest, Jake's body couldn't physically function, from his compromised immune system to his failing gut.

No matter how many Mountain Dews he was downing.

But mostly, Mark served as a witness to this usually stoic man, knowing that allowing him to unload was probably the best medicine he could offer. When he sensed Jake was done for now, he took a deep inhale and let the breath escape slowly. "Do that with me, once."

"Do what?"

"Count to four while you take a breath in, hold the air for another four, then breathe out slow."

Jake mirrored Mark, riding his exhale with a tinge of insecurity. "I kind of did this last night, with Jessica, before I saw what I saw. Calmed me down a little."

"Breathing exercises work. Good thing to go back to when you get anxious."

"Look, I don't mean to be bringing you down—"

"You're not. In fact, I think maybe we could give each other a hand up."

"How?"

"I'll give you a call tomorrow and explain. Go home to that beautiful wife of yours, and find some gratitude. Fear shrinks in that kind of light."

"I was actually feeling a little of that last night, too. Before, you know. . . . Anyway, I'll try."

"There is no try, only do."

"Huh?"

"Yoda. *Star Wars.* Never mind." Mark scratched numbers on a prescription pad. "And here's my cell. Use it. Anytime."

He sensed the whiff of apprehension in Jake's tentative acceptance of the folded piece of paper. "Listen, Jake . . . everything you talked about stays with me. You know that, right?"

Jake nodded and got to his feet. Mark headed to the office and had just hit the lights when he heard the deadbolt unlock and the bell clang against the clinic's front door.

He called into the darkness as he walked down the hall. "Car's around back, isn't it?"

"Jake?"

But the waiting room was empty, the two chairs returned with backs to their usual wall, as if no one had faced each other at all.

———

Jake cranked the ignition, pumping the gas pedal until the Tercel finally coughed to life in the alley behind the clinic. The chaos in his head had barely calmed . . . and he felt a little better, but not *enough* better. He could make a call, right now, and probably get what he needed to wash the noise completely away. Jessica had stashed two twenties in the ashtray for emergencies, which was enough to get enough better.

She'd know if he came home high, but there was an easy solution for that . . . a brief staycation in the back corner of the Sonic parking lot.

He fumbled through his coat pockets, searching for his phone with a twisted sense of rationalized pride. If the doctor wouldn't help him, he'd help himself. He pushed both feet into the floorboard, straightening his legs to cram his now frantically probing hands into his jeans. He'd just do a few pills, and save the rest for when he really needed them. He opened the car door and crawled onto the asphalt, to check under the seat for the lifeline of plastic and glass.

Damn it.

He never went anywhere without his phone.

Damn it.

Jake was still on his hands and knees, straining to push himself back up into the car, when a shadow darkened the Tercel's front fender.

He closed his eyes and dropped his head, until his chin touched his chest.

Busted.

He flopped on his butt and squinted into the fluorescence spilling from the light perched above the clinic's back door. Jake reached into the glare to accept the silhouetted hand, allowing the fingers to wrap around his forearm and pull him to his feet. He noticed an infinity tattoo on the exposed wrist as he steadied himself against the car door and made a mental note to ask Mark about the ink's origin story.

"Thanks, Mark. I . . . I just . . . I—"

Headlights swung into the alley, harsh halogen blinding Jake and exposing the two men in what looked like a drug deal. Jake expected to see a cop car, but the throaty rumble of a diesel engine told him this was no sedan. The driver's side window rolled down as the truck pulled up, and Jake faked a smile. "We're good here."

"We? Jake, do I need to start worrying again?"

Jake took a step back.

"Mark?"

"You came through the back door, then left through the front. I was just making sure you remembered where you'd parked."

"But—"

Jake turned in a circle, a tiny ballerina in a toy music box, dancing with no one. His confused gaze fell upon a piece of glass surrounded by plastic resting on the step leading to the clinic's back door.

He heard Mark's brakes squeak as the truck started to roll. "Looks like you dropped your phone. Get home safe, Jake."

He watched Mark ease out of the alley before navigating to the pool of fluorescent light. Jake bent down stiffly and picked up the phone, turning the device over and over in his trembling hand as he clamored back into the driver's seat.

He would've heard his phone land on the concrete step if it had fallen out of his pocket. And he'd put off buying a protective case, so the plastic or screen would've cracked. How did his phone get on the step, then? Had someone been messing with him? Who? Did the same person help him up?

The phone couldn't have moved on its own, right?

He didn't know the right question to ask. And he didn't really want to know the answer anyway.

Jake opened the glove box, shoved the phone under the car manual, slammed shut the compartment door, and pointed the Tercel toward home.

———

Jessica checked the clock over the kitchen table.

Jake's doctor's appointment was taking a long time. She tried hard not to add the qualifier of *too long* to her observation, but she couldn't help the bubble of anxiety that surfaced every time he left.

She watched Hailey coloring on her canvas of choice, a brown paper bag from Walmart. Every detail about her daughter stood out to her tonight, from the tiny bows holding her pigtails to the tiny trickle of spittle that sometimes escaped from the corner of her mouth when she was really concentrating.

And this is what she loved doing most with Hailey, in these quiet moments between housework and dinner.

Drawing.

Her own creativity hadn't been encouraged when she was a kid. Neither of her parents were "artsy-fartsy"—their dismissive description of the Bob Ross painting shows she begged to watch on public television. She'd loved getting lost in whatever scenes her imagination allowed, even if her mom and dad didn't put the results up on the refrigerator.

She wasn't going to make that mistake with Hailey. Her artwork covered the fridge.

"What are you drawing, honey?"

"Daddy."

"Can I help?"

Hailey nodded and Jessica sat down next to her only child. She breathed in the twisted band of light between them, many-hued and undulating, the tether of deep love that would always keep them connected.

They drew.

And drew.

And drew.

So bonded in ritual, that Jessica didn't even hear the Tercel door slam, signaling her husband's arrival home.

———

After a mostly silent meatloaf-and-potato exchange, Mark's mother announced her progressively earlier bedtime and headed upstairs. He made his way to the living room, where he sat back in his old man's easy chair with a PBR.

He took a swig and dug his notebook out of his briefcase. Twirling a new Dixon Ticonderoga pencil between his fingers, he looked over his notes on Jake.

The latest episode in the alley behind the clinic was a little concerning . . . he'd seemed so disoriented and confused. And maybe Jake had been hallucinating, or maybe he'd fallen asleep in his car a couple of nights ago and had a nightmare, but regardless, a demon-ghost wasn't behind the epidemic of chronic disease running through Jake and his family. And this community, for that matter. There had to be a more scientific, medical reason.

He fanned the pages away from Jake's story, landing on a word circled in the margins of an earlier thought.

Water.

Could be the water. There'd been a landmark class-action suit settled not long ago against DuPont, who'd been accused of wrecking an entire town's health after dumping toxins into their water supply. Jake's whole family, besides Jessica—who hadn't grown up on that farm— had health issues, and they were all drinking the same well water. Had been for generations.

But that was too broad a spectrum of disease, from ulcerative colitis to leaky gut to Parkinson's to leukemia to dementia, to be blamed on something in the water. And besides, Jessica had been drinking from the same well for as long as she and Jake had been married.

Still, could she hold a clue? She seemed to be the only healthy person around.

What made her different?

He turned to a new page and wrote her name at the top, and then *Water* again, and circled them both.

Absently flipping through the pages, he noticed that he'd also written *Food* and *Air* in the notebook margins. For good reason—the scientist in him knew that inputs mattered, so something these folks were breathing or eating or drinking could be at the root of their health issues. He rewrote *Food* and *Air* on the new list, under *Jessica* and *Water*.

Maybe there was some sort of cumulative effect, a buildup over time of . . . what?

What was Jake using a lot?

Drugs.

Not helpful. Not everyone in this equation was an Oxy addict.

Wait a minute.

Not everyone was using drugs on *themselves,* but this was farm country, and they sure were using drugs on their crops . . . potent chemicals . . . to kill insects and weeds.

A stretch, maybe, but worth adding to the list.

Rx (Agriculture)

Also worth a text to Jake.

Hey, man, can you take photos of whatever you're spraying and send them to me? I don't know that world as well as you do and want to see the labels and do some research.

He watched his phone for a minute, waiting for the three wavering dots that would tell him Jake was responding, before tossing it on the floor next to the chair. Didn't matter. He wasn't going to find the answer tonight.

Mark stared into the flames licking the walls of the woodstove, the warmth reminding him of the optimistic endgame he'd had in mind for his failed cold-field visualization attempt with Jake. He didn't play down the mind-body-spirit connection like some of his colleagues did. Maybe that demon-ghost image was Jake's perceived external manifestation of his own setbacks and problems.

Or an incarnation of his conscience, there to scare him straight.

Bottom line, the human brain was still powerfully misunderstood, and Jake might believe that what he'd been seeing was actually real.

He'd try to keep that in mind when he called Jake tomorrow to talk about how they may be able to help each other.

His gaze drifted back to his journal, and the newest addition to the list.

Jessica.

Couldn't hurt to talk to her, too.

—Wednesday—

Mark pulled up in front of the garden to see Jessica on her knees in the dirt, sweat drenching her spine and soaking through her sports bra.

"Oh, hey, Mark! Jake's not here. Sent him to Walmart for groceries. It's my day off."

"Hi, Jessica. I'm not here for him, actually. I was wondering if I could ask you a couple of questions."

"Everything okay?"

"Yeah, that's kind of the point."

She pushed to her feet and took a long slug from a water bottle. "Huh?"

"Well, you seem to be the only person around here without major health problems. Don't you think that's strange?"

She shrugged. "I never thought about it."

"You went away to college, right?"

"Yeah, Oklahoma State."

"Did it change you?"

"Not really. I didn't graduate. My parents got divorced my sophomore year, and tuition money dried up. And Stillwater isn't exactly Hollywood."

Mark eyed the patch of ground where she'd been pulling weeds. "Have you always had a vegetable garden?"

"I loved playing in the dirt as a little girl, if that counts. But this is my first real attempt at growing my own food. I've been feeling a pretty strong drive to nurture and take care of something alive, I guess."

Mark focused on a single green shoot, thriving in the center of the garden. "Almost like you're mothering the land, which is a healthy way to deal with—" Mark clipped the thought, immediately regretting the observation.

She bailed him out of an impossible recovery. "I do put a lot of love into this place."

Mark pivoted the best he could. "Yeah. And into Jake. He wouldn't have made it this far without you."

"In sickness and in health, right?"

"That's what they say." He turned back to face her. "So, you've been feeding Jake out of this garden, huh? Makes sense, him losing all that weight."

She threw her head back and laughed. "God, no. He's meat and potatoes, Doritos, and Slim Jims. I cooked separate for him, until recently."

"Separate?"

"Yeah. Started when we were dating, and I tried to put a black-bean burger in front of him. He looked at me like I'd shot a puppy. So, up until the accident, I'd make him what he'd eat, and then usually make a salad with these greens and some of these vegetables for me. I'm not afraid of meat, but I don't eat it as much as he does.

Trying to get him healthier, though. You know that. He even had one of those black-bean burgers a couple nights ago."

"Yeah, he's doing a lot better. But you didn't find out about black-bean burgers around here."

"No, I guess that's at least one thing I learned in college."

"How to make them?"

"Just that other food existed besides what was at the Sonic and Walmart in Guymon."

"Will he eat anything out of that garden?"

"If there's enough butter and salt on it. But it's mostly been just for me. I rotate stuff around. Greens, corn, beans, squash, tomatoes, carrots . . . everything does alright with some attention. I do have to stay on top of the weeds, though."

"That's what you were doing when I showed up."

"Yeah."

"You don't spray for them?"

"No." She surveyed the quarter acre and wiped a fly from her nose with the back of her soiled hand. "I don't know. I guess it's not a huge piece of ground, so I can stay ahead of the weeds. And we have a compost pile, thanks to the mares, so I spread some of that around for fertilizer."

"HGTV would love you. I'll let you go. . . . Sorry I just dropped by unannounced. I called your cell a couple of times, but it went straight to voicemail. I was heading this way to Guymon, and—"

"Don't apologize. You're always welcome. I hardly ever have that thing on, let alone in my pocket."

"That's interesting—most people worry there'll be some kind of emergency, or some important call they'll miss."

"I suppose." Jessica seemed to size Mark up before she kept talking. "Have you ever noticed that there seem to be two kinds of people in the world?"

"How so?"

"People that get it, and people that don't."

"Get what?"

"In this case, get the concept that all this technology might be delivering a slow kill-shot to humanity. Like with these cell phones. Maybe we're not supposed to be able to hear voices outside of earshot, let alone on the other side of the planet. Via our fingers and a screen."

Mark offered a small, confused smile. "And that would be because . . . ?"

"Think about it. We've been on the planet for what? A hundred thousand years?"

"Closer to two, they say. Took evolutionary biology as an undergrad."

"Well, we evolved as a species without knowing what was happening a thousand miles away. What mattered was what was happening here, now, with those around us. That's how we're really wired. In my opinion, at least."

"So you don't buy the idea of digital tribes, with technology connecting all of us?"

"God, no. Do you? Are people better off with their heads at right angles to their phones? With their chins stuck to their chest?"

Mark felt the weight of his own phone, pressing against his thigh in his jeans pocket. "Probably not. Most of what they're consuming— social media, exaggerated commentary passed off as news—just raises cortisol levels for no good reason."

"Stress hormone, right?"

"Yeah."

Jessica knelt back into the dirt. "All the more reason to be with real people, around my dining room table, or at the Masonic lodge, or at church. That's the only reason I go there on Sundays, actually—religion isn't my thing—but everybody in the community gathers in one place for a couple of hours, which is kind of nice. Otherwise, you'll find me here in the dirt."

Dirt.

Mark slanted his eyes. Imperceptibly. Tilted his head. Barely. Pressed his lips together. Subtly. "Listen, can I take a handful of your garden soil before I go? Random, I know, but I want to take a look at it under a microscope."

"Sure, there are Ziplocs in the kitchen, in the drawer next to the fridge. I'd go in and grab them for you, but I don't want to track this garden through the house."

He emerged with two bags, filling one with dirt from the edge of the wheat field bordering the backyard, and another with garden soil.

And a word no one within a hundred miles would likely understand fell off his tongue, as he walked back to his father's Chevy Duramax, late for the oil change he'd scheduled in town.

Microbiome.

———

Jake doom-scrolled through his phone as he waited in the longest possible line at Walmart. He didn't know why he bothered with the news on social media anymore, since he couldn't tell what to believe, and it was all bad. But still, here he was, thumbing around for what already felt like too long, just so he could be even grumpier than before. Wasn't much else to do in these quiet moments, though.

Toxic pacifier, according to Jessica.

Probably was.

The screen lit up with Mark's number, and Jake checked how many people were in front of him before answering.

"Hey, Mark."

"This a good time? I'm in Guymon getting an oil change and have a few minutes."

"Not really. I'm in line at the Walmart."

"Let me buy you lunch at Frank's across the street. I'll walk down there."

"How about the Arby's instead?"

"What would Jessica say?"

"How do you know what Jessica would say?"

"I'll explain. Headed your way now."

"Alright, I'll meet you there after I check out and put these groceries in the car. Good thing I brought a cooler with me. Can't turn down a free lunch."

Ten minutes later, they were posted up with lean turkey sandwiches on rye on actual plates, a far cry from the two foil-wrapped Arby's French Dips that Jake had planned on secretly getting for the drive home. The lunch rush was on, and the diner was packed with folks staring down at their phones, waiting on their orders.

"I swung by your farm earlier because I had a couple questions for Jessica."

"What kind of questions?" Jake scoffed, trying to hide his insecurity. "You got designs on my wife?"

"Yeah, right. Though I do have some designs on figuring out why she seems to be the only one in three counties without some sort of health crisis."

"Unless you count *me* as her health crisis."

Mark waved his sandwich in agreement. "True. But you know what I mean."

"Yeah."

"Anyway, I wanted to talk to her, because of what I said yesterday about giving each other a hand up. I really think there's something deeper going on here with people's mental and physical health, and she seems to be an outlier."

"Outlier?"

"Different."

"She's different, alright. She any help?"

"I think so. Nothing solid yet, but a couple of light bulbs went on."

"Good. She probably appreciated the company. Stuck way out there, and she don't even turn her phone on."

Mark glanced at the diner clientele, buried in their screens. "Yeah, I think that figures in somehow. And the fact she spends so much time in the dirt."

"And this is what you wanted to talk to me about?"

"Not really. Don't take this the wrong way, but everything going on with you—"

Jake interrupted through a mouthful of bread and bird. "There's nothing going on with me. Only divertic-ulcer-colitis-whatever-you-call-that, and obesity, and a drinking-turned-drug problem . . . and the fact that I'm seeing demons."

Mark caught Jake's eye. "Well, that's what I'm getting at, actually. You encompass so many of the problems I see in the clinic every day. I thought maybe I could ask you a couple more questions about how you've been living and draw a through line that could explain where you are now."

"Which is fucked."

"No, no. Okay, maybe a little. But you've turned a corner, and you know it."

"Yeah. I've been pretty short with Jessica, and kind of on edge trying to come off the Oxy. Doing better, though. Speaking of that, sorry about yesterday. I shouldn't have come to you looking for drugs. And then to talk your ear off like that; it's not like me to—"

"No, I'm glad you did . . . got me thinking. That demon-ghost you saw . . . has that ever happened before?"

"I don't know."

"You don't know?"

"I mean, there was kind of a weird thing, back when I was a kid."

"What happened?"

Jake took a break from demolishing his sandwich and stared down at the almost-empty plate. How much to reveal? "Just thought I saw a shadow in the wheat, that's all. Freaked me out a little."

"Same thing you saw the other night?"

"I'm not sure. That childhood memory is mostly a blur now. Sometimes I wonder if it even really happened . . . like maybe it was all a dream. But Monday night . . . that was different."

"Well, even if what you saw wasn't real, maybe the message is."

Jake's shoulders stiffened immediately, and he felt the premature crease between his eyebrows deepen in defense. That wrinkle was usually the first sign of his temper's hair trigger, and he tried to calm himself down with a shallow breath. "What I saw was real."

"Sorry, that didn't come out right. I'm not saying what you saw wasn't real." Mark scrambled to recover. "But maybe the message it's trying to communicate is something you should listen to."

"Oh, yeah?"

"Sometimes these types of visions are actually manifestations of what we fear. The brain—"

"Visions?" Jake threw his napkin on his plate. "Is that a nice way of saying hallucinations? How about this for a message? Find another subject to use as a lab rat for your theories."

He pushed back from the table and stomped out, punishing the pavement with his boots all the way to the Walmart parking lot. He'd let himself be so vulnerable, only to not be believed. And he got the sense Mark had been hitting on his wife, too—or was that just another "vision"? Whatever. He didn't need Mark's help. Or anyone's. Sure, Jessica was helping him right now, here and there. But he could handle his own business, even with some of these recent setbacks.

And he was damn sure he'd seen what he'd seen.

He drove toward home with both hands gripping the wheel, as if the slightest breath of wind might knock the Tercel into Texas County. What he hadn't told Mark—thank God—was that he'd been seeing that demon-ghost every harvest season, twice a year, for both wheat and corn, for the last decade.

And lately, all the time. Standing in the corner of their bedroom at 3:13 a.m. At the top of the stairs, after one of his evening drives around the front pasture. Behind Jessica's chair, just as she was sitting down at the dinner table. In the backseat of the Tercel, when he was pulling out of the driveway today on the way to Walmart.

But the figure had only appeared as a shadow, before a glint of sunlight or the flip of a switch would burn it away. Except for that night he'd tried to kill himself, and two nights ago when he'd tried to run it over. Both times, its face had become more defined before melting into a napalm-like soup.

That was new.

Coming off the Oxy wasn't what had put him on edge. The constant expectation of turning a corner to see the hollow body standing there, skin dripping off bone like melting butter, beckoning, demanding some unknown thing from him . . . all the time, everywhere?

He wasn't even on edge anymore. He'd fallen off the edge into a debilitating sea of severe fear and anxiety.

And now he was drowning.

Only one sure way to float.

Jake pulled a U-turn on the interstate just outside of town, and ten minutes later he was standing outside McGill's, heart in his throat. Just one drink wouldn't hurt. Only to settle his nerves and keep him from doing what he really shouldn't do, which was to head farther across town and make a buy in the parking lot behind the Sonic.

He'd just have one.

An hour later, he stumbled out of McGill's, scrolling his phone for the number he'd thought about calling last night, the number he told Jessica he'd deleted, the number he'd really meant to never dial again. Relief washed over him when he found the code-named contact, grateful he'd be able to get himself well, just one more time.

Probably not what the doc had meant by finding gratitude, but drunk beggars couldn't be choosers.

He pushed the green *Call* button, tripped into the driver's seat, and veered in long arcs to the Sonic back parking lot, where he waited for the high school kid to slink out from behind the dumpster.

Twenty minutes passed before Jake got out of the car to see if their signals had gotten crossed. He turned the corner of the metal bin and abruptly stopped, suddenly stone-cold sober, before falling, falling, falling into opaque arms stretched out in embrace, smile widening into a gaping abyss, hair burning to ash, skin dripping off bone, eyes disintegrating into hollow sockets.

Face into face.

———

Mark turned from the kitchen window and checked his phone for a response from Jake.

Nothing.

The thunderheads building in the west looked to be more than a passing rain, and he silently wondered if the basement still flooded in bad weather. He'd been going through the stacks of shelved boxes down there, trying to lighten the inevitable packing load that his mother would eventually have to bear. She'd mentioned more than once that living in this house alone wouldn't be good for her. Too many memories, too few people.

Hard to argue with that.

And so, pieces of his past, from high school yearbooks to *Star Wars* action figures, were scattered across the basement floor, in fierce competition with one another to be packed up safely and treasured or tossed into a trash bag. He flipped the switch at the top of the stairs and headed down to clean up, just in case the rain hit before dinner.

He opened an unlabeled box, hoping to find space for the action figures, which were near the top of his never-getting-rid-of list. This dank basement had been their home since he was a kid, the thin area rug next to the workbench their battlefield during the awkward afternoons when his mother sat without expression on the living room sofa, waiting for his father to come in from the field.

Mark looked to the corner behind the water heater, where he'd read with his back against the warm metal cylinder on the winter nights reserved for whatever sports his old man was watching on TV. Nobody had been down here in a long time, or at least paid much attention, because the Pendleton blanket was still balled up under the stairs. Probably right where he'd left it, in fact, after sleeping there as a teenager. Sometimes he'd play an adolescent version of house and spend the night down here, pretending this was his own apartment and he could be who he was supposed to be.

Not who his father wanted him to be.

He peered into the box to make sure there was room for Yoda and friends, his heart quickening at the sight of a few college notebooks fighting for air. A heart was drawn on one cover, a game of hangman on another, spelling out "I Almost Love You."

They were both first-year premed undergraduates, and he usually managed to find a seat in class within talking distance of her. Not that he ever worked up the nerve to say anything. She shined like the sunrise gleaming off their fields after a night rain . . . and was totally out of his league.

He'd never been the most confident kid, and by the time he got to college, he hadn't even been on a proper date. But every time he saw her, he got a knowing.

Not a feeling. A *knowing*.

He dreamt about her at arm's length, until she asked him out for a beer one night after a study group. She softly kissed his cheek midway through that long night spent traveling across acres and acres of common ground, which had evolved into a magical, endless landscape by the end of the semester.

She didn't give him her home phone number on their last morning together, saying she'd be gone on a ski trip with her family until school was back in session. And so he walked into class the Monday after Christmas break, expecting to see her smiling face waiting at her usual desk. The seat was empty, and he called her from his dorm room that afternoon, but the phone rang unanswered. Neither of them had bothered much with other friendships at school, since they'd spent almost every waking moment together. Nobody else even knew she was gone.

And that's how she stayed.

Gone.

He'd thought about looking her up every once in a while, especially when the Internet started making most people findable with a few clicks. But he'd told himself these things happened for a reason, a weak excuse in place of the truth that he was afraid of what he'd find.

Maybe she'd passed away unexpectedly, maybe she'd gotten swept up into something sinister, or even worse, maybe she'd met someone else over Christmas break, and was now living happily ever after with a beautiful husband, a new baby, and a black Labrador, in a converted Sprinter van on a never-ending adventure.

Or even worse than that. Maybe she simply didn't want him.

She wasn't the only one he wasn't good enough for. His father had frowned on medical school's steep tuition, begrudgingly cosigning student loans while telling Mark he'd be better off learning the family business. And even when he'd graduated and was working on breakthrough chemo treatments, his old man couldn't be bothered with the details.

"Not too late, son. Come on back, and I'll teach you the trade."

He didn't think his quiet, submissive mother really loved him for who he was, either. Her love was more a consequence of giving birth than a decision rooted in deep appreciation of his essence and character.

And that's why this love as a choice, *her* love, had felt so different, maybe even more sacred, because the expression of that emotional connection was voluntary.

Not hardwired.

He wanted that again, so badly.

The first patter of rain hit the window in the upper corner of the basement wall, shaking Mark out of the familiar remember-when spiral and into the present, which was about to get really wet. He grabbed a trash bag from under the workbench and hurriedly shoved every sentimental remnant into the plastic cocoon, which he then stuffed back under the tools.

Except for the action figures. He laid those carefully on the notebooks, secured the lid firmly in place, and set the box on the highest shelf. Halfway up the stairs, he gave the basement floor a once-over for anything that couldn't survive some water, before turning off the light, shutting the door, and heading to the kitchen to make dinner for his mother.

———

The demon-ghost vanished almost immediately, dissolving into Jake before he exhaled, and pushing him into a recoil that landed him on his back. He rolled onto his side, just as the high school kid rolled by, saw the commotion, and kept right on rolling.

He lay there, on the asphalt with a side-angle view of the guy begging near the drive-through order window. Tall and skinny, with a flat-billed hat, baggy jeans barely held by a belt around his thighs, and an oversized parka two seasons too late, making the same hand motion to each car passing by. The easy smile he offered to the only agreeable donor reminded him of his brother, who'd gone from partying to partying too much to completely off the rails—all before he was even out of high school.

Jake had stopped giving him money a couple of years ago, and what was left of the text communication had dried up once Jake got a habit of his own. . . . By then, his brother had become an inconvenient mirror to Jake. Last he'd heard through the feed-store grapevine, his brother was couch-surfing between towns, not really living anywhere, and not really caring about much of anything except meth first and maybe food a distant second.

Jake's brief contemplation about where his brother might be now, maybe dead, probably high, drifted into who might have seen what just happened. He knew he'd only been on the asphalt for a matter of seconds, but this was a small town, and somebody was bound to recognize him. His struggle to push himself to his feet was mercifully interrupted by a backlit forearm dropping into the frame, offering him a hand up. He pushed to his butt and raised his own arm in the direction of the shadow framed against the fluorescent drive-through lights.

A vaguely familiar grip wrapped his forearm and pulled him to his feet. Jake's eyes focused on the neck tattoo crawling from the Good Samaritan's tank top, and then on the huge jacket hanging off his frame.

The beggar guy.

"Hey, brother. Nice car."

Jake squinted into the guy's face. "Adam?"

"In the flesh, if you could call this skin bag I'm wearing flesh."

Jake rooted his work boots in the asphalt, as if all of this would go away if he stood still and maybe closed his eyes. He couldn't take care of himself right now, let alone his brother. And if his mom and dad saw Adam like this, their hearts might break into tiny, unfixable pieces. Adam had always seemed to do no wrong in their eyes, until that night his dad turned a shotgun on him in the utility hangar. That night . . .

"So, Jake, buy your brother a burger. For old time's sake."

Too drained and shocked to do much else, Jake followed Adam to the walk-up window, where his brother ordered almost the entire menu. Jake got a coffee, not sure his stomach could handle much else. They walked back to the Tercel, where Adam spread out his feast across the hood.

Jake let him demolish most of the first burger before asking what he already knew to be true. "You're following me, huh?"

Adam stopped chewing and offered a surprised cough. "What makes you say that?"

"That was you in the alley yesterday, helping me up."

"How do you know?"

"Same grip, same infinity tattoo on the inside of your right wrist."

Adam crumpled the burger wrapper and threw it against the windshield, waiting until it had ricocheted back down with the rest of the food. "Okay, yeah. Word got out last year that you got a habit and—"

"Where did you hear that? I'm not like a junkie or—"

Adam held up his hand. "Whoa, bro. Relax. This is a small county, and even smaller town. You think you're the only one that high school kid is selling to? He probably told you he's just raiding his mom's medicine cabinet every once in a while. But he can get whatever you need, across three counties. I should know."

Jake looked down at his coffee. That *was* what that kid had told him.

Adam picked up his next course, a chicken sandwich. "I came back because I thought maybe we could help each other out."

"You want me to buy you drugs?"

"No, no. I haven't used in almost two months. And besides, I wasn't buying at the end. I was cooking."

"Are you fucking kidding me? You mean like making meth in the bathtub?"

"Basically. Remember those first couple episodes of *Breaking Bad*? That was pretty much me, without the RV and chemistry teacher. My dealer and I worked together."

"How did you get out of that? You can't just walk away, can you?"

"My dealer's own problem got a lot worse than mine. Easier to walk away when your partner is up for three days and sleeping for four."

"You don't look like you haven't used in two months."

"Yeah, well, my radiant beauty isn't going to come back overnight."

Jake's coffee had finally cooled down enough to take a sip. "What do you want from me, then?"

"A reintroduction . . . maybe a little help smoothing things over."

"A reintroduction? To what?"

"The family."

"The family isn't what it used to be, Adam. Dad's got Parkinson's and Mom's mind is starting to go. Jessica and I aren't in the best of places, and Hailey—"

Adam shifted from one foot to the other. "Hey, man, sorry about her."

"Thanks. But you're not here to talk about that. I just don't know what you'd be trying to get out of the family. The last thing they need is you asking for anything."

"Don't hate a guy because he's trying to make a change."

"A change? Is that what the neck tattoo's about?"

Adam started to gather what was left of his food. "Forget I said anything. I'll see you around."

Jake took another swig of coffee. "Hang on. You still owe me a few explanations. I just spent almost twenty bucks on all this crap for you. Well, Jessica's twenty bucks."

Adam turned and leaned against the hood. "Whatever. What kind of explanations?"

"How did you find me behind the clinic?"

"Followed you from the farm. I borrowed a friend's Ford Ranger to get here. Well, I guess he's more an acquaintance than a friend. He won't even know the truck's gone."

"Drug buddy?"

"Dealer I was telling you about. I put my Civic, which was actually worth something, up as collateral for his bail when he got arrested. Bondsman took that when he skipped. Figured borrowing his piece of shit truck was a fair trade."

Jake looked past Adam and across the parking lot for the Ranger, keying on the older short bed with a camper shell in the corner of the lot. "Is that where you've been sleeping? Back of that truck?"

"Yeah. Speaking of, where's your F-150? I didn't expect to see that little Toyota pulling out of your driveway."

Jake hesitated. He didn't want to give too much away. "Just an accident. Driving a loaner now. So, you've been staking me out."

"Pretty much. I was just trying to figure out the right time to approach you."

"Then why did you disappear after helping me up yesterday?"

"I don't know. Still nervous about showing my face around here, I guess. I thought I was ready, but as soon as those headlights lit up the alley and you got distracted, I ran. Left your phone on the ground by the back door. I swiped it from your jacket pocket in the waiting room, while you were with the doctor."

Jake slammed the Tercel's roof with a closed fist. "You haven't changed, motherfucker."

"I gave it back, didn't I?"

"Have you been following me today, too?"

Adam took a long chug of Mountain Dew. "No, I spent the day trying to make a few apologies to some people I've burned bridges with. Didn't go great. I get it, though. I'm an asshole."

"Yes, you are." Jake let the sentiment hang in the air for a couple of seconds. "And then tonight—"

"I was just standing by the drive-through order window, trying to get somebody to buy me a burger, when I saw a guy hit the deck in the parking lot. Happened to be you. What was up with that?"

Jake eyed his brother. Was he really trying to change? Or was this just another bait-and-switch, one that Adam had perfected to get what he wanted?

"I was pretty drunk, and I tripped."

"That's not what I saw. And you might reek of whiskey, but you sure as hell aren't drunk right now. I know what that looks like."

"What did you see?"

"You got out of the car—I didn't know you were you, since you're moving like a broken old man—and walked around the hood toward the dumpster. Then I thought somebody pushed you backward, hard enough to take you off your feet. That's why I came over, to break up whatever was going on. Except I didn't see anybody else, just you on the ground. Who pushed you?"

Jake paused again, uncertain of how much to share. He'd never talked to Adam about what he'd seen as a kid, and he assumed his brother hadn't experienced anything. Adam was the talking type and would've said something.

"Did you ever see anything weird out in the wheat?"

Adam leaned back. "What the fuck are you talking about? And why are you changing the subject?"

"Just answer the question. Ever see anything on the farm that creeped you out?"

Adam's eyes narrowed with suspicion. "What do you mean? Like a ghost or a dead body or something?"

"Just something that you couldn't explain."

Adam scoffed. "No. Are you trying to tell me you're seeing things? Because listen, man, I've seen a lot of crazy shit when I was high, too. A lot. And if you think you're seeing something real . . ."

It was Jake's turn to start clearing the debris from the car hood. Mark's first reaction had been this same suggestion, that he'd been high and hallucinated. Nobody believed him. And this is why he'd never talked about it . . . reactions just like this. Whenever he tried to be vulnerable, this is what he got. Including, especially, as a kid, when he'd tried to talk to his dad about what he'd seen in the field. "We're done."

Adam tried to back him down. "Hey, bro, all good. I didn't mean nothing."

Jake piled the wrappers and what was left of the food into the Sonic bag. There was a reason his dad wouldn't talk to him about it. And he was going to find out, right now. "Stay away from Mom and Dad, alright?"

Adam followed him around to the driver's side, stepping back to avoid the slamming door. "Don't you want to know how I could help you?"

Jake hit the ignition and chirped the tires as he floored the Tercel.

Adam spanked the rear window glass. "Remember, I said maybe we could help each other out?"

But Jake was already pulling away, out of the parking lot and onto the interstate, where he kept the little car going as fast as she allowed, past the big rigs and their continuous stampede of chrome and exhaust, all the way home.

The sun was resting on the horizon, caught between threatening clouds and dry prairie, as he pulled into the farm driveway, banked left toward the old elm, and stopped in front of the bunkhouse. His mom was staring blankly at the window, as if she couldn't see past the glass.

What was he going to do about her? For her? With her? What was the plan, as her dementia dug its talons deeper into her everyday life?

Not now, not now.

His dad was slumped in the main room of the bunkhouse, which they'd converted into a space mirroring their old living room. Same easy chair, TV, coffee table . . . even the same paint on the walls and the same linen drapes. An episode of *Judge Judy* had apparently been more of a sedative than intended, because his dad was snoring like a pirate.

"Dad? Hey, Dad."

He nudged his dad's elbow, which graduated to shaking his shoulder. "Dad!"

"Huh? What? What did I do?"

"Nothing, Dad. It's me, Jake."

"Jesus, son, where's the fire? And what the hell happened to you? You smell like a distillery."

"Sorry, but I need to talk to you about something."

"The birds and the bees?"

His dad's hand tremored uncontrollably as he slapped his knee in self-amusement, the spasmic rhythm punctuating a dry cough and hack.

"I'm going to have Mark come and check you out. That cold isn't going away."

"Just this goddamn Parkinson's."

"I don't think it's just that. And no, I don't need to know about the birds and the bees. I want to talk about what I saw."

His dad coughed again. "Seen a lot, I would think."

"The man in the wheat, Dad. When I was a kid."

"Why you gotta bring that up?"

"Why don't you want to?"

Another hack. "I told you before . . . everything turned out okay. Don't need to shake that tree."

"Really? You have an obese, addicted son who tried to kill himself, a granddaughter with leukemia, you've got Parkinson's, and Mom is starting to go dark. Everything turned out okay?"

"Everybody's got some kind of burden they're carrying. We got ours."

Jake stepped closer. "That's what you think? Is that your way of deflecting my question, like those politicians you love to hate?"

His dad turned off the TV. "I suppose I did feel a little shame in not . . ." His voice trailed off in hesitation and landed in a wheeze.

"Not what?"

"Well, not paying enough attention. Any attention, really." He looked at the TV, as if Judge Judy was going to bail him out of a difficult conversation.

"That's pretty vague. Attention to what?"

Another cough. "I've kept a secret for a long time, son."

"What's that have to do with what I saw?"

"Hold your horses, for Christ's sake. This isn't easy for me. Like I said, things were going alright. And I wanted to keep them going alright. We had bills to pay, this place got so big . . . momentum, I guess. And I didn't really know what to make of it."

"Jesus, Dad, get to the point. What to make of what?"

"Well, I saw that thing, too."

"What?"

The answer rode the back of a violent hack. "The man in the wheat."

"*What?*"

"Shh, keep your voice down, boy."

Jake knelt in front of his dad, hissing an angry whisper. "How could you have never told me? I've been carrying this my whole life, thinking nobody else would understand. And my own father . . ."

"I guess I just put it away somewhere. Didn't pay it no mind. As I got older, I chalked it up to being a nightmare. Figured you would, too."

"Yeah, well, I didn't."

Cough. Cough. "You should."

"What about Adam? Did he ever tell you about seeing anything?"

Cough. "No, but I don't think that boy could see his own nose, even if he knew where to look."

"I saw him today."

His dad visibly tensed up, his hand tightening against his knee. "The man in the wheat?"

"No. Well, yeah. But also Adam. He was at Sonic."

"What's he doing in town?"

A little white lie wouldn't hurt. "I don't know. Didn't say."

"How did he look?"

"Like shit."

"You didn't give him any money, did you?"

"Nah, just bought him something to eat."

"He means well, he just—"

He lost his dad's rationalization in the frayed fabric of the old couch. He and Adam had picked it up, already well-used, at a farm sale before Jake was even legal to drive, and time had reduced the worn threads to barely connected tendrils. "Go to bed, Dad."

Jake turned and headed out of the bunkhouse, shaking his head as he slowly stepped down the porch stairs. He'd thought redemption would have felt a little better than this.

———

Steady rain was hammering the galvanized roof, and a biblical rush of water had already flooded the dirt driveway. Mark found the storm almost meditative as he swung in the porch chair hung from the soffit.

That is, until he noticed the downpour falling through the truck window he'd left open.

He ran across the porch and cleared the stairs, landing in the new mud river that used to be the driveway. A few slogs later, he hit the ignition with the key he'd left in the cupholder, shut the window, and reversed course back to the house.

He wiped his feet on the front mat in vain, before opening the screen door with the *No Shoes In The House* sign tacked to the frame.

He kicked at his heels, smearing mud across his socks.

Dirt.

His conversation with Jake this afternoon and the pre-storm daydream about *her* had overshadowed his one-word epiphany when he left the farm.

Microbiome . . . an army of microorganisms, really—bacteria, fungi, and viruses. Mark knew that the gut microbiome protected humans against germs, broke down food to release energy, and produced vitamins, among other functions. A highly diversified gut microbiome was critical to even decent health, and that diversification came from inputs in the environment. Food, sure. But what people breathed, what they touched? That was even more important.

Jessica was working in the soil almost every day, growing what she ate, with dirt under her fingernails, streaked across her cheeks . . . and she was healthy.

Jake was riding in an air-conditioned sealed cab, spraying chemicals on his fields, eating processed food . . . and he was not.

Soil had a microbiome, too. All living ecosystems did.

Walk it back, walk it back, walk it back.

To the source.

Which was waiting in two Ziploc bags on the truck passenger seat.

———

Jessica stood with arms folded, her glare piercing the streaked living room window.

A trip to Walmart shouldn't have taken Jake five hours.

The Tercel's headlights finally lost their rain-refracted life in front of the bunkhouse, and she watched Jake lumber out of the car and up his parents' porch stairs.

He doesn't even know which house is his.

After a few minutes, she saw his trudging shadow leave his parents' place and lurch toward home, until she could make out his thinning hair sprouting in random directions, eyes bloodshot and tired.

Disheveled and disoriented. Awesome.

She kicked open the screen door and stormed onto the porch. "Where the hell have you been?"

"Jessica, I—"

"Jesus Christ, Jake, you reek."

"I know, I—"

"You what? Had a few whiskeys and a shag with that Johnson girl before driving home?"

"No, I mean, I—"

"I'm not doing this anymore, Jake. I've been so supportive, so nurturing, so caring, through everything. The drinking, then the pills, then the 'accident,' then the recovery, and this is what I get?"

"But I—"

"Now you want to talk? That's funny, because the only talking you like to do is when you bitch about what I'm making for dinner. Barely a thank-you. You run away to the fields like you're hiding something, and when I ask what's going on, you say *nothing*. That's what it always is . . . *nothing*. Well, that's what you're going to be left with. Because I'm done."

Jessica spun and stormed back into the house. She flew up the stairs and was pulling one of the suitcases from under the bed when Jake finally made his way into their room.

"Jessica, listen, I—"

"I'm taking Hailey and going to Beth's."

"What do you mean, *taking Hailey*? Jessica, she's—"

"Don't talk. You've dug a hole plenty deep already."

———

Jake paced between the kitchen and living room as rain pummeled every glass windowpane in the house. Shame and fear were closing in on him like a vise, and he'd just called Mark for a lifeline when a soft knock sounded.

Jake rushed across the room, his heart sinking guiltily when he opened the door.

"Oh, hey, Mom. What are you doing out there?" His first thought was that she'd started to wander, but he couldn't go there. Not now.

She retreated off the porch, into the rain. "I heard you."

"Heard me what?"

"Talking to your dad."

"About what?"

"About that man in the wheat."

"Don't worry about it, Mom. Nothing to be scared about."

"Nobody paid attention."

Jake walked out to meet her, pulling the back of his shirt over his head for some minor protection. "Let's go inside, Mom."

"Not your dad, or his dad. They never even read 'em. I did, though. I read 'em. I read 'em all." One of her hands clutched a strange bulge protruding from her nightgown, and she seemed to be talking nonsense again, which he was trying to get used to.

But it still made him so sad. Soon he'd be watching one small piece of her die at a time, if he wasn't already.

He stared straight ahead as the unmeasurable weight of everything rose from his belly to his chest to the back of his throat, until a single tear tracing his cheek led to two, then three.

When he was a kid, his mom told him that rain was God crying.

He stood there in the torrential downpour, an arm's length away from her, and gave God a run for His money.

———

Jake's mother reached under her nightgown, placed the bundle on the darkened top stair, and turned to her son. He was afraid; she knew this much.

Of what?

Maybe the answer was in the package she'd just left on the porch, or something else. She couldn't remember if he'd told her what scared him, or why she'd brought the package out in the first place.

But her son was afraid, which his father didn't allow. She let him cry sometimes, though, only when her husband wasn't looking.

She turned her head from side to side, searching for her husband across the land she barely recognized, but not because her quickly fading memory denied her a reference point. A starkness reigned over the barren recesses of the farm, clouding what used to be, when she was a girl still being courted by her husband.

She remembered the warmth of the spring sun resting on her shoulders the afternoon he brought her up these very stairs to meet his parents.

How the porch smelled of new paint before the rot took hold.

How the lawn surrounding the house was neatly clipped before the grass was eaten by gravel.

How the wheat towered over the farmhand in the afternoon light before her husband started using the seeds fixed in a laboratory and the wheat only reached her waist.

These memories were wagon ruts running deep through the dirt of her mind, ingrained long enough ago to not be swept away by the cruel wind of time.

After one more glance around to make sure her husband wasn't watching, she took her son into her arms.

This she still knew how to do.

She absorbed the convulsions of his small sobs into her shoulder, as the awareness of what was happening to her crept in between them. She sensed, even in these sundowner moments when the world got increasingly less familiar, that she was steadily losing her grip. On everything. Except him. Right now.

And so she held her son even closer and let herself cry her own soft release into his chest, as his arms tightened across her back, her confused soul tangled with his, their tears lost in the drenching rain of the Oklahoma prairie.

———

Mark struggled to find gaps between the frenetic windshield-wiper swipes, parsing through worst-case scenarios as he drove to the farm. Jake had sounded frantic, almost manic, on the phone a few minutes ago when he'd asked Mark to come over.

He passed what looked like the Tercel on the side of the road, just seconds before he turned into their driveway. Two shadows stood against the farmhouse, silhouetted by the light spilling from the open front door. Mark pulled up slowly, until he realized Jake was hugging someone. Looked like Jake's mom.

He turned off his headlights and rolled down the window. "Jake! You good?"

Jake's mom lowered her head and scurried toward the bunkhouse, as if she'd been caught stealing. Mark opened the truck door, holding the front page of the town newspaper against the rain. "She alright?"

"Yeah, she's just embarrassed, I think. Isn't very comfortable with her situation."

"Come on, let's get inside."

Jake followed Mark into the house and stood dripping in the hallway while Mark hunted for a towel in the laundry room. He'd noticed that Jake's eyes were bloodshot, and he smelled like the bottom of a bottle. Mark was about to ask what happened when Jake stated the obvious.

"I fucked up."

"It's okay, Jake."

"It's not okay. She left me."

Mark handed him a dry T-shirt, the closest thing to clean he could find. "What happened?"

"I fell off the wagon. Hard. I just don't know how to deal with this anymore. Got nowhere to turn."

"You've got a lot going on, man. You can always talk—"

"No, no. I haven't told you the whole story. Haven't told anyone. But I think I should."

———

Jessica sat slumped over the steering wheel in the driver's seat of the Tercel, staring at the pool of leaked-in rainwater gathering on the floorboard.

How? How? How?

She'd been on the shoulder of the interstate a few hundred yards from the farm for over an hour, sobbing and pounding the dashboard with a clenched fist, until a spiderweb of shatters radiated through the sunbaked plastic above the speedometer.

This was so far from where she wanted to be, where she'd thought she'd be by now . . . here, on the side of the road, one Tercel backfire from a failing farm, facing the truth she'd been running from for the last five years: This wasn't what a marriage was supposed to look like.

Only two things seemed to honor the love she offered: Hailey and the garden. What love she put into them, she got out tenfold . . . the opposite of the dynamic with her husband.

Hailey was always with her.

But if she drove away now, she'd have to leave the garden.

Her frustration morphed to anger as she imagined the vibrant life in the soil, life she'd nurtured, life that had nurtured her, life that would die from neglect. Without her there, it wouldn't take long, not more than a couple of weeks, for the quarter-acre to wilt into a graveyard of shriveled carcasses.

Jessica looked up from the steering wheel at lightning crashing in the east, dropped the Tercel into first, and whipped a U-turn.

She wasn't leaving that garden.

———

Mark looked past Jake at the dim headlights barely making their way through the living room window. "Hang on, Jake. I think you have a wife about to come up the front stairs."

Before Jake could respond, Jessica burst into the house. "Evening, Mark. Jake, don't even look at me. I'm not going anywhere. But you are. Sorry, Mark, but we have a situation here."

Mark took a step backward into anonymity. "Maybe I should go."

Jessica pointed to the door. "You should, and you should take Jake with you. He's not staying here."

Jake stepped in between Mark and Jessica. "Wait a minute. This is my family's house. I'm staying."

"Not if you ever want me living here again, you're not."

Mark took Jake by the arm. "Hey, Jake, why don't you stay with me tonight? We have a guest room."

"No, I'm—"

"Come on, let's go."

"But I need—"

"What you need is sleep. Things will look different in the morning."

Mark put his arm around Jake, holding his jacket like a cloak against the rain, and led him through the open door, down the porch stairs, and to the passenger side of his car.

Jake resisted Mark's gentle push into the seat. "I belong here. On this land."

"I know. This isn't forever, just for the night."

Maybe Jake was too exhausted to fight anymore, or maybe he'd resigned himself to the inevitable, but all Mark heard were the same three words as Jake slumped into the car.

"I belong here."

———

Jessica watched as the two men seemed to have a temporary stand-off. Jake must have relented, but she couldn't tell if he was sobbing or shaking with anger as he fell into the seat and Mark shut the door. She stared through the warped glass of the living room window at the taillights pulling out of the driveway, their damp red glow illuminating what looked like a few books starting to get soaked on the top porch stair.

———

The ride back to his parents' house was silent. Mark let Jake be, figuring he'd talk when he wanted to talk. And if he didn't want to talk, that was fine.

Mark put a finger to his lips as they took their shoes off on the porch and stepped inside. He showed Jake the guest room, which had its own bathroom, and softly encouraged him to try the breathing exercise he'd shown him.

"Just a four count in, hold for four, and a four count out. Tell you what, why don't you take a shower, and leave your clothes here in the hallway. I'll wash them, and—"

"I don't need you washing my clothes."

"Shh. Not so loud. I'm doing a load anyway."

Which he hadn't really planned on doing, but he wouldn't mind being up for a while and letting his wheels turn on this medical mystery of small-town sickness.

Mark listened for the guest room door to close before he went downstairs and sank into his father's easy chair in front of the woodstove. Hopefully Jake would settle down by morning, because if Jessica left . . . well, he didn't want to think about that.

He took his notebook from the coffee table, thumbed through to his most recent entry, and added *Dirt* to the list.

Jessica
Water
Food
Rx (Agriculture)
Dirt

Dirt.

That's right. The microbiome.

His train of thought had been derailed by the frantic phone call from Jake, who hadn't even noticed he was sitting on two Ziploc bags in the passenger seat.

Mark waited until he heard the shower shut off upstairs, the bed creak under Jake's weight, and the soft snore of a hibernating bear, before slinking outside with the truck keys and starting the engine. He slowly backed out of the driveway, navigated a few sections of washed-out highway, and ten minutes later, he was at the clinic, looking at the farm dirt and Jessica's garden soil under the microscope.

Hypothesis confirmed.

Jessica's soil was alive with a diverse microbiome . . . bacteria, fungi, the occasional not-so-micro earthworm. Her dirt was teeming with life. Jake's dirt was dead by comparison, even though the samples came from virtually the same land.

There was something else about Jessica's soil, though, that kept Mark staring through the microscope.

Something that looked strangely familiar.

After a few minutes of trying to pinpoint what he recognized, he rushed back into the clinic office to search through the last year of boxed-up chemo research, where he pulled an imaging printout of the latest therapy he'd been working on.

Whoa.

One of the carbon molecules in Jessica's dirt looked a lot like this cancer-killing chemo.

Which could mean that her soil contained something that looked a lot like pretty powerful medicine.

The drive home seemed to take only seconds, accelerated by theories and thoughts spinning through his head. He climbed the stairs stealthily, grabbed the clothes piled outside the bedroom door, and headed back down to the laundry room, where he started the load and found a blanket for the couch.

Jake didn't need to know there wasn't really a guest room.

———

Jessica's index finger traced the frayed edges of the black-and-white photograph she'd found in the folds of the last journal.

Unreal.

She'd been able to salvage them from the top porch stair before the driving rain had done any damage. Her first guess was that Jake's dad had left the journals there after knocking on the door and getting no response from an embarrassed son.

An entire pot of coffee later, she'd read every entry. She'd stepped back in time, to the old ways, when needs were few and the creek by the elm was running clear, into a scene of indigenous tradition and family . . . and then witnessed the ripping away of a child from that tradition and family—into a forced and tragic assimilation.

She'd watched the three sisters of corn, squash, and beans devolve into cash crop farming and the Dust Bowl. She'd felt the deathbed regret of the blind pursuit of money, power, and revenge, in the shakily scrawled final plea to descendants.

> *My greatest regret, and gravest error, is that, in trying to honor my father, whose picture I have left here with this page, I turned away from him. And in turning away from him, I turned away from our great mother, who returns to us what we give to her.*

All the ancient family stories were here, woven through five decades of a man's life . . . the second generation to farm the place. Jake's great-grandfather, if her genealogical math was right.

She held the picture to the dining room light, wondering if she was the first person in over a century to look at this faded image of a small field alive with the interwoven tangles of corn, beans, and squash, surrounding a stoic man with beautiful braids draped over his shoulders, wearing a deerskin breechcloth and a fringed leather shirt.

She probably was.

—Thursday—

Muted light seeped through the curtains, casting the room in unfamiliar shades of gray.

Where was he?

Jake sat up quickly, his head pounding in protest at yesterday's bender. He stared around the room, taking in the relics adorning the childhood shrine.

A space caught in time, that's where he was.

Above the small desk hung yellowing posters, not of rock bands or *Sports Illustrated* swimsuit models, but of the solar system and planets and stars. The wall opposite the bed was plastered with spelling bee participation certifications and math club awards.

Jake squinted, trying to make out the name.

That's where he was.

Mark's room.

Yesterday began to creep back into Jake's consciousness, and he reflexively built a dam of deflection to stem the tide.

Not now.

Jessica, McGill's, his brother.

Couldn't think about that now.

He focused on the buckets of rain being thrown against the window and pulled himself out of bed, looking for his clothes. The floor was bare save for the shag carpet that must have been older than him. A quick hit of panic startled him into damage-control mode . . . he didn't want anybody to see him like this, a real-life Jabba the Hutt torn from the poster above the dresser.

He cracked the bedroom door and peered down the hall. The toilet peeked out from an open threshold, and the only other door was closed. Mark's mother must be in there, if he was in Mark's old room.

So where was Mark sleeping?

Focus, Jake. Focus. These details mattered not. Clothes mattered.

Maybe the dresser held a random pair of sweatpants he could fit into. Unlikely, but worth a look.

He dropped his gaze, as if staring at the carpet might soften the door's closing, and there, folded outside the threshold, were his shirt and pants from yesterday. Even his socks, married in the same ball Jessica made when she was doing laundry.

This Mark guy was alright.

Jake met the smell of coffee halfway down the stairs and found Mark taking a sip at the kitchen table. "Sorry, Mark. I usually don't sleep in like that."

Mark set his mug down. "My professional medical opinion was that you needed some rest, so I stayed as quiet as I could."

"And thanks for washing the clothes."

"No problem. Hopefully the aura of booze, sweat, and Sonic isn't lingering anywhere else. That *was* Sonic I smelled, right?"

Jake held up both hands in defense. "Yeah, but not my food. My brother's."

"Your brother? You never talked about having a brother. What—"

Jake turned to the counter, in search of the coffee maker. "Not now, please . . . maybe later. And listen, about last night—"

Mark pointed toward the other side of the kitchen. "Get some coffee, over there, then a plate. Eggs are on the stove. We're going to take a little trip, so we'll have plenty of time to talk about last night and your mystery brother."

"Where are we going?"

"Stillwater."

"Like five hours away Stillwater?

"Yeah. Oklahoma State."

"Why?"

"For one thing, I doubt Jessica's ready for you to come crawling back. Also, you don't have a car, or anything better to do." Mark returned his attention to the pencil in his hand. "But I'll explain the real reason on the way."

Jake chased his breakfast with black coffee while he watched Mark feverishly write in a notebook, filling two pages before Jake was done with his first cup. "What's that all about?"

"Been going most of the night, sorting through theories and checking a few things out online. Couldn't really sleep. But I think I have an idea about what's making both you and the land sick."

"That so?"

"Yeah, we can talk on the drive. Leave your dish in the sink."

They hustled outside to the truck, rain pounding the windshield as they pulled onto the highway. Jake nursed his coffee and was surprised to hear Bison Bridge on the stereo. "You listen to this guy?"

"Is it a guy? Or a band? I don't know his story yet. A friend at work shared the album with me. You?"

"This was the soundtrack to me trying to kill myself. Had to dub the songs onto a cassette to play on the old truck radio. Really, just one song."

Mark reached for his phone to change the playlist, but Jake blocked him with his free hand. "It's alright. This is fine." He took another swig of coffee, sat back, and let the music dominate the drive, happy to not have to talk.

As soon as they passed the city limits sign for Woodward, Mark turned down the radio. "Here's some trivia for you. Sonic basically started here, in this town we're passing through."

Jake's love for Sonic was well documented, so this was an interesting development. "Really?"

"Yeah, the first franchise location ever was in Woodward. It was called the Top-Hat Drive-In Restaurant back then, in 1956. They changed the name to Sonic Drive-In when they found out 'Top-Hat' was already trademarked."

"And how do you know this?"

"While you were asleep, I fell down a few rabbit holes researching inputs."

Jake watched the last buildings of Woodward dissolve into bleak, drenched prairie, the thick blanket of clouds mirroring his not-yet-cured hangover. Coffee hadn't lifted the painful fog, and while his track record for getting meds from Mark wasn't stellar, it couldn't hurt to ask.

"You got any Advil? Assuming that's legal?"

Mark pointed to the glove compartment. "Not really, but I'll make a rare exception since I'm dragging you to Stillwater. Look in there. And drink some water."

Jake found the ibuprofen, took four tablets out of the bottle, felt Mark's disapproving stare, and put two of them back. He washed the Advil down with an entire bottle of water and belched. "Sorry for the conversational detour. What do you mean by 'inputs'?"

"Inputs influence outputs. Garbage in, garbage out."

"You sound like Jessica."

"Well, she's right. You took in a decent amount of bourbon last night, and you feel like shit this morning. A more scientific way of saying the same thing might be that you introduced a toxin to your body . . . most notably acetaldehyde, from the oxidization of ethanol and—"

Jake's smirk devolved into a groan. "I get it. Inputs influence outputs. Garbage in, garbage out. But I'm guessing we're not driving to Stillwater because of a hangover."

He watched Mark fumble with the Walmart bag perched on the console between them, and just as he was getting around to offering his assistance, Mark succeeded in pulling out a sandwich. With one hand on the wheel, he used the other to pry apart the Saran wrap. "Actually, in a manner of speaking, we are. Before I explain, though, it's your turn. Tell me about your brother."

———

The pounding was incessant, abrasive metal rapping so hard against the glass that Adam bolted upright in the bed of the Ranger and slammed his head on the truck shell roof. He looked toward the tailgate and saw a head framed by two cupped hands, nose pushed into the tinted rear window.

He slid open the rear side window. "Can I help you?"

The figure, folds of neck flesh burying his uniform collar, trudged around the truck, holstering his .38. "You better."

Adam's patience for law enforcement had run out long ago, right around when the cops had nothing better to do than raid their cornfield circle-ups back in high school. "Is that really necessary? Pulling your gun out?"

"Just used the butt to wake your ass up. You're not allowed to be parked here overnight."

"Yeah, well, looks like morning to me."

The cop took a step back. "I'm not in the mood. Get out of the truck."

"I'm not in the mood either. Find someone else to hassle."

Unnecessary backup arrived within a few minutes, and Adam's journey from sleeping bag to cop car was even quicker. He yelled through the barely cracked window to the officer, who was rubbing bellies with his esteemed colleague. "You want to tell me what you're arresting me for?"

"Grand theft."

"What?"

"Ran those plates, came back stolen."

"Oh, for fuck's sake. I borrowed this truck."

"Apparently you're the only person aware of that."

He didn't have a phone anymore, which is why he'd very briefly stolen Jake's, but he'd committed a few numbers to memory . . . well, really just two—his home phone number growing up, because he had to as a kid, and his dealer's, because he had to as an occasional adult. "Let me out of these cuffs, and I'll call the guy. We're friends."

"That's not how this works."

"And how does this work?"

"I take you to the station, you get processed, put in a cell, and if you can find someone to bail you out, you leave."

Adam took a closer look at his captor. This was a small town.

"Wait a minute. I know you."

"That so?"

"Yeah, you were friends with my older brother when I was little. I don't forget a face."

"I know. I saw the last name on your ID. But you don't look like your brother at all."

"Sleeping in the back of a Ford Ranger will do that."

"I doubt that's the only reason. Good chance that whatever led you to grand theft might be contributing."

"I didn't—"

"Me knowing your brother doesn't change anything. We're just waiting for the tow truck to show up. You'll get to make a call from jail, like everybody else, and when bail's set, they can post for you."

Adam slunk back into the vinyl seat.

He always had the shittiest luck. Except luck was getting harder and harder to blame.

———

Mark took a bite of his sandwich and chewed slowly on Jake's hesitant revealing of his brother Adam's issues. Sounded like Adam had discovered harder drugs through partying and had quite a good time until that silly reality of physiological addiction took over.

Jake had been introduced to opioids via a prescription pad. Back injuries, complications from surgery, debilitating arthritis—there were a lot of people in a lot of pain. And there was a place for opioids. Hell, he'd want morphine too if he'd been in a wreck and had to be stitched and sewn and stapled back together . . . but Purdue Pharma's flooding of hospitals and doctors' offices, and eventually the streets, with their miracle drug?

Borderline criminal, fueled by marketing like the pharmaceutical world had never seen, despite knowing the incredibly addictive nature of their brainchild.

Jake shook Mark out of his mental indictment. "So, back to this thing about us going to Stillwater because of my hangover . . . "

Mark considered how best to explain his theory, which was mostly rooted in science, but not without some speculation. He pushed the first word that came to his mind through his full mouth. "*Mfffmphhlphhn.*"

"Huh?"

Mark swallowed, set the sandwich on his lap, and took a big swig of lukewarm coffee from his travel mug. "Sorry. Inflammation. Your body's immune response to the toxins in alcohol can lead to inflammation, which can cause headaches, malaise . . . basically, your hangover."

"Which still explains nothing about why we're driving to Stillwater."

"Easy, easy—there's more to the story." Mark watched Jake dig through the Walmart bag, probably hoping to find his own sandwich. Which, of course, Mark had made while Jake was hibernating. "So even though you feel like crap right now, inflammation's actually a protective mechanism, where your body sends white blood cells to defend against outside invaders—some of the more dangerous bacteria, viruses, toxins, stuff like that."

Jake offered a slight smile as he pulled out the wrapped sandwich, but Mark knew he was happier about the sandwich than the explanation. "Uh-huh. That sounds like a good thing."

"Crucial, actually, until that inflammation becomes chronic and the immune system gets triggered over and over and over, often when there's not even anything to defend against. Chronic inflammation is at the root of a lot of disease, including your ulcerative colitis."

"What causes it?"

"Well, that's why we're in the truck right now. I'd like to chase down some answers at OSU about what causes the kind of chronic inflammation I'm seeing in my patients. And in you."

Jake smirked. "What, are we going to uncover some medical mystery in Stillwater? Should we call a news crew to meet us there? Thank God you washed my clothes last night. I'm going to be on TV." He shoved half the sandwich in his mouth and pulled his phone from his jeans pocket.

Apparently, they'd had enough science talk for now.

Mark turned up Bison Bridge on the radio and sailed through the storm, eyes focused on the spaces between the rain until he saw a lone horse on the rise to his right. Mark watched, for as long as so many miles per hour would allow, this animal with such power and strength, such grace and speed, choosing to stand still in the downpour.

As if the horse was waiting for the weather to pass through him, instead of wasting his energy outrunning the storm.

As if this knowledge and experience already in his blood dwarfed the intentions of these dry humans, moving at their unnatural speed along the wet asphalt river, careening toward their own destruction.

As if.

———

At first, Jessica didn't recognize the ringing sound.

Was that the landline? Nobody called that number anymore, which had been the same since Jake was a little kid.

She left the dishes soaking in the sink, dried her hands on her jeans, and picked up the receiver mounted to the wall.

"Hello? What?"

———

Jake's father turned off *Judge Judy* and studied his withering hand, barely able to grip the remote.

Rainmaker, huh?

Used to be.

He'd never been the most reflective guy, but lately he'd been thinking about the past more. Who knows, maybe because he was dying. And his wife was fading.

She was getting a lot worse, and fast. She'd been able to handle the cooking, and pretty much everything else, up until a couple of months ago. Now, he sometimes wondered if she even knew who he was. He'd been trying the best he could to make meals for them, but there was only so much he could do with a hand that wouldn't stop shaking.

He hadn't told Jake how bad she'd gotten, but he probably knew. Seemed like he had his own problems right now.

Some had to do with him, maybe. He shouldn't have dismissed Jake when he wanted to talk about that man in the wheat, back in the day. And he still wasn't sure what he'd seen, but he'd had no trouble lying about it. Even last night. He hadn't just seen that thing once.

No, he'd seen it twice a year, around harvest time. Seemed to really start happening a year or two after he'd almost killed himself, right around when this place really started taking off. He'd managed to find a good working schedule, between tilling and planting and spraying, double-cropping for yield . . . the farm was so damn productive.

So why pay too much attention to a shadow?

His wife had told him his grandfather's journals had something to do with it. She'd read them all, she said, and had practically begged him to do the same. But what good would that do? Nothing was going to slow him down—oh no, got to keep on moving, just like the esteemed advice from that early eighties song.

Nothing was going to slow him down, especially whatever ghost story she'd hinted was in there.

What a crock.

She didn't say much back then. Never had, really. Jake had gotten his quiet from her. Adam had probably gotten his loud from him. Which one was worse, he was starting to wonder.

He flinched against the lightning strike and braced for the coming thunder.

Goddamn rain.

———

Jake scrolled through his endless Facebook feed, then switched over to Instagram, not wanting to admit that he was slightly intrigued by Mark's science-guy scavenger hunt. Not looking up from his phone, he tried to hide his curiosity in impatience. "So, you're chasing this chronic inflammation thing. You want to tell me why I'm here?"

"What's with the newly discovered crappy mood? You're welcome for the sandwich, by the way."

"Sorry. Thanks."

"Maybe it's that damn social media you default to instead of sitting with your thoughts for a minute. Garbage in, garbage out, remember?"

"I said sorry, alright? Who's the grumpy one now?"

A grin surfaced behind Mark's grimace. "Just busting your balls. So, you want to know why you're here? Other than letting Jessica have the day to realize how much she misses you, you're here because of one word: soil."

"Soil?"

"Yeah."

Jake tucked his phone back in his pocket. "Here's the part where you explain."

"Right, right. I realized something last night at the clinic."

"What? When did you go there?"

"After you took a shower and went to bed. I had a hunch . . . and I was right. I looked at samples of your farm dirt and soil from Jessica's garden under the microscope. Her soil had a lot more organic activity . . . a *lot* more. Best word I can think of is 'alive.' There's even something that looks like medicine in there."

"And that's because . . . ?"

"She doesn't use much in the way of manufactured chemicals—if any—and I think there's a connection there. Because when I looked at your dirt—"

Jake finished his sentence. "Let me guess. It was dead."

Mark glanced at Jake before he hit the accelerator, risking the wet road to pass a semi. "Well, yeah. Probably comes down to inputs again, this particular one being about what you're adding to your dirt. Something is killing the life in there, and my theory is that dead dirt's contributing to the chronic inflammation at the root of your health problems. Not to mention the issues you're having with your land. And it's not just you. If most farmers are treating their land the same way, the scale could be large enough to contribute to a human health crisis."

Jake took a breath, trying not to be offended. "You're saying I'm poisoning people?"

"No, no. Not intentionally." Mark's eyes were still on the semi, finally in the rearview mirror. "But maybe something you're spraying or spreading is damaging the soil somehow. And I'm not just talking about chemical inputs, but also what and when you're planting, and how you're working the fields. I really don't know yet, and I could be way off. But you and Jessica are opposites, from your plants to your health, and the soil is a key difference, so I want to chase that idea down."

Jake bristled. "I don't like where this is going."

"Understandable, but wouldn't you want to know if you had the power to make a significant change? I'm not just talking about woo-woo abstract health, Jake. You could be making a lot more money with better yields. And spending less on inputs."

Jake closed his eyes. "I guess."

"That's why we're driving to Oklahoma State. I talked to the head of the Ag Research department, and he said you guys can have a conversation about how you're running your operation. He'll give you whatever related current research they have."

"What will you be doing?"

"I'll be across campus at the medical library. We'll cross-reference that Ag research with whatever studies I can find about how environmental agents might cause chronic inflammation in people. Eating, drinking, breathing . . . those kinds of inputs."

"Can't we just do this with an Internet connection?"

"Actual humans can be more helpful sometimes, especially when sorting through a huge mass of data. Kind of like asking an old-school librarian who's been around the block for help instead of digging through a card catalog all afternoon. I want to explain what I'm thinking to the lady in charge of the medical library. Her assistant told me she'd be in by noon."

"Do I really need to talk to the Ag guy? All this stuff you want me to tell him is common knowledge in our world. Not that you would know, of course." Jake hadn't meant to sound derisive, but combating vulnerability with passive-aggressiveness had become almost second nature.

Mark was quiet for a moment, and Jake guessed that he'd hit a nerve. "Oh, really? Do you know exactly how that weedkiller works? Tell me, what metabolic mechanism does the chemical compound use to drain life from the weed? Does that chemical compound stay in the dirt? For how long? What does it do to the soil while it's there?"

Jake stared at the passing winter wheat fields. Stems rose from the standing water, like antennae surfacing on a submerged submarine. His dad had leveled most of the natural contours out of their land, too, and they had the same issue. Both he and his dad had dedicated their entire adult lives to their farm and knowing every inch of field, every piece of machinery, every chemical used, and how much and when . . . but he sure didn't have those kinds of answers. And there was no way his dad did, either.

Mark's tone softened. "Listen, look at the Ag guy as that librarian who's seen and read a lot and can maybe make connections you might not think of. New research, who knows?"

"Whatever. Google would be easier."

"Yeah, well, the Internet isn't always right."

———

Adam sheepishly accepted the Ziploc bag holding the extent of his personal belongings: an empty wallet. Empty, except for his state ID, which he somehow had miraculously not lost in the haze of the last few years. . . . Otherwise, he probably wouldn't have been bailed out.

He turned the corner from the discharge window and saw his sister-in-law sitting on the wooden precinct bench. "Hey, sis."

Jessica looked up from her lap and pushed to her feet. Adam went for the hug, but she flattened her hand against his chest. "Not yet, Adam. Not yet."

They walked in silence toward the Toyota Tercel parked in front of the jail. Jessica balked as Adam reached for the passenger side door handle. "Wait a minute. How do you know this is my car?"

"Jake told me the truck got in a little fender bender."

Jessica stopped halfway around the car. "What? You talked to him? I thought you said—"

"I said he didn't know I was in jail. But I saw him yesterday driving this little guy. I'll explain on the drive."

Jessica cranked the ignition, coaxing the engine to life. "Drive where? Where am I taking you?"

"Well, I got nowhere to go. Up to you."

"You can't stay at the farm."

"I know. I get it." He put on his seat belt. "Listen, I'm not looking for a handout, or anything like that. Let's grab some lunch somewhere, and I'll tell you why I'm here. Nobody believes me, and I don't expect you to, either. But at least we'll have something to talk about."

Jessica scoffed as she pulled out of the parking space. "You're not looking for a handout? That's cool—what are you going to be buying lunch with, then? Your charm?"

"You'd be surprised. The shit I got away with when I was growing up, flashing a smile or winking an eye? Criminal. Literally. Neck tat doesn't help my case these days, though." He rolled down the window, grateful to not be inhaling cement and steel. "I know sincerity doesn't have much cash value. But how about I pay for lunch with some unexpected honesty?"

Jessica shot him a sideways glance. "Fine. But we're going to Frank's, not Sonic."

Another breath of fresh air, in and out. He caught himself just before making that trademark wink. "Sweet. A sandwich for the truth."

———

Jake squinted at the two huge stacks of paper on the desk in front of him. "All of this?"

The Ag Research department head glanced at him over his glasses.

Jake was surprised at how, well, normal the guy looked . . . not the stuffy academic type he'd been expecting. "That's not even half of the studies we have about that weedkiller compound in particular. Lots of buzz lately. And you're not just using it for killing weeds, are you?"

"No." Jake studied the creases in one of his palms. The conversation with Mark on the way here had got him thinking that he might be doing some damage to his dirt. *Might* be. Nothing proven yet. But the fact he had to basically wear a hazmat suit to prep the mixture was starting to feel a little suspect.

"Didn't think so. Using it as a desiccant?"

"Yeah."

"And you're double-cropping with corn, using that company's GMO seeds resistant to their weedkiller, right?"

"I am."

"And spraying even more, I'm guessing, to try to get rid of the weeds that have figured out a way around the herbicide."

"Yeah. Pigweed doesn't seem to care, though."

The Ag guy frowned in agreement as he jotted down notes on a yellow legal pad. "We're seeing a lot of those weeds that have developed resistance. Superweeds, I call them. Last question. No-till?"

"No, I clear the land after each harvest. Always have."

"Alright. I think I know what your doctor friend is trying to get at. Hang tight a minute."

The Ag director disappeared into the stacks and returned in less time than Jake had to get his Facebook fix on his phone.

"Based on what you told me about your operation, this is what he's looking for." He dropped another phonebook-thick stack of papers on the counter between them. "I threw in some of the patent info, too, in case he needs it."

"Thanks. Not sure what he's after, to be honest, but I know he's trying to sort out why folks seem to be falling apart."

The eyes across the counter lit up, just enough to show approval.

"Well, good for him. And maybe for us. I'm sure he'll let on soon. Come back with me to the copier room. We got a lot of Xeroxing to do."

They stood side by side, feeding handfuls of documents into the machines. Jake had just been lulled into mechanical meditation when the Ag head broke the conversational seal. "I was friends with your dad, you know. Even held you in these tree-trunk arms, when you were in diapers . . . before I moved here for undergrad."

"Yeah? How do you know who I am?"

"I needed your name to get you clearance. That's really the only reason I pulled all this info for you . . . because I knew your family. How's your dad these days? Still blasting Tim McGraw from the combine?"

"Not really, actually. He's got Parkinson's."

The Ag guy paused stuffing the document feeder long enough for Jake to think that maybe his dad had shared a beer or three with him. "Damn. I'm sorry to hear that."

"He's hanging in there. Still early."

"Well, all the same. Give him my best, would you?"

Jake started pouring the copied files into the Walmart bag that had held their sandwiches. "Yes, sir. I will."

"Life sure is short, huh? But your dad's had a pretty good run."

Jake lifted his focus from the pile of papers in his hands, and in the tiny fleck of time before his eyes settled on the cracked plastic cover of the copy machine, he saw his dad.

Faint forehead lines amplifying his excited anticipation as he watched young Jake open the giftwrap hiding one of those fancy Apple computers on Christmas morning.

Deepening wrinkles hiding his cautious pride as he shook teenage Jake's hand after finishing his first solo lap in the combine.

Sagging cheeks lifted by pure joy as he held Jake's little girl for the first time.

And a creased brow furrowed with finality, barely disguising his anguish a year later, when the farm-town physician gave him what amounted to a death sentence.

Which we're all up against. Most of us just don't know the timing.

Jake's eyes found the floor as he took a measured breath to steady his response.

"Yes, sir. It sure is. And yes, he has."

———

Mark had been slouched so long in the rigid plastic chair that he'd resorted to finding asbestos constellations in the texture of the seventies drywall.

The click of high heels on polished concrete—*high heels?*—reached a crescendo with the downturn of the door handle, and Mark instinctively held out his right hand as he stood up.

He stopped, still bent at the waist, when his gaze caught her fingers.

Her fingers.

Her fingers.

"Hey, stranger."

And her voice.

Her voice.

Her.

"Hi. Sorry. I, uh, I . . ."

Her cupped hand found his chin, gentle pressure guiding him up to eye level.

"Hi, Mark."

And a freight train of release rushed through him, engine stoked into motion by this living, breathing remember-when. A flickering, fluorescent-lit *here* was left in the wake of its wind, where *here* was his father's passing, his mother's quiet sorrow. *Here* was everything he thought he'd be by now. *Here* was *her*.

All this that he had not cried for, he did now, burying his tears in the fabric of her blouse, trying to mask his emotion in an embrace, but unable to hide the shaking and surging in his body.

He pulled back when he had nothing left and focused his wet eyes on the concrete floor, embarrassed by what she probably saw as over-emoting. This wasn't the second first impression he wanted to make.

She placed her hand on his trembling chest and lifted his chin until her eyes found his. "We have a few things to talk about, don't we? Tell you what. Let's make a deal."

"What kind of deal?"

"You're going to owe me an OSU football game for helping you."

"Okay."

"And dinner."

"Fine."

"And maybe a beer."

"Of course."

"That's when we'll talk."

"But . . ."

She pressed an index finger to his lips. "This is a much longer conversation than either of us has time for right now, Mark."

He took her wrist and pulled her hand to his heart. "I have all the time in the world for this. You never left here. You never—"

"Not now. Later. You want to take another minute before we dive into why you're here?" She dropped her hand to her side.

"You mean why I *thought* I was here."

"Mark . . ."

"Fine. If there's one thing I'm good at, it's compartmentalizing."

"Alright. Get to compartmentalizing, then. And tell me why the message from my assistant was so cryptic. Something about a secret that's killing people?"

"That does sound a little dramatic, I guess. I don't know if I used those exact words, but I've been playing around in unexplored human health territory, at least unexplored to me, and got kind of excited."

She rolled her eyes. "You never seemed to be prone to conspiracy theories . . . let alone making up your own!"

"That's why I'm here. I'll tell you what I think might be going on, and you can prove me wrong."

"I accept your challenge gladly. Debunking myths before they have a chance to spread misinformation to an unassuming public sounds like community service."

She walked around the oversized office desk and eased down into her chair, with the same gentle flop Mark remembered from the lecture hall. "I had my assistant pull some studies together based on what you told her, and I have to say, as an MD, I'm a little leery about the diversity of diseases you want to link together."

"Which is why you called me a conspiracy theorist."

"Well, Parkinson's, diabetes, autism, leukemia, dementia, gut disease, even obesity . . . "

"Those are all conditions I've seen in our little farm town clinic, and I just think there may be a common thread between them."

"And that thread is . . . ?"

Mark went for the low-hanging fruit first. "We can agree that the medical community has established and embraced systemic chronic inflammation as being at the root of many diseases, right?"

Her slow nod showed a hint of reluctance. "I'll give you that."

"Maybe if we walk it further back, there's a common denominator causing that systemic chronic inflammation."

"That's a stretch, but not entirely absurd."

"Whew. Finally, a crack in the armor."

She smiled and pushed the stack of papers to the side of the desk. "What put you on this particular path?"

"Sort of a perfect shitstorm, I guess. I'd been working in chemo research for a long time, which wasn't as fulfilling as I'd hoped, and then I had to go back to Guymon—"

"Why? You always said you were never going back there, no matter what."

"My father was dying. Cancer, of all things."

"Oh, Mark, I'm sorry."

"Thanks. Maybe we can talk about that later, too. My mother isn't much of a sounding board these days. Anyway, I went back home, and my old man said something that both pissed me off and got me thinking."

"And that was . . . ?"

"He claimed that I wasn't really working on a cure for a disease . . . that cancer was more like the symptom of something else going on. Something bigger."

"Where did he get that idea?"

"I'm not sure. Maybe too much Art Bell and *Coast to Coast* on AM radio."

"That's where this 'walk it back' approach is coming from."

"Yeah, those were his exact words."

Her sea-green eyes softened as she tucked a few loose strands of auburn hair behind her ear. "Go on."

"I stayed in Guymon to help my mother and started working at the small clinic in town, where almost every day I have patients coming in with these chronic diseases. They want me to prescribe some pill they see advertised on TV in between *Judge Judy* segments or episodes of whatever other show they might be bingeing."

"And that's wrong?"

Mark chose his words carefully. "I don't know. I just think we've built this behemoth, based on disease treatment, that focuses more on drugs to alleviate symptoms, especially for chronic disease, instead of considering—"

Her fingers, clasped around her knee, stiffened slightly. "Mark.

Come on. That approach may have a few flaws, but when patients are struggling, they need help. We're trained as doctors to combat disease."

"Yeah, but we learn way more about combat than ways to prevent the fight in the first place. And we're using the same mentality for trying to cure the disease as we are for alleviating symptoms. More drugs, synthesized and sold by humans."

"Which often work, by the way, to great effect. Are you trying to tell me that you have some magical, better way that nobody has thought of before?"

Mark hedged his response. "No. But this established way of practicing medicine has so much momentum—history, money, societal inertia. I mean, look at me. I was developing new chemotherapies, thinking I was going to save the world—never thought twice about what I was doing. Ten thousand drugs to treat ten thousand symptoms was normal to me, and to all my colleagues."

"So, what changed your mind?"

"Dirt."

"Dirt?"

"Yeah, dirt."

She gathered the studies from her desk and stood up. "Now we're veering into cuckoo land. Let's walk and talk."

They headed out of the office and deep into the stacks, where Mark tried to take the crazy down a notch. "It's simple, really. Take any system . . . outputs are a product of inputs, right?"

"Well, yeah."

He struggled to keep up with her blistering walk. "And if you strip a system of its beneficial, medicinal inputs, and replace it with harmful ones, the outputs are going to reflect that."

"Fine."

"I looked at samples of dirt from my friend's farm and his wife's garden, and it didn't take a medical degree to see that the farm dirt is being stripped of life."

"That sounds like an agricultural issue, not a medical issue."

Mark grabbed her forearm so she'd stop for a minute and look at him. "It's both. Agricultural *and* medical. You know as well as I do that the gut microbiome is playing a way bigger role in health than we ever imagined. Biodiversity in the gut microbiome is crucial, and it's heavily influenced by our environment, including the soil microbiome. Plus, those soil outputs encompass our food system. And we are what we eat, right?"

"This isn't *Sesame Street,* Mark."

"Sheesh. Tough crowd."

"Sorry. I'm a data girl. You know this."

"Well, that's why my friend is at the Ag department now, collecting research on what kind of impact mechanical and chemical farming might have on soil. And why I'm here in the medical library, with you."

She stopped in front of a shelf stuffed with file boxes and side-eyed him. "That so?"

"Well, I would've come to clean the toilets if I knew you'd be here." He tried to plead his case without sounding desperate. "Look, like I told you, I'm not trying to push some conspiracy theory. I want copies of peer-reviewed studies that show strong causality between systemic chronic inflammation and chronic disease, research on disease incidence, that kind of thing. And whatever you think might help as far as environmental toxins and human health. I sent your assistant the list of what my friend uses on his fields."

"You probably could've found this on the interwebs."

"I'd rather have someone who knows this world point me toward what's irrefutable and away from what's not."

She handed him the stack of papers she'd brought from the office. "Well, here's everything we could find about those different disease incidences—when they ramped up and to what demographics—going back almost a hundred years. That's as far as my assistant got. And a medical study in *Nature* was recently published connecting systemic chronic infection, chronic disease, and the environment. I think it mentions social and lifestyle factors, too. We might be kicking off this whole adventure with your holy grail."

She pulled out one of the file boxes.

"Should be in here. Yeah . . . check this out."

Mark's excitement rose just seeing the title. "'Chronic Inflammation in the Etiology of Disease Across the Life Span.'"

"Right. Just read the abstract for now."

He squinted at the tiny print.

"'Although intermittent increases in inflammation are critical for survival during physical injury and infection, recent research has revealed that certain social, environmental and lifestyle factors can promote systemic chronic inflammation (SCI) that can, in turn, lead to several diseases that collectively represent the leading causes of disability and mortality worldwide, such as cardiovascular disease, cancer, diabetes mellitus, chronic kidney disease, non-alcoholic fatty liver disease and autoimmune and neurodegenerative disorders.'" Mark flipped through the study. "All diseases that I'm seeing in my clinic."

"Like I said, could be the holy grail for you as far as linking chronic disease to chronic inflammation, using how people eat and live, not to mention what they do with and to the environment. Anyway, moving on."

She took off down another aisle, talking over her shoulder as Mark tried to catch up. "My world isn't in the soil microbiome, but there's actually a good National Institutes of Health study linking the soil microbiome to the gut microbiome. And there's a lot coming in about how disrupting the gut microbiome has drastic impacts on our health. You might not be entirely crazy. But that dinner just got a lot more expensive."

"From what I remember, you're worth it."

———

Jessica pointed to a booth near the window at Frank's. "Take a seat; I'm going to wash my hands. If the server comes by, get whatever you want. I'll have the Cobb salad."

She headed into the bathroom and ran the water, looking at herself in the mirror for the first time that day. Jake would be beyond pissed if he knew about her bailing Adam out and taking him to lunch, especially on their dime. The truth always seemed to rise to the surface sooner or later, and he'd find out.

But with her in-laws' health fading, time was short. Maybe Adam just wanted to say goodbye, and then be back on his way again . . . whatever that way was.

She slid back into the booth, wiping her hands on a paper towel. "Alright, newfound-honesty guy. You're up."

Adam leaned against the backrest. "First, agree that you'll hear me all the way out. Delay judgment as long as you can, until I'm done."

Jessica took a quick, silent inventory of the collateral damage Adam had caused. "I'll try."

His head was turned toward the rain-streaked window, the gray light exposing the sores scattered across his face. He caught her staring as he scratched at the inside of his forearms. "Meth mites."

"What?"

"Meth mites. I still scratch at them, kind of compulsively I guess, even though I'm not using."

"They're not real, right?"

"Nope. Sure thought they were real, though, when I was high. How about I start there?"

"Where? Getting high?"

"Yeah. This'll be quick, because I don't remember a ton. But what I do remember, nobody in the family knows about."

Jessica waited for the server to set the food down and walk away before encouraging him to continue. This was a small town. "Go on."

"Well, no secret that my muse was meth. Wish I could tell you I started using for some nobler cause, like staying up to study or work, but I just liked the high. Opioids slowed me down too much. . . . Meth made me feel like Superman." Adam chased a bite of his sandwich with water and shrugged his shoulders. "Partying was fun."

"Really? That's all? You didn't have some self-awareness of wanting to escape or quiet the noise? Sorry, not trying to be a therapist . . . just curious."

"Ask whatever you want. You're buying lunch. And no, I wasn't consciously trying to forget about problems; I just loved the feeling. The euphoria and the hyperalertness were mind-blowing to me. Which makes me look like even more of an asshole, I know, because I had a good gig. Solid family, friends—I wasn't born into an abusive family or anything. Some of the stories I heard at rehab—"

"Wait, you went to rehab? I didn't know that."

"Yeah, a few times. A lot of those people were thrown into fucked-up circumstances that they had no hand in, and they kind of deserved empathy, know what I mean?"

Jessica thought of Hailey, sick through no fault of her own. "I do."

"Well, that wasn't me. Hard to feel sorry for a kid that just wanted to party and let it get out of hand."

"Is that what happened? Just got out of hand?"

Adam teased a melody under his breath, muttering something about doing a little, but a little not being enough.

"Thought that band was before your time."

"Time doesn't apply to the greatest rock band of the last thirty years. Axl Rose knew what he was singing about in 'Mr. Brownstone.' Different drug, same story."

They sat in silence for a moment, Jessica picking at her salad and

Adam devouring whatever it was he was eating on thick slabs of white bread. Pastrami, maybe.

"Why did you go to rehab?"

"Court-ordered after a couple of possession offenses. Felt like I was getting loved to death."

"Loved to death?"

"Yeah, I mean, nobody was really holding a mirror up to me and saying, 'Look what you're doing to yourself and your family. You're a fucking asshole,' if that makes sense."

"No, not really."

Adam stared at the infinity tattoo on his wrist. "I appreciated the support of the program staff at both facilities I went to, but I didn't need somebody holding my hand, over and over and over, until I overdosed. Sitting around in a circle, searching out and dissecting my deepest demons, didn't make me want to stop using. That's what I mean by getting loved to death."

Jessica's nurturing side rose up in defense. "Well, I'm sure some patients in those programs do really want to be there, and they stay clean. Those facilities exist for a reason."

"I suppose. Just telling you that I went through treatment with a group of guys also there on court order, and most of them didn't really want to stop either. And because of that, they probably ended up in the 85 or 90 percent or whatever that relapse."

"*Whatever* isn't really an exact statistic, Adam."

"Look up the numbers yourself. I'm not lying. And I didn't mean to start a debate about rehab. . . . Just letting you know where I'm coming from, which will also help you see why I'm really here, back in town."

"Which is?"

"Hang on, I'm getting there. All this I'm telling you about happened after I moved out of town, because this place is way too small to get lost in. I was in Oklahoma City most of the time. In between rehab and short jail times, I'd sneak back here and steal from my parents to feed the habit, until my dad pulled a gun on me and told me to never come back. That's when I really started stealing from whoever I could, which got me in a lot more trouble. In rehab they'd talked to us about getting high as a way to escape from problems, but I was more trying to escape the next withdrawal. I liked getting high a lot, and pretty soon I lost control. Doesn't have the childhood trauma of a good Netflix documentary, but that's my story."

"I would think most people's addiction problems are rooted in trying to escape from really bad situations, though."

"Probably. Just speaking for myself. Same as rehab. Wasn't that way for me."

Jessica studied Adam's eyes. She couldn't decide whether to believe that his way of having fun got out of hand, until he physiologically couldn't stop, or if he just hadn't done the work to look at what else was driving his drug use. She settled on somewhere in between. "You've clearly given this some thought."

"Yeah, well, you get time to think when you're in prison. Last stint was six months."

"For what?"

"Burglary, while I was in outpatient rehab. I walked straight from the sharing circle that afternoon into a house I'd been staking out. I thought no one was home. I was wrong."

"Jesus. I had no idea things got this far, Adam."

"Nobody does. Paying for my sandwich in truth, right?"

"Yeah, you can have dessert too, at this rate."

Adam laughed, a welcome break for both of them. "Maybe I will. I'll get off my soapbox, but I think if somebody wants to get off this shit, they have to *want* to, and sometimes that means hitting rock bottom. For me, being locked up for that long made me realize I didn't want that life anymore. Not saying prison works for everybody, but it sure as hell worked for me."

"How long have you been clean?"

"Going on two months. Cut all those ties I could, including my dealer and business partner."

"Business partner? What do you mean?"

"Let's just say I learned a lot about chemistry."

Jessica's eyes widened as she leaned into the table. "Are you telling me you were cooking meth?"

"*Ssssshhhhh*. Yeah. I made the product; he distributed. And since I'm paying for lunch with honesty, I didn't exactly tell him I was taking his truck. I hot-wired it in his driveway."

"So you *did* steal his car."

"Technically, yeah. He owed me some money, and I just assumed he'd understand the trade. Figured he wouldn't even know it was gone, since he never left the house. At least, that's what I told myself."

"You committed another crime to come back here, so you could work your way back into your family's life?" She saw Adam tense against the borderline accusation and caught herself. "Sorry, I didn't mean it like that. Your mom and dad aren't doing that well. Probably a good thing you came back when you did."

"And here's where we get to why I'm really here. I did tell Jake I'd appreciate a reintroduction to the family, but I didn't get a chance to tell him the real reason I came back."

"Which was?"

"Him."

Jessica did another mental inventory, this time of what Adam might know. He couldn't have heard about the suicide attempt. Only she knew about that. She was about to put her careful feelers out when Adam offered some clarification.

"I'd heard he was using, and I wanted to stop him."

Jessica put her fork down next to her plate and tried to push down the tears riding up from her tummy. "Stop him?"

"Yeah, he always looked out for me when we were kids, and I was already a handful as a teenager. Even when I started to really go off the rails, he tried to help. I owe him one. Probably more than one."

"How were you planning on stopping him?"

"I don't know. Just thought the first thing to do would be to get here, see how bad off he was, and then figure it out. Especially when I found out he was using Oxy, which is getting harder to find. Dealers are turning to counterfeit pills made with fentanyl. Not good."

Jessica used her napkin to hide the small tear escaping from her eye. "I just don't know what to believe, Adam."

"Understandable. But I'm his brother. And I've been there."

"You better not be pulling some manipulative bullshit."

The warning signaled the end to lunch. She left a twenty on the table, slid out of the booth, and headed toward the door, expecting him to follow her to the Tercel.

Which, of course, he did.

———

Jake sank deeper into the worn leather couch in the medical library lobby, watching the rain wash over the quad outside. He'd never been on a college campus, and he tried to imagine the pretty coeds walking by in their stylish, but not too stylish, clothes on their way to lectures they didn't pay attention to.

Not a positive take on academia, but he knew his opinion was tinged by jealousy. He hadn't really been a book-smart kid, and coming to a place like this had never, ever been an option. And he still didn't completely understand why he and Mark were here. Mark seemed to be running around like Tom Hanks in that *Da Vinci Code* movie, trying to uncover some secret that had been held for a long time by important people with a lot to lose. Which felt sort of sinister, as if they could be in trouble if the wrong folks found out.

Or maybe he'd just been watching too many true crime documentaries on Netflix.

But he was here because Mark represented his last chance at redemption. Jake didn't know who else could help him get better, and he was willing to see this wild goose chase through if it meant getting Jessica back.

Almost an hour of listless digital bottom-feeding had passed when Jake looked up from his phone again to see the dim gray of twilight creeping through the windows.

His eyes traveled across the quad, searching for fleeting signs of human activity. Most kids were probably home for the summer, but nobody would be out in this kind of storm anyway.

Except for over there, under what looked like an elm.

A man, standing with his hands at his side, staring in Jake's direction.

Strange, that he didn't just come inside the library.

Takes all kinds, I guess.

And Jake returned to consuming the bountiful feed from his phone, which he knew would somehow leave him hungry for more.

Better than just sitting here, though.

A conspiracy theory about a demon hovering above the White House had already rolled across the screen before he realized that a very real one was waiting for him outside, under the elm.

———

Mark checked his watch as the Xerox machine in her office spat out the final photocopy.

"Shoot, I gotta run. That guy I was telling you about is waiting for me. Listen, I don't know how to say goodbye. Or if we need to? We never really did that."

"No, we never did. And I don't want to keep you in the dark, but like

I said . . . this is a longer conversation, and you deserve to hear the whole story. For now, know that it wasn't you. It was me."

Fingers of defensiveness crept up from Mark's gut. He was the victim here, and he wasn't going to let her get away with ghosting him again. "So all I get is a bad rom-com line?"

She turned abruptly from the copier to face him. "How about I met you in the middle of a perfect shitstorm, I left to handle the cleanup, and by the time I was done, I was embarrassed and ashamed for not telling you, so I figured you were better off without me? How about that?"

Mark took a step backward, but kept pushing. "Doesn't make much sense without context and details."

"Yeah, well, that's why I didn't want to start this now. We don't have enough time to finish it."

Their serendipitous connection had shifted from playful reunion to tension in the space of a few sentences, and Mark didn't want the afternoon to end this way. "Okay, I get it. Sorry. We'll talk later. This is just all a little weird, right?"

The creases at the corners of her lips softened. "Not as weird as I thought your mission was when we started pulling this research. And now I think you could be onto something." She added the last study to the expanded file folder and handed him the volume of research.

"Thanks for the vote of confidence."

She took his arm and walked him toward the library lobby. "I'm a numbers girl, but I'll allow this simple line of reasoning: Chronic disease is caused by systemic chronic inflammation, which, in turn, could be caused by environmental toxins. And lack of proper nutrition in poorly grown and processed food, for that matter."

"Walk it back, right?"

"Right. Also, I had a thought about how those toxins might get into the human bloodstream."

"And that is?"

"I want to do some research on my own first. Your friend is wait-ing." She stopped before the lobby and slipped him a corner of paper, torn from one of the studies. "Here's my cell number. I remember how shy you were, but now you officially have a reason to call."

"Maybe I want to come back, instead of call."

"You will. For dinner and a football game, remember?"

"Yeah, of course. Pick a game this season, any game."

She leaned into his shoulder and whispered in his ear. "The very first one."

Mark couldn't contain his giddiness as he hustled into the medical library lobby and almost ran over Jake, who was standing in front of the nearest plate glass window, seemingly hypnotized by something across the quad.

"Jake! Sorry, man. Took longer than I thought. But I got what I needed, in more ways than one. Let's get home before this storm floods out the roads even more."

Jake didn't move, and Mark thought maybe he had his wireless earbuds in. He touched Jake on the shoulder and felt a slight tremor.

"Jake?"

He raised his hand and pointed.

Mark followed his outstretched index finger.

"I don't see anything."

"You don't see that?"

"No. What is it?"

"There, under that tree."

"Jake, I don't see anything." Mark grabbed the Walmart bag full of research papers at Jake's feet. "Come on, let's get you in the truck."

"It's following me."

"What's following you?"

"It's following me."

"Well, whatever it is can follow us all the way back to Guymon if it wants to."

Mark headed toward the opposite lobby door that opened to the parking lot, almost dragging Jake by the wrist. He thought he heard Jake whisper something indecipherable under his breath, as they fought the rain on the way to the truck. "What did you say?"

"It will."

———

Jessica watched the slow crawl of water move across the driveway, absently twisting her hair into a braid while turning over the dirt of her life, plowing over how it is and under how she thought it would be.

Adam's words in the diner circled through her head, about addicts having to hit rock bottom. How was attempted suicide not rock bottom for Jake? And then going on a bender, after all she'd done to help him. . . . Should she just leave? Friends from college had stayed in Stillwater and could probably help her get a job somewhere other than Walmart.

She paced through the dining room and looked out the window, where her garden was underwater, save for the taller leaves barely breaking the surface.

Probably won't make it through this storm.

She walked into the kitchen and saw Hailey, coloring at the table.

Would any of them?

Jessica picked up one of the journals she'd left by the coffee maker and sat down next to her daughter. She traced the edge of the soft leather cover with her index finger, and her eyes lost focus as she thought about what she'd read last night.

A lot of history here.

In this land, this house, this family. Seemed like the further away they'd gotten from respect for all three, the worse the existence. And her heart hurt with the realization that Jake kind of epitomized the endgame . . . addicted, diseased, apathetic. The land, too, now that she thought about it. Addicted to whatever chemicals he was spraying, diseased with the weeds and bugs that had developed resistance, and apathetic in not producing much of anything these days.

Maybe they needed a new start, somewhere far from this legacy defined by trauma. "Do you like living here in the country, Hailey? Or do you want to go to the city, where the hospital is?"

Jessica flipped through the pages of the journal, now as familiar as her own, and waited for her daughter to respond. "Don't worry, honey. You're going with Mommy no matter what."

A voice sounded over her left shoulder. "Man, I needed that nap. Who are you talking to?"

Jessica froze, horrified.

She looked to her left, where Hailey had been sitting just a moment ago.

She was gone.

Not in her chair.

Not in the kitchen.

Not in the house.

Gone.

Like she had been.

For over a year.

She'd known all along—of course she had—but this was the only way she . . .

Jessica heard the voice again, this time on descent into the chair next to her.

"Jessica? You okay?"

She gently laid her head on the table, cheek pressed into the pine, and finally surrendered.

———

Mark eased the Duramax onto Highway 51 and headed out of Stillwater. Bison Bridge had filled the first few minutes of the drive while he'd waited for Jake to get off his phone and actually say something, but even as they hit sixty-five miles an hour, all was quiet on the passenger front.

Which was fine with him. He was watching the compartmentalization he'd said he was so good at rapidly unravel, in between the torrents of rain hurrying across the road.

Nothing had changed. The butterflies dancing in his stomach when he saw her, the superpower of invincibility he gleaned by being close to her, the knowing while he was with her. Nothing had changed.

He skipped through the playlist until he found the song that said what he couldn't and turned up the volume.

We met in the rainstorm of being twenty-five
Halfway from being born to finally being alive
But you can't stop a rainstorm or hold back the tide
Some waves are going to form and all you can do is ride
My daddy likes to say I'm two decades too late
But I feel fine
Right on time

"Why are you smiling like that?"

Mark snapped out of his daydream. He'd been imagining the first breaths of next fall drifting through the OSU campus and her taking his arm as they walked into the stadium on their rediscovery date. "No reason."

"You're full of shit."

"Maybe."

Mark let a few mile markers pass before he broached the elephant in the truck. "You want to tell me what you saw back there?"

"You're not going to believe me. You didn't before, and you won't now."

"Try me."

———

Adam sat down next to his sister-in-law, confused and concerned. When he'd woken up from his nap on the couch, he'd found her at the kitchen table, talking to the air. And now she was face down on the table. "Jessica? Are you alright?"

A single tear traced her cheek and absorbed into the pine. "Yeah. I was talking to Hailey."

Adam put his hand on her shoulder. "I'm so sorry, Jessica. I can go in the other room . . . whatever you need to do. I get it."

"No. Stay. I'll tell you what I need."

"Alright. But how about you pick your face up from the table first."

She smiled weakly and pushed back into her chair. "I have to give in. Surrender."

Adam was still confused. He tried to search her eyes, but they were trained on the table. "Surrender? To what?"

She shifted her body in the chair until she was facing him. "Reality, Adam. Reality."

"I have no idea what you mean, but I'll help however I can."

"At the diner, you told me what happened over the last few years. I listened. Time to return the favor. Same rules apply. No judgment, just hear me out. Only difference is that I probably need to tell myself more than you."

"Okay."

She inhaled deeply and breathed out slowly. "They've gotten a lot better with treating pediatric leukemia, but Hailey was one of those increasingly rare cases that nobody could get a handle on. We spent her last six months at the Oklahoma Children's Hospital at OU, probably around the same time you were in Oklahoma City. I lived in an apartment across the street from the hospital, and Jake came whenever he could."

Shit. He was probably tweaking out of his mind while Jake was here at the farm, taking care of the fields and their parents instead of being with his dying daughter. "I don't know what to say, except—"

Jessica held her hand up. "You don't have to say anything. I'm talking. For me. We spent Christmas there, and Hailey hung in there for a while. She made thank-you drawings for the nurses and twirled around the playroom in her do-rag and oversized gown, until her legs couldn't hold her up anymore. That's when doctors moved her into a private room, where I slept on a cot at her bedside. Until the end."

Adam swallowed. "I was off in Neverland. I mean, I don't know what to say. Was Jake there at the—"

"Yeah, he was there at the end, Adam. And please don't make this about you."

"Right, sorry."

Adam couldn't put his finger on it, but Jessica seemed to be morphing somehow. Not physically, just the way she was speaking. The shakiness was all but gone from her voice. "Since she died, I've been living two lives. One, fairly sane, the other, not quite sane at all. Only way I could find to function was to pretend like Hailey was still with me, especially around the house. Eventually, those moments didn't feel like pretend, and I started to believe Hailey really was here with me. That's what you just walked in on."

He'd stumbled onto something even more sacred than he thought. "Whoa."

"Yeah, whoa. I did a whole lot of self-diagnosis courtesy of Dr. Google, and I think this has something to do with a coping mechanism. Pretty basic stuff—a loved one dies and somebody left behind doesn't want to let them go."

"I know I sort of shat on rehab, but don't you think you should go see someone about this? Like a therapist?"

"Probably. Haven't been ready, I guess. I don't want to know what might happen if I stop seeing Hailey in our most treasured places, like coloring at the kitchen table and playing in the garden. I mean, if that illusion is shattered, my fragile grip on normalcy probably will be too. Scares me."

Adam was awestruck. Jessica wasn't so different than him—she'd been doing whatever she could to survive, too.

Jessica paused to reload. "I also thought that if maybe I put all my mothering into the garden, where I could nurture and help something grow, I'd be able to deal better. But that hasn't worked—it only makes Hailey visit more often."

"Saying 'visit' sounds creepy. No offense, but—"

"None taken. And listen, this doesn't happen all the time. When I'm away from the house, on my morning walks or at work, I don't see her. I carry a ton of sorrow and longing throughout the day, of course, but I can manage without separating from reality. Here at home is another story."

"Not my business, I know, but how have you and Jake stayed together through this? You both are battling separate shitstorms. Like, major ones."

"He's actually been calling me out, but very gently. I know when he's trying to get me to break character, so to speak. But I get super defiant or deflective and just shut him down."

"So, he's had to tiptoe around a wife who seems half-on, half-off the rails, and hasn't been able to talk to her about what had to be the biggest trauma of his life, too." Adam was surprised by his defensive tone. She was being vulnerable with him, and he'd promised to listen.

Jessica didn't seem offended and actually agreed with him. "Right. A wife who's still setting the table for three every night."

"So, if you know this is a problem, why don't you stop it?"

Jessica lifted an eyebrow. "Really? Was I the only person in the conversation at Frank's a couple of hours ago?"

"Yeah, sorry. You have to really want to stop. And you don't."

"Bingo."

The desperate aloneness Adam had assumed would always be his calling card retreated, just a little. "I know what I need to do for my situation. Stay clean, make amends. Do you know what you need to do?"

"Not really. Maybe acknowledging this out loud is the first step. Toward what, I'm not sure. But you finding me like this. . . . I guess something does need to change."

Late-day light was struggling to come through the kitchen window, battered by rain. Adam thought Jake would've been home by now, and he was already thinking of an escape route. He couldn't be here when Jake got home. "Speaking of needing to change, where's my brother?"

He watched Jessica fumble through the drawer under the coffee maker and return with an old-school flip phone. "His doctor's house, as far as I know. I'll explain. But first, I'm sure you know how to work these things better than me. Tell him to come home."

———

Jake shoved his phone in his pocket and adjusted the truck heater vent. "Remember when I told you that I saw something in the wheat yesterday? Your first reaction was to ask me if I was high."

Mark was hesitant to walk the line between Jake's reality and fantasy. He wasn't that well versed in the hallucinations and delusions associated with psychosis, and he also didn't want to believe that this deeper mental disorder might be surfacing in Jake. "What I also said, you may recall, was that I believed that *you* believed what you were seeing, and that was enough."

Jake shifted his gaze back to the constant river of soaked plains running past the truck, and a small seed of frustration sprouted in Mark. "Why do you care so much if I believe you, anyway?"

"Great. Now you sound like my dad, who also pretty much told me I was making this up. And you know what he told me yesterday? After all these years of me thinking maybe I was crazy? That he'd actually seen—"

Jake's phone vibrated in his pocket, and Mark was grateful for the chance to prepare a better response while he answered the call.

"Hey, Jess . . . Wait, who is this? . . . What are you doing with her phone? . . . What? . . . Why are you there? . . . No . . . I told you to stay away . . . I don't give a shit if Jessica says it's okay. You better be gone when we get back."

Jake ended the call and threw the phone on the floorboard. "Motherfucker."

Mark killed the radio. "Something I should know?"

"Just get me home."

"We don't have to talk about that. But you started to say something about your dad—"

"Just drive, please?"

The next three hours slipped into silent oblivion, which was fine with Mark. He had a whole new world to dream about, and he picked up right where he left off, walking with the love of his life on his arm into the OSU football stadium on an early fall afternoon.

———

The exposed west side of the farmhouse was now under attack by machine-gun-assault waves of rain. Jessica stood protected behind the dining room window, her gratitude for the safe haven tempered by apprehension. As soon as Mark's truck headlights swept into the driveway, she steeled herself in anticipation, knowing that she needed to harbor Adam from the storm that would be his brother.

Like this glass was doing for her.

Jake was going to be pissed. Understandably. Without turning from the window, she yelled to Adam, who was drifting around the house. He'd tried to get her to take him into town, but she'd wanted to be here when Mark brought Jake home.

"Hey, Adam? Why don't you go upstairs for a minute? Just hang out in Hailey's room while I calm Jake down."

She could hear the relief in his voice, already coming from halfway to the second floor. "Thanks, Jess."

Jessica walked to the small foyer at the bottom of the stairs, ready to be a human shield if words didn't work. She heard the truck door close and steps ascend the porch stairs, and she waited for the front door to swing open, likely with the same ferocity she'd used about this time last night.

Screen door creaking.

Soft knock.

Jessica tilted her head.

Another soft knock.

She hit the door latch and pulled.

"Mark?"

"Hey, Jessica."

"I thought you were bringing Jake back."

Mark waved toward the Duramax. "I did. He's in the truck."

"Why?"

"Told me he didn't want to do something he'd regret."

She couldn't hide the relief in her own voice. "He's just going to stay out there?"

"I don't know. He hasn't said much for the last three hours, except just now when he asked me to come get you."

"Me? Not Adam?" Jessica looked past Mark at the truck idling in the driveway.

"Don't worry, Jess. I think he just wants to talk. I'll hang out here. Maybe introduce myself to Jake's brother."

"He's upstairs." She grabbed her rain jacket from the rack and stepped onto the porch, holding the door open for Mark. The distance to the truck was a matter of a few strides, but she managed to get soaked to the bone, even through her coat. She opened the passenger door and almost sat on Jake.

"Whoops. Hang on."

She hurried around the hood to the driver's side and climbed in the seat, then slammed the door and turned to her husband. "Ready to come home?"

She couldn't tell if Jake was smiling or not, since he was backlit against the porch light. "I guess. And I'm too tired to be mad about Adam, so you don't have to worry about me killing him."

"Well, that's exactly what I was worried about. Mark mentioned you haven't said a word for the last few hours."

"A lot turning over in my head, which probably took more out of me than this hangover I can't shake."

Jessica started peeling her coat off. "Is that why you wanted me to come out here? To talk about what's turning over in your head?"

"No, no. Well, actually, kind of. After being pissed off about Adam for a little while, the main thing I kept coming back to on the drive here was how sorry I am. And how lame that sounds."

She stared straight ahead, but still caught his eyes in the windshield reflection. "Yeah, the begging for forgiveness thing is getting old. I love you. You know that. But I can't live like this."

"You shouldn't have to. And I'm going to—"

"Hang on, Jake. I need to apologize too."

"For what? You haven't done anything wrong."

"Maybe not wrong, but not right, either. Especially in relation to you."

"I don't understand—"

She turned and reached across the console, taking his hand in both of hers. "I'm sorry I've been so shut down about Hailey. I know

I created this fantasy world where I could still be with her, I know I brushed you off when you tried to step in, and I know you were trying to help me. I know all these things. What I don't know is how else to deal with this. But shutting you out isn't the answer."

She felt his hand tighten into a fist, and expected a response, but none came.

"Jake?"

His fingers started to tremble, ever so slightly, and then his forearm, until his shoulders were lightly shaking.

Jessica climbed over the console, wrapped herself in Jake's arms, buried her face in the stiff denim of his Carhartt jacket, and let her own floodgates open.

———

"You must be Adam."

The skinny guy in the corner of the upstairs bedroom, sitting with his back against the wall and arms wrapped around his knees, looked toward the door, his face caught somewhere between fear and confusion. "Uh, maybe."

"Don't worry. Your brother's not here. Not yet, anyway."

"Who are you?"

"I'm his doctor. His friend, too, I guess. Name's Mark."

Adam pulled himself up. "I'm Adam. But you probably knew that."

"I didn't even know you existed until very recently."

"Yeah, that's been the tendency around here. I'm like Voldemort in those *Harry Potter* movies. No one's allowed to say my name."

Mark smiled. "Never saw the movies, but I read the first book. You don't look too evil to me."

"Nah, not evil, but not at the top of anyone's Christmas list, either. Didn't Jake tell you about me?"

"Not really. Just that you partied a lot, left home, and only came back to beg or steal."

"That's a pretty good description. Adding *addict* and *convict* would round out my Tinder profile nicely."

He was funny. Charming, even. Mark knew guys like this in high school and quietly resented them. Probably because he couldn't be one of them, but also because consequence never seemed to catch up to their cavalier behavior, from smoking weed behind the gym to skipping class. Cavalier to him, at least . . . a high school kid not so far removed from the kindergartner who'd been afraid to color outside the lines.

Mark had never considered extending the ramification timeline out a little further, to what these guys' lives might look like later down the road.

Because this skin and bones standing in front of him was one of the cool kids.

"You still with me?"

Mark twitched his head. "Sorry. Got lost in a daydream there for a minute, thinking back to whether I could remember you from high school. I think I was already gone by the time you got there."

"You wouldn't have liked me—I was a cocky asshole, which has obviously worked out really well for me."

Mark was taken aback by the parallel between his mental chatter and Adam's self-awareness. Any residual resentment for what Adam represented from Mark's past evaporated into the stale bedroom air.

"Are you trying to get clean?"

"Have been, almost two months now. Didn't come back to beg or steal—I'm here for Jake."

"How so?"

"Small-time dealer here in town said that he'd been selling to Jake for quite a while. I thought maybe I could scare him straight. One look at me would probably do that."

"You don't look that bad."

"Are you kidding? Have you seen my teeth?"

Mark sat down on the bed. "I didn't know Jake was using that much."

"From what I heard, he definitely has a problem. Or had. He told me he got in an accident. Maybe he was fucked up and that knocked some sense into him."

"I'm not sure that was an accident."

Adam tried to sit in the kid's chair next to the dresser, but only succeeded in barely wedging his hind end between the arms. "Damn, I thought I was skinny enough for this. Wait, what? Not an accident?"

"He knows that land like the back of his hand. Even if he was high, I just don't see how he would ever hit that old elm head-on, unless he meant to."

"Jesus. I mean, the Hailey thing was probably devastating. But suicide?"

"There are ripple effects from that, I'm sure, but there's a lot more going on. This place isn't producing like it used to, and his physical health got pretty bad. I think those two are related, actually."

"I think I know where you're heading. Garbage in, garbage out. I'm living proof. Barely."

"Those were my exact words to Jake. Garbage in, garbage out."

"If I'd graduated from high school, that would have been the quote next to my senior picture."

Mark laughed, in spite of himself. "Sorry. But yes. Same idea with the land. If your inputs aren't healthy, you're not going to get much of anything healthy out of it."

"I get it. Not only was I putting shit into my body, I was making it. I know all about inputs."

"Making what?"

"The product. This probably sounds weird, but I really liked it. Getting high, yeah, but I'm talking about the chemistry side. That was the only subject I ever got an A in, which is probably why I thought I'd be good at cooking meth. That, and I'd be making my own supply. And I was good. Really good."

"You may be interested in this, then. My bet is the land's problems revolve around too much aggressive chemical and mechanical farming. Key word is *aggressive*. Over-tilling, double-cropping, overusing pesticides and fertilizers, that kind of thing. Those are the inputs."

"So, we're killing the soil, basically. Like I was doing to my body. I siphoned a lot of anhydrous ammonia from fertilizer when I was cooking meth, actually. Kind of ironic. Or is that a paradox? I don't know the difference."

Mark got the sense this kid was a lot smarter than he let on. "Doesn't matter. You get it."

The thud of a truck door closing sounded from the driveway, which seemed to draw Adam toward the bedroom window. "And Jake's kind of been doing both. Killing the soil and his body."

"Not on purpose. But yes. I'll keep you in the loop as I chase these ideas down on the chemical side, if you want."

"It was fucking ugly, man."

"What was?"

"Manufacturing that shit. What went in it, the fumes that came off it, everything. Not to mention what it did to my skin and teeth and pretty much everything else when it went in me."

Mark headed out of the bedroom and down the hall, expecting Adam to follow. "Well, imagine something similar going into the dirt that your food is coming from."

He was already halfway down the stairs when he heard the words repeat, faint and faraway, their source presumably still standing at the bedroom window.

"Fucking ugly, man."

———

"Let's go inside." Between crying in front of his mom last night and his wife just now, Jake was done with being vulnerable.

"Alright, but promise me you'll lay off Adam."

"Why are you on his side all of a sudden?"

Jessica let him go and moved back into the driver's seat. "I'm not. I mean . . . I just think maybe he's actually trying to make a change, and a night won't hurt."

"You invited him to stay the night?"

"Not yet. I more meant a night without him worried about hiding from his brother."

"He's not worried about that. I saw him yesterday. He's the same old Adam, not afraid of the things he should probably be afraid of."

"Well, whatever. Let's just get you inside, fed, and in bed."

Jake still wasn't moving that great, and he took forever getting out of the car and even longer lumbering to the house. Jeans, jacket, shirt, even his socks were soaked by the time he got to the porch stairs. He slid the Carhartt from his torso and left the jacket on the mat, before pushing the front door open just as Mark and Adam were coming down the stairs.

"Hey, Mark. Adam."

He headed to the back porch, stripping the rest of his clothes off along the way. "If you don't want to see an overweight, pasty man in motion, don't watch."

Jake found a pair of sweatpants and a T-shirt in the dryer, and he emerged to find Mark and Adam at the dining room table. "Night."

Jessica called from the kitchen. "Sit down, honey. I'm making you something to eat, remember? Might as well feed everybody."

Jake grudgingly shuffled to the head of the table but didn't take a seat. "What's going on here with you two? Are you best buds now?"

Adam motioned toward the kitchen. "Just waiting on some eggs your wife was kind enough to offer. Then Mark's taking me over to his place for the night. Don't worry—you won't have to deal with me."

Jake pointed a finger at Mark in warning. "Hide your valuables."

Jessica called again from the kitchen. "Jake, you promised. I can hear you."

"Fine." He migrated out of the dining room and into the stove's orbit.

Jessica nudged him with her hip as she cracked eggs into a bowl. "If you're not going to talk to them, how about telling *me* why you went off the rails last night."

"I thought a drink would help me from spinning out. I didn't know what else to do."

"Why were you spinning out?"

Jake picked at the grout on the kitchen counter. "I don't know. Been anxious about bills, the farm, you, Hailey . . . everything."

She hummed softly under her breath, a telltale sign to Jake that she knew he wasn't telling the whole truth. She did that whenever he lied, probably without even knowing it. On cue, she turned to face him. "If you don't want to lose me, you'll tell me what else is going on. Now."

Sometimes, there really is nothing left to lose.

"Okay, Jess. I've been—"

A shadow appeared on the linoleum. "You guys need any help in here? I was on KP duty in jail. I can clean a mean dish now."

Jessica turned back to the eggs. "We're good, Adam. Relax. Actually, check out some of those journals on the table. They were your great-grandfather's."

"Whoa, cool."

Jake waited to hear his brother's chair scoot out and back in. "Can we talk about this when there's nobody around to interrupt?"

Jessica took a step closer to him. "He'll be able to occupy himself for a minute—"

Adam walked back into the kitchen. "Who's this?"

Jake dropped his chin to his chest. "See what I mean?"

Jessica looked at the faded photograph Adam was holding out between his thumb and forefinger. "Jake's and your great-great-grand-father. Seemed to be kind of the patriarch of the family. Full-blood Choctaw, far as I can tell."

A dagger of confusion and fear pierced Jake's temple, sending a shrill siren through his brain. "Let me see that."

He brought the small picture closer with his quivering fingers.

No.

No.

The front door was the only way out. The keys were in the car—Jessica always left them in the cupholder. He bolted from the kitchen faster than he'd moved in years and spilled out of the dining room, onto the front porch, and into the Tercel.

He heard nothing. Not his wife's escalating pleas for explanation leaking through the screen door, not his brother's expletive-laced pro-test echoing off the porch roof, not his doctor's concerned warnings to slow down. Nothing, except the high-pitched siren of madness, screaming behind his eyes at first, and then out loud into the wet night.

———

Jessica and the doctor looked at each other, frozen in shock for the first few seconds, until the Tercel's engine finally turned over.

Adam was already gone.

He ran out the door just as the single taillight cast a receding reflec-tion in the huge puddles of standing water in the driveway. What could he do? Follow him. That's all he could do. He eyed Mark's truck and sprinted to the driver's side, praying to a God he wasn't sure existed that Mark had left his keys in the console, like most folks did around here.

He stepped on the brake and hit the start button, and the huge diesel engine roared to life. Adam threw the truck into drive and stomped on the gas pedal, sending a wave of gravel and water all the way to the porch as he peeled away. He could barely make out the dim red dot of the taillight turning through the farm, toward the northwest.

Adam did a rapid search of his unreliable memory to plot a route that might cut in front of the Tercel. He hadn't broken his focus on the single red taillight since he got in the truck, and he gained on Jake quickly before veering slightly more west and punching the gas pedal even harder. Adam piloted the lifted Chevy Duramax directly across the field, mowing through stands of winter wheat that made it tough to see the Tercel to his right, haphazardly navigating the flooded dirt road on the field perimeter.

A few hundred yards later, the truck exploded through the wheat and surfaced in front of the little car. Adam looked in the rearview mirror and saw Jake suddenly bank right.

Shit.

Adam floored the truck in the same direction, struggling to see through the torrential rain blanketing the chest-high wheat.

He was losing him.

A frantic breath later, the truck was an airplane, busting through thick clouds of wheat into clear air and back onto the frontage road. Adam checked his side mirror and saw the Tercel headlights fifty yards behind and to the right.

He looked back through his own windshield, just in time to see the huge, gnarled elm come into the frame.

Jake was going for the tree. Again.

Adam flattened the accelerator to the floor and pointed the truck straight at the elm.

Only question now was who was going to get there first.

———

"He better not be going to McGill's, Mark."

"I don't think that's his plan."

"You think he's—"

"Yes."

Jessica paced another lap around the dining room table before going upstairs to see if she could get a better view from the second floor. Hailey's room faced the northwest, which was where, in the distance, the old elm stood by the creek.

Through the window by the nightstand, she saw bright flashes of beamed light, two light sabers battling in the distance. She shuffled closer to watch the lightning show, only to see that the activity was much lower to the ground.

Like, on the ground.

Headlights, out by the dry creek.

———

"Come on, *come on!*"

Adam yelled at the Duramax to give him more, as the distance between the truck and the Tercel barely closed. Jake wasn't slowing down, and in a moment that stretched into eternity, Adam knew what he had to do.

———

Jessica rushed down the stairs and out onto the porch.

"Jake! *Jake!*"

But she knew he was too far gone, driving too fast toward the sacred place where everything, including almost and maybe him, was already dead. Because she'd already solved the mystery of what had been buried out by the elm, with the help of a pot of coffee and those century-old journals.

Three generations had been laid to rest there, under a burial tree that might as well be a magnet.

———

Adam cranked the steering wheel to the right, crushing the Tercel's front fender and sending it back into the wheat. He took his foot off the gas, hit the brakes, and braced himself just as the left corner of the truck clipped the tree and spun backwards, toward the dry creek bed.

The truck settled halfway down the bank, the tailgate resting against the creek bottom and headlights catching the upper branches of the elm. Adam forced the door open against gravity, crawled out, and scrambled up the slope, searching the wheat horizon for a sign of the Tercel.

Dim headlights barely refracted through the wheat to his right. He ran to the driver's side of the Tercel, where Jake's body was convulsing uncontrollably. Adam didn't know what to look for as far as serious trauma, but he opened the door, knelt next to Jake, and started feeling around his torso. He'd just started to wonder if this was a good idea, that maybe instead he should run back to the house and get Mark, when he realized that Jake was sobbing violently.

Maybe he wasn't hurt. Physically, at least.

"Hey, hey, *sshhh*. It's alright, Jake. It's alright."

"It's not. It's not."

"Where are you hurt?"

Jake put his left hand over his heart.

"Your ribs? Your clavicle? What? Shit. Never mind, doesn't matter, I wouldn't know what to do. Hang on. I'll run back to the house to get Mark—"

"No, Adam. No."

Jake reached into the chest pocket of his T-shirt and pulled out a small piece of paper, shaking in his hand. At first, Adam couldn't tell what Jake was holding, but he steadied his brother's hand so he could make out the tattered old photograph of their great-great-grandfather. "What's the problem?"

"I have to end this. Nobody else can help me."

"I think I might've just saved your life. Try me."

"You don't understand. This is—"

"This is what? Jake? *Jake?*"

Adam checked his brother's wrist for a pulse and took off running for the house.

———

Mark closed the travel medical kit that he kept in the truck for house calls. He was still catching his breath from sprinting behind Adam all the way here. "He's okay enough. When he wakes up, he can tell us if there's acute pain anywhere. But, big picture, I think he's alright."

Jessica had been hanging on Mark's every move from the Tercel passenger seat. "This isn't a coma or something like that?"

"No, I think he just shut down. He's so tired, on every level, and his nervous system is probably shot. Hard to say, but Adam said he was alert when he found him, and his vitals are fine."

Jessica opened the car door and set her feet on solid ground, hoping to settle herself down. "What happened, Adam?"

Adam pointed toward the creek. While Mark was tending to Jake, Jessica had mentioned she'd learned about the burial tree from the journals. "Apparently he was bent on visiting our ancestors under that old elm tree."

"More like joining them."

Adam tossed the small photograph on the car hood. "Yeah. Something about this picture really upset him."

Jessica tucked the picture into her jeans pocket. "But he didn't say what?"

"No, he passed out before he could tell me. What should we do now, Doc?"

Mark surveyed the Duramax, which from here amounted to beams of light pointing up at a forty-five-degree angle from the creek bed. "We're lucky that my medical kit was easy to get to in the back seat. I think we're going to need a winch to pull that thing out, though." He peered into the rear window of the Tercel. "Jake's a big boy, but there are three of us. Pop the hatch and let's try to get him in the back so someone else can drive back to the house. I can't believe this little car is still running."

Adam opened the hatchback. "This thing is a miracle. They don't build 'em like they used to, huh?"

"No." Jessica touched the photograph in her pocket. "They don't."

———

"Jake?"

Someone was saying his name, from a land far, far away. Jake forced his eyes open and looked to his left at his wife, sitting on the floor next to him, holding his hand. He hadn't seen her looking that way at him in a long time. There wasn't an ounce of accusation in her face.

Just . . . love.

"Hi, Jess."

"Anything hurt?"

"Everything. Nothing. I don't know."

"Mark says he doesn't think anything's broken."

"Adam shouldn't have saved me."

"What are you talking about?"

"That old photograph."

Jessica squeezed his hand. "You're not making any sense. Help me out here."

He repeated himself. "That old photograph."

"Of your great-great-grandfather?"

"That's the problem."

"What's the problem, honey?"

"I've been seeing him everywhere."

Mark pushed up from the couch. "Are you saying that's the man in the—"

"Yeah."

Jessica dropped Jake's hand and got to her feet. "What are you guys talking about? Is there some secret here that you don't want me to know about?"

"I didn't want to tell you. You wouldn't believe me. Probably think I was using again."

"Tell me what?"

Mark helped Jake up from the floor and walked him the few wobbly steps to the couch. "Tell her, Jake."

Jake eased onto the cushions, sitting upright because that was the only position that didn't hurt. "I started seeing a shadow figure back when I was a kid. Didn't think anybody would believe me then, either."

"You mean, like a ghost?"

"Kind of. Always looked the same, until recently. It got way darker and scarier. I started to think I was, like, damned or something, and—"

"Damned? Jesus, Jake. Were you high every time you saw this thing?"

"And this is why I didn't want to tell you."

Mark touched Jessica's shoulder. "Just let him talk."

Jake shifted his weight on the couch. "Where's Adam, by the way? He was here, right?"

Mark pulled a chair from the dining room over to the couch. "He seems to think he can redneck my truck out of the creek bed."

"Of course he does."

Jessica sat back down next to Jake and put her hand on his knee. "Don't change the subject. Tell me about this thing you're seeing."

"Not much more to say. Used to look sort of like an old Indian, but lately it's a horror freakshow. Skin melting like candle wax, eyes bulging out of sockets. And I can't make it stop. Only sure way I know *not* to see it is to not see *anything* anymore. So, when you showed me that photograph, and I realized that this thing is one of my ancestors, I—"

Jessica covered her mouth with an unsteady hand. "Oh my God."

"What?"

"The journals."

"Huh?"

"Those journals on the table."

Jake followed her eyes, straining his neck against the rigid pain. "What about them? Never seen them before."

"They belonged to his son."

Jessica approached the table cautiously, as if the leather and paper could suddenly shape-shift into the demon-ghost. Jake half hoped that would happen, because at least then, someone would believe him.

She sorted through the journals until she found one of the earlier volumes—she seemed to be searching for a particular page as she turned back to the couch.

Earmarking an entry with her finger, she handed the journal to Jake. "Here. Read out loud, so Mark can hear, too. Wait, never mind. You can barely see straight. I'll read."

June 27, 1908

Yesterday I found my father on boughs gathered by the creek bank. His long, graying braids were draped over his shoulders. I thought he was asleep.

But he was not asleep.

His last words to me were about the past. He told me that he was not happy, because people are forgetting the old ways. But I told him that the white man calls these new ways and machines "progress," and they taught me this is the way forward.

He rebuked me, but gently, as always. He said that the earth gives to us what she offers, and we cannot take more from her, and that his shilombish had shown him a grave future. I did not understand this word shilombish, and he told me that we all have a shilup and a shilombish: a shadow and a spirit. He said that while he slept, his shilombish had traveled to another place, and had seen what is coming. Sick people. Sick earth. And this was why he was sad.

I asked him what he wanted me to do, and he said that when he died, his shilup and shilombish would leave this body. His shilombish would stay for a moon, resting for the journey to the Land of Ghosts. He wanted me to keep a fire burning by his body for four days, so his shilombish would have comfort.

His words were even stranger when he talked of his shilup. He told me that his shilup may haunt this land for many moons, in warning of what is to come. He told me to honor the earth, and his shilup would have peace and retreat.

Yesterday my father's voice was silent, and I wept, and I prepared the fire for his shilombish. But I did not keep the fire burning by his body for four days. Only until dawn. Because I have much to do. And I no longer believe in such spirits.

Jessica walked back to the table and picked up the journal where she'd found the old photograph. "I can't say I believe in ghosts, but I mean, listen to this farewell entry. The very last one. From 1936."

> *My body will soon be returned to the earth, and my greatest regret has been that, in trying to honor my father, I turned away from him. I have seen his shilup in the wheat, haunting this land, a ghost whose face turns so frightening that I cannot recognize him as my father. I did not heed his warning or follow in his path, but whoever reads this must, or they will suffer the fear of his shilup's presence and the wrath of an angry earth.*

Jessica pulled the photo from her pocket and handed the faded image to Jake. "I can't believe I'm suggesting this, but maybe you've been seeing his shilup."

The great-great-grandson of a forgotten farmer turned the delicate parchment over and over in his trembling hands, until he found a whisper of breath and locked eyes with the pinprick pupils of the man in the photograph.

"What do you want me to know?"

The strongest torrent yet hit the dining room window, a million tiny birds of water slamming into the glass. Jake watched their hydric entrails dripping down the pane, suddenly illuminated by a flash of headlights in the driveway.

Mark stood up. "No way." He circled the couch and headed to the living room window.

Jake heard the truck door slam and a solid thump on the porch. He'd cleared the stairs in one leap. Adam always did that.

Mark opened the front door, and Adam slid into the foyer, shaking like a wet dog.

"Did you see that geyser of rain just now? Just when I thought the storm was letting up a little. I gotta get out of these clothes. Don't mind me if I strip down. We're all family, right?" Adam's pants were already dropping like a detonated building—too late for protest.

Jessica headed to the back porch in search of clean pants and a shirt that might fit Adam, who was now walking toward the couch in his skivvies and nothing else. "Your truck has an aftermarket winch, Mark. You know that?"

"No, that Duramax was actually my father's. I don't even know what a winch looks like, only what it does."

Adam sat down next to Jake. "Clearly you didn't get stuck in the mud as much as I did in high school. I wrapped the cable around that elm tree, and the winch pulled her out enough to get the rear wheels turning. She made the rest of the way pretty easy in four-wheel drive. Nice truck."

Jake eyed his brother's naked body. "Jesus, you're skinny."

"Name's Adam, not Jesus. Although it's easy to confuse us. And yeah, this enviable figure is what a solid year of meth for breakfast will do to you. Who needs a Peloton?"

Mark sat back down on the dining room chair he'd borrowed from the table. Jake could tell he was trying to navigate the seriousness of an attempted suicide and the levity of Adam's humor. "It's okay, Mark. You can laugh."

Mark clasped his hands in front of him, frowning. "I'm just telling you right now, as a medical doctor, that while Adam's approach clearly has proven quite effective, I can't endorse meth addiction for weight loss. Not yet, anyway. As soon as a huge global pharmaceutical company tells me it's perfectly safe, though, I'll order you a truckload."

All three of them laughed, in spite of the darkness.

Or maybe because of the darkness.

They could finally find a light.

—Friday—

Jessica nudged Jake. "That was a long day yesterday, huh? And night."

How he'd managed to get up here, after what had happened last night, she had no idea. He'd gone to bed downstairs in the guest room, where he'd been sleeping since the accident—the first one, anyway. She was going to start calling those two late-night forays into the elm tree "accidents" now. Because maybe, hopefully, that's what they really were.

She'd gotten up around midnight to pee, and he was here, next to her. She hadn't even felt him get in bed. They were all so tired. So, so tired.

A couple of minutes ago, she'd felt him kick his legs under the sheets, which usually meant he was awake. His response to her question was one of his patented bear snores, and she knew he'd be out as long as she let him.

He probably did need to hibernate, actually. There'd been a lot more going on with him than she knew how to handle. Enough to make him want to relapse, enough to make him want to kill himself again.

How could that possibly be fixed? How would he get back to *okay* again? How would they?

She silently slipped out of bed and dressed, taking soft steps down the stairs so as not to wake Adam, asleep on the couch. She'd offered him Hailey's room, which he'd declined, saying he'd spent enough time up there yesterday hiding from Jake, and it had kind of creeped him out.

Jessica stopped midway on the staircase, turned around, and headed back up. From the top stair, she could see the dawn poking through the door ajar into Hailey's room. So many mornings, she'd stood right here and seen that same quality of light, treasuring those moments before she'd wake her daughter with a kiss on the forehead.

Her beautiful, beautiful daughter.

She tried to keep her tears quiet as she passed the master bedroom and made her way to the end of the hall. This walk was the verse to the most beautiful song ever written. And this pushing open of her door, the first words of the chorus.

Jessica stood in the threshold.

Maybe the best way to help her husband was to help herself.

And write a new song.

———

Hi.

You've been watching my mommy, too.

My name is Hailey.

I love my mommy and daddy, and our horse, Annie.

I wish I could be with my mommy and daddy and Annie again, but I got too sick to be there. It's okay though, because one of my grandpas is here with me. He says he's even older than Daddy's daddy. He's nice. His hair is so long. Longer than even Mommy's. His name is Aki.

I like to draw, more than anything in the whole world, and sometimes I try to help Mommy draw pictures, even though I'm here, and she's there. I put Aki in some of the pictures, because he says nobody knows who he is anymore. That's sad. We should remember him. He really is nice. He's there, in the new picture on the refrigerator.

Anyway, since you've been watching my mommy, too, could you tell her that I'm okay? I can't talk like I used to, but I want her to know there are no scary needles here. No masks or gowns. Only green fields as far as I can see, rivers running to the sea.

As far as I can see.

I'm going to go walk along the river with Aki. I don't

know when I'll be back, so please, could you tell Mommy
that I'm okay?

> *She doesn't have to worry anymore.*
> *Okay.*
> *Bye.*

———

Mark took his first sip of coffee.

The first sip was always the best. Without fail. Every morning.

He'd slept long, deep, and dreamless, exhausted from yesterday. He'd thought they'd just take a drive to Stillwater, get some curated information, and come home. But what had actually happened had been straight out of a movie. A dark, romantic, dark, suspenseful, dark, mysterious, but mostly dark movie. With a hint of humor at the end.

Still didn't feel real.

Strange, how a day like any other ends up being anything but.

His mother was asleep, not due to wake up for another hour. Her internal clock was shifting more and more toward alarm signals. He was going to let another couple of weeks pass, and then get more aggressive with finding her help. Mourning and grieving were vital, but the weight was starting to sink the whole ship.

Kind of like Jake. That guy had nine lives, with only two of them gone. He might've busted a rib or three, but there was no way to know without an X-ray. And even then, nothing to give a broken rib but time. The rest of him, Mark wasn't sure about. A relapse, a second suicide attempt—hard to have a worse night, to say the least. He wasn't sure what Jake needed now. And he had to admit, when Jake said that the Native American in that old photo was the man he'd been seeing in the wheat . . . and Jessica had read those journal entries . . . as much as Mark's scientific mind wanted to dismiss the notion of a haunting, or any kind of ghost story, he knew enough to know that he didn't know everything.

Maybe there was more to what Jake had seen than what could be touched or counted or weighed. Metrics. Measurable units. Precisely quantifiable findings, the kind he'd become a master of in that chemo lab. Because what he'd felt yesterday, when he'd seen *her* again, had nothing to do with math or science. This was another kind of force, an energy that could not be touched or counted or weighed.

So powerful.

So, so powerful.

But he knew science, and he still believed there was a connection between inputs and outputs.

Garbage in, garbage out.

He set his coffee cup on the kitchen counter and walked out to the truck. The rain had finally stopped sometime before dawn, and sunlight glistened off the droplets on the hood. Stray strands of water shook free from the door handle as he opened the passenger side to get the Walmart bag filled with the Ag research. The studies they'd pulled at the medical library were in his briefcase, in the back seat next to the travel medical kit.

Time to walk it back.

———

The soft, contented clucking of hens down in the yard pulled Jake from the hardest sleep he'd had in years. Only his eyes moved toward the sunlight filtering through the lilting linen drapes. He knew that deep slumber had locked his limbs, tendons, and muscles into tenuous pain-free positions, and the slightest twitch could ruin this relative peace.

From this temporary reprieve, there was space to question what he was thinking last night.

He knew, of course.

He'd built a fragile house of cards the last few months . . . resisting his physical therapy until he grudgingly complied, just to get Jess off his back . . . complaining about healthier food, until he was hungry enough to eat anything, and would sneak out to get that anything—all while flat-out refusing to get treatment for his addiction and paying no attention to his mental health, despite Mark's repeated pleas.

And seeing that shadow figure around damn near every corner.

No surprise that photo brought the house down.

But this time, he hadn't failed to kill himself, like he seemed to fail at everything else. Somebody had cared about him enough to risk their own life to save his. Of all people, his brother.

He still wasn't sure he deserved that kind of sacrifice. But if somebody else thought his life was worth saving, well . . . maybe it was.

He tensed and relaxed every muscle he could, starting with his toes all the way to his jaw, trying to gently break in the pain before he got out of bed. He'd come up the stairs more than half asleep, driven by a longing to be next to his wife. So much time spent alone lately. She was good for his heart.

But he was anticipating the worst, as far as his body was concerned. He swung one leg off the bed, and then the other, bracing for a hurt that didn't come. One step, okay. Two steps, alright. Well, maybe not alright, but no worse. He maintained the pattern in his boxers and socks across the bedroom and into the hallway.

He started to turn toward the stairs, but a shadow caught the corner of his eye.

His heart leapt into his throat.

The man in the wheat.

Jake slowly turned his head toward the shadow. He couldn't run down the stairs, which was his first instinct. He was trapped.

The backlit figure in the doorway came into focus.

Jessica. Facing away, into Hailey's room.

Damn.

He assumed she was pretending to wake Hailey up or something. He shuffled toward her, waiting until he was a step away to put his hand on her shoulder.

"Jess."

She didn't jump or seem startled. She only drew her fingers from their resting place on her heart and placed her hand on top of his. "Morning, honey."

"Are you—"

"No, Jake. I'm not. Come on, let's go downstairs and get some breakfast. Butter's plenty soft by now, after sitting on the counter all night. I'd just started making you some food when all hell broke loose again, remember?"

He kept his hand on her shoulder for support as they moved toward the staircase. "I'm tired of hell breaking loose."

"You and me both."

Jake started the coffee while his wife went outside to collect more eggs for breakfast. He was waiting by the coffee maker, mug in hand, when she knocked at the door with her foot. "Those hens sure are happy the rain stopped."

She set two handfuls of eggs on the counter. "I was thinking . . . and if you don't want to talk about this, forget I said anything . . . but I read those journals, right? I could give you a quick summary, and you could see if anything stands out. Maybe get a line on what your great-great-grandfather might have been worried about, why he might have threatened that his shilup would come back."

Jake welcomed the opportunity to talk about anything other than trying to kill himself again, but he was wary of anything remotely related to the man in the photograph. "Let's eat something first, yeah? I don't need to go back there right now."

"Back where?" Adam's head poked up from the back of the living room couch.

Jake sighed. "You're still here."

"Oh, you mean the motherfucker who saved your life last night? Yeah. Still here."

Jessica took two more mugs down from the cupboard. "You allowed to drink coffee?"

"That depends who you ask. If you're asking me, the answer is absolutely."

Jake sat down at the kitchen table while his wife poured two cups and took one to his brother. Adam accepted the mug with one hand, while kneeling on the couch and putting on a shirt with the other. A way-too tight shirt, with sweatpants that fit him like leggings.

"What the hell are you wearing?"

Jessica sat down at the kitchen table. "Your clothes were like a circus tent on him. So he's wearing my stuff."

Adam paraded around the couch and into the kitchen, one hand on his hip, the other holding the coffee mug. "I kind of like this look."

Jake tried to kick him as he danced past the table. "Stop. Sit."

The suggestion came out more like a demand. Which was probably what he intended. Jake touched Jessica's hand. "Give us a minute, will you?"

She got up from the table. "You give *me* a minute. I have breakfast to make."

Adam pulled out Jake's chair. "Come on, bro. Let's get some sunlight on that white-ass face of yours."

They walked out to the porch and down the steps. Adam stretched out his T-shirt as best he could and squinted into the sun. "We're both vampires. Who knew we'd be afraid of the sun."

"You're worse than me. At least I'm outside for a living."

"If you call listening to Kenny Chesney inside that combine being outside."

He had a point. But that's not what Jake wanted to talk about. "Listen, about last night."

Adam sat back against the hood of the Tercel. "Sorry about this little guy's front fender. But I wasn't going to let you hit that tree."

"That's what I wanted to talk to you about. I know we haven't always been on the best of terms, and you've come to me for help, and I've turned you away—"

"Whoa, whoa. You were right to do that. Money to buy meth is not the right kind of help."

"Yeah, but I guess I always felt like there was something more I could be doing. After a while, I just gave up. Maybe that's why I'm saying sorry."

"So, you wanted to tell me you're sorry?"

Jake looked at his feet. No, that wasn't what he'd wanted to tell him. He lifted his eyes until they met his brother's. "I wanted to say thank you. For saving me from myself last night."

"You've been trying to do that for me as long as I can remember."

A stray green leaf, divorced too soon from his tree, drifted between them, pushed by the early summer breeze coda to yesterday's torrential symphony. Jake watched the leaf flutter past them and was thinking of what else to say when two arms wrapped around him. His brother brought him close, and they held each other for longer than they ever had.

His mom, then Jessica last night, and now Adam. . . . Jake wasn't all that comfortable with this much embracing. "You better not think I'm going to tell you I love you."

Adam pushed him away. "You better not think I'm going to either."

A whiff of butter, biscuits, and coffee floated down the porch stairs, carried by the breeze. Adam looked toward the house. "Race you inside, old man."

Adam turned and cleared the steps with his trademark leap, leaving Jake to walk slowly toward the porch with the sun on his back.

For once, he actually noticed it.

———

She watched the two men from the bunkhouse window. Her sons. She knew those were her sons.

The one, she knew better. He was around here all the time. They had just been together yesterday, or maybe the day before. The other, she hadn't seen in a long time. Something bad had happened with him. She couldn't remember what, but her husband had been so angry. So, so angry.

But holding each other, like they were doing, made her heart happy. She was always looking for reasons now for her heart to be happy, because one moment was lost to the next so quickly.

Maybe this one would stay for a while.

———

Mark went into his father's office to get a piece of computer paper. He had an idea—several, actually—and needed a blank canvas. The fine blue notebook lines of his journal were interfering with the threads he was trying to draw.

Threads, because after only an hour sorting through the Ag and medical research, he was already spinning a circular spiderweb pattern, connecting separate branches of the same tree.

He listened at the bottom of the stairs for signs of his mother stirring in her bedroom. She was either sleeping, or wishing she still was.

Mark sat down at the table and set the clean 8½-by-11 sheet in front of him, a buoy in the sea of mixed-font print and study headlines. At the center, he drew a crude picture of Jake and around the perimeter of the paper, boxes labeled with what he thought might be impacting Jake's health, both physical and mental. His diet, relationships, the farm, pharmaceuticals . . . and in turn, what might be affecting those things, according to all these studies. Environmental toxins in his diet; dishonesty in his relationships, including with himself; bad dirt in his fields; addiction to pain pills.

Walking it back.

The spiderweb took shape, with Jake at the center, as he drew lines connecting the concepts and labeled the threads. Mark flipped the page and did the same thing with a scribble of a plant in soil, surrounded by its own cadre of influencing factors.

He sat back and realized that he'd made a mistake. The two sides of paper looked almost exactly alike.

Jake and the dirt belonged on the same page.

———

Jessica put plates of eggs and homemade biscuits down in front of Jake and Adam. "Jake, you mind if I give Mark a call and have him come over? I'd like him to take another look at you, just to be safe."

"Yeah, that's fine. I got something to say to him."

He shoved a forkful of eggs into his mouth while Jessica made the call from the landline. Waiting for Mark to pick up, she put her hand on Jake's shoulder. "You sure we can't talk about these journals? They're pretty cool."

"Nah."

Adam lightly punched him on the arm. "Why not? Nothing wrong with a little family history. I could use the introduction."

Jake punched back, not so lightly. "Fine. I'll tune out if I want to."

Jessica hung the phone receiver back on the wall and sat down next to Jake. "Mark is on his way over. Adam, looks like this recap may be more for you. But, Jake, I hope you listen. Your great-grandfather wrote about how his father—who, remember, is your great-great-grandfather in that photo—homesteaded the land and subsistence-farmed on a small scale. His father planted different crops at the same time, all next to each other, and called them the 'three sisters.' Corn, beans, and squash."

Jake smirked at the primitive technique. "Why would anyone want to plant those crops at the same time together? They'd be growing all over one another. You could only harvest by hand."

Jessica tilted her head in mock confusion. "Wait—I thought you weren't listening? And anyway, I think that was kind of the point. They had a symbiotic relationship."

"Nobody plants that way anymore. One thing I actually know about."

She held up her hands. "Point taken. But back to the journals . . . he wrote that when he was growing up, his father showed him how the big squash leaves covered the ground, which protected the soil from heat beat-downs, and the cornstalks gave the beans something to grow on. Kind of ingenious, really. Each thing was helping the other. And in a way, it's what I've been doing with my garden, without knowing the three sisters story. Everybody else around here was already starting to use tractors in the late 1800s to plant cash crops, but his father was hanging on to the old ways."

Adam took another sip of coffee. "So that's what you meant by symbiotic. Each thing was helping the other."

"Yes, that's what I meant."

Jake exhaled and softened, just a little. "So what happened next?"

"The son got sent away to boarding school as part of an assimilation program."

Adam reached for another biscuit. "Wait a minute. They took him away from his father? They were allowed to do that?"

"Apparently." Jessica frowned, went to the stove, and slid a couple of eggs onto her own plate. "That's when he started writing in these journals. He described life at the school, which sounded awful for the most part, and wrote about missing his mother and being mad he didn't get to say goodbye to her. By the time he came back a decade later, his father was dying too."

Jake mopped his plate with a biscuit. "This is starting to sound like a TV show."

"If the TV show is an incredibly dark family history, then yes. Barbaric government policies, the killing of a culture, war, alcoholism, domestic abuse—"

He had enough to worry about with his own problems. He didn't need to take on the past too. "Do we have to get into this now? The morning was starting out so . . . normal. Except for Adam sticking around."

Jessica reloaded Jake's plate with the last of the eggs. "We've avoided it for long enough, don't you think?"

Adam grabbed the last biscuit. "And maybe that's part of the problem?"

Jessica nodded. "So, after his father died, his writing became more and more angry. Like he was resentful of white people because of what had happened to him and wanted to wage some sort of silent war on them—show them he was better than them. He thought he could buy revenge, so he traded horses for a tractor and focused on a cash crop."

Finally, subject matter that actually mattered to Jake. "What did he plant?"

"By then, autumn was coming, so he went with winter wheat."

"Makes sense. That's what we do now."

Jessica crossed her arms. "Don't you get it? He pretty much abandoned the old ways. And he sure didn't sound like a happy guy in his writing, but he did have some success, keeping the farm going until the Dust Bowl killed the dirt and . . ."

A glimmer of recognition flickered in Jake's memory. "Wrong."

Adam slouched in his chair. "Huh? Who's wrong?"

Jake pushed his plate away. "The Dust Bowl didn't kill the dirt. I watched a Ken Burns documentary about this when I was laid up in the hospital. Plow up all the topsoil, pile on a few years of drought and wind . . . that's what killed the dirt. The Dust Bowl happened *because* of that. Didn't *cause* it."

Jessica raised her hand in oath. "I stand corrected. Way to move the story forward, Jake. The last journal entry ends the day before he dies of dust pneumonia. And that's the super short version."

Jake heard a rumble outside the open front door and turned his attention to the billows of dust coming straight for the house. He closed his eyes for barely longer than a blink and saw dirt clouds as tall as skyscrapers, as far as he could see, barreling down on this place, fine pieces of what used to be slamming into that warped living room window.

He opened his eyes, just in time to see Mark coming up the porch stairs, the dust kicked up by the Duramax already settled in the driveway.

———

Mark pulled the screen door handle, entered the foyer, and set the medical kit on the plank floor.

"Hungry?" Jessica's voice drifted in from the kitchen, along with the undeniable aroma of a country breakfast.

"Always, these last few days." He walked through the dining room and took a seat at the cramped kitchen table, where Jake and Adam raised their coffee cups in tandem. "Hey, boys."

Jessica took another cup down from the cupboard and poured Mark some coffee. "Be right back. Hope some eggs are hiding out there. Seems like we've eaten three dozen in the last twelve hours."

She disappeared out the back door, and Mark stood up. "How about we take a look at you, Jake? Step into my office at the bottom of the stairs."

By the time Jessica was back inside, the rudimentary physical was already done. Jake looked pretty good, all things considered. He had his brother to thank for that.

They sat back down at the table, and Mark noticed Adam's wardrobe for the first time. "What the hell are you wearing?"

"Just opening up to new ways of expressing myself, Mark. Don't hate."

Mark shook his head. "Oh, Adam." He surveyed the brothers. "How's everybody doing after the world's longest day yesterday? I know Jake is on his third of nine lives."

Jake shifted uncomfortably in his seat. "Listen, Mark, I wanted to tell you something."

Adam pushed his seat back from the table. "I gotta go to the bathroom. Jess, you look like you have to go to the bathroom too." He reached around her to turn off the stove, and ushered her by the elbow out of the kitchen before she had a chance to respond.

Mark waited until they were out of earshot. Adam's instincts with people were good. That kid could've been something. Maybe still could. "So. What do you want to talk about?"

"Well, Jessica harps on me about being thankful, and you said something about finding gratitude back when we first met. But that went in one ear and out the other."

"You've had a lot on your plate."

"Yeah, well, I put it there. No excuse. I just wanted to say thank you. Doesn't seem like enough."

"Adam's the one you should be thanking."

"I already did. But you've actually given a shit for the last few months."

Mark was surprised. Jake was starting to show more and more vulnerability, which had to be pretty hard.

On cue, Jake reached over and gripped Mark's forearm. "I'm not going to hug you, though. I've had more of that than I'm used to these last couple of days. And listen, I know I'm not all good in my head right now. The way I reacted to seeing that photo last night . . . something just snapped."

"If I'd been haunted by some demon-ghost thing my entire life, and finally realized that it was an angry ancestor, I probably would've snapped, too. I might not have tried to kill myself, but who knows. Can't imagine being in your shoes."

Jake relaxed his fingers. "I'm just saying . . . I know I need to, you know, see somebody about all this shit."

"You want to know what I think?"

"Well, of course."

"I think you should take a breath, eat some breakfast, and get the rest of the story first."

"What do you mean?"

Mark shifted and crossed his legs. "You have to know the whole story, so you can know how to start living a different one."

"Living a different story?"

"Yeah. You need to change your story." Mark thought he saw a light of understanding wash over Jake. "Looks like I just saved you thousands of dollars in therapy."

"I can change my story."

"Is that a question or a statement?"

"Both, I guess."

"Yes, and yes."

"So, what's this rest of the story that I need to know first?"

Mark paused. "The rest of the story revolves around the real reason this ancestor is scaring the shit out of you."

Jake stared at his plate. "That shilup thing."

"Yeah. From that journal entry Jessica read, we know he's pissed because you're not doing right by the land, which is also feeding your own health issues. So, to get the whole story, we need to know exactly what you're doing that's making him so mad."

"And then change what I'm doing."

"Right. Live a different story. I've gone through those studies we got yesterday, and I'm learning a lot about the scientific and medical side of what might be making you sick. I don't have *that* particular whole story yet, but I think I'm getting there. And you may not be all that happy about what I'm finding, because I think there are some unforeseen negative impacts from the chemical and mechanical side of farming. But that's one way you could change things."

"Like what?"

"We can talk about that later. I want to get my head completely wrapped around the research first. For now, maybe you should check out those journals that Jessica read from last night. That was some powerful shit. Excuse my French. I've said shit twice already, and it's barely breakfast. I don't know what's come over me."

"Jessica wanted to revisit that family stuff this morning, and I didn't want to. But we did kind of start talking about it."

"Well let's bring those two back from their bathroom break and finish what you started."

———

Jake's father hacked up a good one, wiping the phlegm from his chin with his collar. He didn't know if this cold was somehow tied to his Parkinson's, but it wasn't going away. Seemed to be getting worse, if anything.

He moved past his wife at the sink, who was doing the dishes. She could still manage that kind of stuff, probably because she'd been doing it for so long. He put the leftovers back in the Tupperware container and returned the food to the freezer, where Jessica had stockpiled a few weeks' worth of meals for them.

How Jake had landed her, he still couldn't figure out. And why she was still here was a mystery. Who knows, maybe she saw something in him that he didn't.

Not that he didn't love his kid. Both of them. But Adam had always been so much more fun to be around. Jake seemed borderline morose growing up, and getting him to socialize with other kids was like pulling teeth.

Adam's personality may have gotten him into a little trouble, and maybe he'd made a few mistakes. But who hasn't made a few mistakes? Even his being a druggie was probably a bump in the road. Although that last time he'd caught Adam stealing fertilizer from the utility hangar, God knows why, he'd gotten pretty pissed. Scared his wife, he'd been so mad. Even broke out the shotgun on Adam. Not that he'd ever use it.

He hadn't seen Adam since that night. Kind of missed him, actually.

A coughing fit hit him as pulled a beer from the fridge and made his way to the couch, where he struggled to pick up the remote with his shaking hand. Some sport had to be happening somewhere, so he turned on the TV and started flipping through the channels with his thumb.

Kind of like the kids these days did with those stupid phones.

He settled on a replay of a classic college football game from the mid-eighties. What a decade.

A dry hack from deep in his lungs failed to produce anything worthwhile, and he sent the spittle back down with a swig of beer.

Adam had a good heart. Still did, he was sure. Just liked to have a good time.

And who doesn't like to have a good time?

———

Jake yelled toward the living room. "You guys done going to the bathroom?"

He heard steps coming down the stairs, and Jessica marched into the kitchen. "What were you doing up there?"

Jessica put a laundry basket full of clothes by the back porch.

"I just was going through some of Hailey's clothes. I was thinking I could take them to the hospital. They take donations for kids who are there for a while."

Jake looked at Mark, who showed no reaction. He didn't understand what a big deal this was. But Jake did. "Great idea. Let me know when you want to go, and I'll drive with you. Where's Adam?"

The hallway toilet flushed, followed by Adam's muffled voice. "I'm in here, I told you. I was going to the bathroom."

Mark laughed. "Is he always like this?"

"Always been funny, if that's what you mean. He made a lot of friends that way. Some good, some not so good."

Adam slid back into his seat at the kitchen table. "So . . . where were we? Were we anywhere?"

Jessica turned the stove back on. "I was making more eggs, thanks to some hens that must be very happy the rain let up. And I'd just given you the short version of what's in those journals."

"That's right. Old guy in the photo did the three sisters thing, his son got sent away to get assimilated, came back pissed, and worked hard to prove the white man wrong. Am I close?"

"Close enough. Forgot to mention, he also was the first one to start using fertilizer. Ammonia pellets, I think I read."

Mark got up to pour himself a cup of coffee. "Looks like I got here in time for the introduction of chemical farming."

Jake noticed a defensive angst rise up from his gut. "Fertilizer works. Still does."

"You're right, fertilizer works. But one of those papers you photocopied at the Ag library yesterday shows how N-P-K fertilizer helps stalk strength and chlorophyll production, which will keep the plant green, but doesn't replace the rest of the nutrients the plant gets from healthy soil."

"So what? If the plants are green, wouldn't you assume they're fine?"

Mark sat back down. "Yeah, most people would. And have for a long time. But if the dirt's stripped of its nutrients, the plant gets weak—like a human who doesn't eat right—which compromises the plant's immune system, making it more prone to viruses and pests."

"But it's a plant, not a human."

"Your opinion of the truth doesn't change it, Jake. This is how living multicellular organisms work."

"Fine. You're the doctor."

Jessica—shifting into what Jake liked to call "mediation mode"—tried to change the subject. "Hey now, let's relax. We're just eating some eggs and talking about farming." She put a full plate down in front of Mark. "Which actually makes me curious as to how this place we call home really evolved. Jake, what about your dad? Did he do anything differently here?"

"He bought more land. And always the latest and greatest in machinery. Used a lot of carbaryl, which really helped with the bugs. Oh, and he was the first to double-crop with corn in the summer. Wheat in the winter, then corn. As soon as the wheat was cleared, he was planting corn in the same field, and vice versa."

His wife finally sat down with her own plate of food. "I'm guessing carbaryl is a pesticide. Anything else?"

"I remember the weeds got a lot worse when I was a kid, so he switched from 2,4-D and started using a more powerful weedkiller. And desiccating with it. I still use the same stuff."

Mark seemed to be almost talking to himself. "So, he was applying a toxic pesticide compound, along with a strong weedkiller, all year long, and wasn't letting the soil rest."

"You want to back off a little? Yields were good, he was taking care of his family and feeding a lot of people."

"Sorry, I meant that as an observation, not a judgment. I'm guessing your great-grandfather did mostly single-crop farming, right?

Probably the first to use a tractor, and then he suffered the consequences of drought and wind on destroyed topsoil when the Dust
Bowl era hit."

Adam twirled his coffee cup in circles with his index finger.
"We were just talking about that before you got here. How did you
know that?"

"I read up on the history of farming around here in the 1930s.
The dead soil of the Dust Bowl demanded that farmers, including
your grandfather, use fertilizer to grow anything. Bad soil meant
weak plants, which made pests more of a problem, which led the
next generation—your dad—to use more chemical pesticides and a
potent herbicide, which just caused more damage to his fields. One
big circle."

Jake couldn't keep the ridicule out of his voice. "What are you,
some hippie MD now? And how would we feed this country without
those bigger yields?"

Mark wasn't sure if he should go there but went anyway. "That's
a different conversation, Jake, but our hunger problem isn't about not
having enough food in the country. We have plenty. It's about having
access to it . . . getting the food to the people who need it. And we
waste so much. I used to volunteer every week at a food bank a couple
blocks from the clinic. The director told me that something like 40
percent of the food in grocery stores and restaurants is literally thrown
away. Finding a way to get that food to people who need it is just one
of the challenges."

"Whatever. This finding fault with how my family farmed—and
still *does*—feels like an assault on our way of life. Not really helping me.
Especially right now."

Jessica touched Jake's shoulder as she headed toward the sink for
more water.

Mark shook his head. "No, no . . . this isn't an assault at all. You're
not to blame. All I'm saying is that your grandfather, father, and you

got locked into this cycle of dependency on chemicals to keep your crops alive. Generations of your family have been suffering with bad dirt for a long time, and you've just been doing what you have to do to make it work. Which is expensive, right?"

"Yeah. Still feels like a blame game."

"I don't know if anybody's really to blame. Some of these bigger agribusiness companies, like the one selling you that weedkiller, may have been a little loose with the truth, though."

Jake wasn't sure whether to be defensive or interested. He decided he was both. "Yeah, well, what you said about the cycle of unhealthy dirt and chemical dependency sounds a lot like what you do too."

Mark's eyes seemed to light up like a proud father's. And his one-word response couldn't hide a strange excitement. "Oh?"

Jake fought through the distraction to finish the thought. "Yeah. I mean, as a doctor. Somebody unhealthy comes to you. Like me. You prescribe a particular drug to alleviate their symptom, so they can get through the day. That drug has a bad side effect, so you prescribe a different drug to treat the side effect . . . until you're not treating the disease as much as you're managing the symptoms with chemicals."

Now Mark was beaming, as if Jake had won a 4-H contest. "I suppose that's true."

And Jake was on a roll. "Of course it's true! Everybody's seen those commercials for some new drug, where half the ad is dedicated to listing the side effects. And I didn't go to medical school, didn't even go to college, but I have a hard time believing that humans evolved over however many years just to rely on a bunch of companies' drugs. Something's wrong with that picture, *doctor*."

Adam landed his coffee mug on the table like a gavel. "Why do I get the impression that Mark was hoping Jake would come to this conclusion on his own? Oh, the look on his non-poker face. That's why. If he ever invites me over for card night, I'm in."

Jake studied the constellation of crumbs on his plate. Had the answers really been right there in front of him, lines of connection just waiting to be drawn?

The plate swooped out of sight, stolen by Jessica's hand. She scraped her breakfast remnants onto Jake's plate and pushed it back in front of him. "Well, I think we can all agree that we're doing the same thing to our land that we are to our bodies. Everybody's right, which is pretty sad. But I don't see any concrete solutions here from any of you."

Jake slid the plate over to Adam, a subtle peace offering. "I'm done. Going to take a nap."

Adam offered a gentle protest. "Why? You just got up!"

Jake lumbered to the back bedroom, flopped on his stomach, and was asleep before the words he'd intended to say about being so, so tired could even gather air in his throat.

———

After the breakfast dishes were cleared and washed, Mark bid a quick goodbye so he could get back to work. Jessica was right—he was pointing fingers, but not offering an alternative to the status quo. A little more time with the research might show a solution or two.

The break in the rain offered relief from the zero-visibility worry of getting in a wreck. Mark pulled onto the highway and thought about calling *her*, but he let his shyness talk him out it. He didn't want to talk just about research with her, and he didn't know how to talk about anything else. Which was frustrating, because there was everything to talk about.

And so he turned to his latest escape, the Bison Bridge EP. Mark cranked the dial and sang along with lyrics he'd already committed to heart. This is why he loved these songs. They told him he wasn't alone.

There's a fire on the mountain
Can you see the light
Burning like a fountain
Shooting through the night
How long do we have now
No one really knows
So gather arms and gather round
Family, friends, and foes
And raise a glass to tenderness
And to reminisce
And pray we get another day
To live like this

He hadn't had that kind of epic day—one he wanted to live over and over—in a long time. But seeing *her* again had sparked this fire of a second chance . . . and if not with her, then maybe with the rest of his life. Could be that coming back home, to where he began, was offering him an opportunity to start over.

To begin again, without the fear of disappointing his father.

And with a few years of living to learn from. Quite a few, punctuated more by lessons in what didn't work than what did, but still . . . gifts.

We gave 'em hell's high water
Darling, we were so young
You the preacher's daughter
Me the sinnin' one
Maybe those days were better
Than we knew back then
We thought we'd live forever
Not for remember-when

So let's raise a glass to tenderness
And to reminisce
And pray we get another day
To live like this

He rewound the song to the line about being aware of the good days as they're happening.

Maybe those days were better
Than we knew back then

Maybe these days are better too.

Mark rolled down the window to let in the late prairie morning and raised an open hand to the dawn-streaked sky, his fingers moving through the quiet air that stood still over the wet road, until a vibration shook him out of his reverie.

His phone lit up from the cupholder.

Of course.

Her.

He tried to sound casual. "Hello?"

"Hey, stranger."

"You used that line yesterday."

A smile shined in her voice. "True. You got a minute?"

"For you? All the time in the world."

"Easy, Romeo. Listen, you told me that, of all these chemicals we researched yesterday, that one weedkiller is the most used, right?"

"By far. Something like three or four hundred million tons a year. Agricultural and residential."

"Well, that's why I looked in my garage. I used that stuff on my driveway last weekend to kill weeds between the pavers, which pushed me to find out more about the active ingredient, since I was handling it myself without any protection. The label says that studies show it's safe for humans, but I think they missed something."

"And that is?"

"The active ingredient works by disrupting the shikimate pathway, and—"

Mark quickly searched his internal encyclopedia and came up short. "Remind me of what the shikimate pathway is. Been a long couple of days."

"Metabolic series of steps used by bacteria, fungi, plants, and other microorganisms to make essential amino acids, three of which are crucial to the protein synthesis in the human body. Phenylalanine, tyrosine, and tryptophan."

Mark vaguely remembered reading about this. "Right. And we don't have a shikimate pathway, so we have to get those essential amino acids from our food, or the bacteria in our gut microbiome."

"Atta boy. So, check this out . . . that weedkiller works by blocking an enzyme in the shikimate pathway, which inhibits the organism's ability to make those essential amino acids, and that's how the organism dies. The company pushed the product as 'safe' with the premise that humans don't have a shikimate pathway, so this stuff wouldn't affect people. But what they didn't understand is that the bacteria in our gut *do* have a shikimate pathway."

"Which is how we get some of these essential amino acids."

"Yeah. And if we're really dumping that much of this stuff into our ecosystem, we're depleting our global reservoir of shikimate-related amino acids."

Mark hit the steering wheel with his open palm. "Depriving us of critical building blocks for proteins throughout the body."

"As well as neurotransmitters responsible for mood stability, sleep quality, sex drive, and more."

That's Jake. Right there.

Mark started connecting the dots. "Lose a few of the essential amino acids, and you end up misspelling a lot of proteins, among the hundreds of thousands of different protein structures that we produce, including scaffolding proteins, enzymes for metabolism and detox . . ."

The other end of the line was silent for a hesitant moment.

"Wait, *misspelling?* What do you mean by that?"

Mark finally had something to impress her with. At least he thought he did. "I think about it like words. If you screw with the vowels of the alphabet, of which there are only five—six if you count Y—you mess up the words you're trying to spell. Same thing with amino acids. Tweak three of the vowels, or essential amino acids, in this case, and the proteins made by them are altered."

"Nice one. Great metaphor. But there's another reason I called."

The butterflies in Mark's stomach woke up. To talk? Like *talk?* "Let's hear it."

"Leaky gut."

Damn. "What?"

"Pull over if you can. I'm texting you a few attachments. You're going to want to see this."

———

Adam gathered his sheets from the couch and skated on his socks past Jessica on the back porch, putting Hailey's old clothes in a cardboard box. He dumped the sheets on top of the washer and headed back to the living room to get the rest of his stuff together. Which wasn't much. He wasn't sure where he was going, especially since his ride was now an impounded stolen truck, but he could ask Jake or Jessica to take him into town. He'd figure the rest out.

He'd just started stuffing his worldly possessions into his backpack when Jake shuffled into the living room. "What are you doing?"

"What happened to the nap?"

"I don't know. Maybe I just needed a twenty-minute-er. Back to you. What are you doing?"

"Packing up, bro. I appreciate you and Jess letting me crash, but I know this isn't forever. A ride into town would be epic, though."

"Where are you going to go?"

"Not sure. Not back to OKC, that's for sure. Too easy to lapse back into that old life. And I have to stay close. Court date for stealing that truck is next week. Somebody in Guymon might need a hand and let me work for them for cash under the table. I'll save up quick without having to pay rent. It's practically summer, and I can sleep almost anywhere."

"I can keep you busy with a hammer and nail, if that's what you want."

"No, man. You guys have a ton of your own stuff to work through. I'm not going to get in the way of that. I'll take the invite for a Sunday dinner now and then, if that sort of thing comes my way, though."

Jessica's head appeared over Jake's shoulder. "What are you doing?"

Jake answered for Adam. "He's leaving. Says he'll get a job somewhere and start building back up again."

Jessica stepped around Jake. "That's ridiculous. Stay here. Jake will put you to work."

Adam shoved his clothes down with his fist and closed the zipper. "Jake already offered. Thanks, but no thanks. I'm getting out of your hair."

Jake leaned against the back of the couch, using his hands for support. "What if I told you that you'd be doing me a favor? I have to start harvesting what wheat we have left, and I'm obviously not in the best shape at the moment. I was telling Mark earlier, while you were in the bathroom . . . my body's a mess, but I know my head's not right, either. I could use the help."

Adam examined the frayed straps of his backpack. "Where would I sleep?"

Jessica pointed down the hallway. "Guest room, where Jake just took the shortest nap of his life. He doesn't need that bed anymore. Right, Jake?"

Jake pushed himself back to standing. "This ain't forever. Just until you get on your feet. And listen, Mom might not know who you are at the moment, and Dad's still likely to shove a shotgun in your face. So, if you stay here, you should probably just let them be for a while."

Adam could tell that Jake was trying to protect their parents. Their dad had always let Adam get away with everything and had probably only pulled that shotgun thing because he'd been drinking. But he respected Jake's intent. "I'll stay away from them. But I haven't worked on the farm since I was in high school, and even then, I was a shitty hand. You'd have to show me what to do."

"I know. You just have to pay attention."

Adam studied his hands, which had only been holding needles and pipes and the occasional fork for the last couple of years. Hands that hadn't held other hands in longer than he could remember, if ever. He'd been the kind of popular in high school that spawned the occasional hookup with the same breed of girl, but never the kind of girl whose hand you'd really want to hold.

He balled his fingers into fists, gripped tight, and released, before holding out his right hand to Jake. "Looks like these things still work. Let's get some dirt on 'em."

———

Mark pulled back onto the highway from the shoulder, trying to process what she'd just explained to him using the attachments. "Wow."

"Yeah, I had a feeling that those tight protein junctions in the gut lining might be directly affected by that weedkiller. It can practically turn the protective membrane into a sieve. And I don't have to tell you, but those protective membranes are all over the body, not just the gut.

That chemical also tightly binds to metals, so it could theoretically shuttle aluminum through the blood-brain barrier. Just in theory. But still. None of this is good."

Mark backed off the gas pedal. He'd already been going ninety miles an hour, without knowing. "Oversimplified question, but why do you think they're selling something so . . . well . . . bad?"

"They probably didn't understand the dangers, at least initially. When this weedkiller was first introduced, we didn't notice a dramatic impact on public health. And I found an EPA study claiming the weedkiller is safe, as well as one sponsored by the company, showing the active ingredient had a negligible direct impact on humans when used in the intended amounts."

"I sense a 'but.'"

"But they weren't looking for the off-target side effects, and they only considered immediate direct impacts, not generational."

"Generational?"

"We have a lot of research showing it can take time for dangerous chemicals, like DDT, for example, to have downstream effects on biology . . . effects that get worse with every passing generation."

"Almost like a delayed, cumulative poison."

"Exactly. Imagine a fetus growing in an environment influenced by a chemical that alters the ability to build a healthy human body. We can expect they'll carry forward the epigenetic injuries of their parents, along with the potential for worsening neurodevelopmental conditions and cancers."

"Which we're seeing now."

"Yeah. We call that generational toxicity."

Mark slowed as he approached his parents' house. "So, the company's finding that their product was safe wasn't entirely false, given the parameters they used. But they didn't see the whole picture."

"Right. They didn't measure off-target effects, and they didn't account for the generational toxicity piece, let alone the protective membrane permeability. Mainstream medicine has only recently started to understand how important some of these things are. I should know—I'm one of the last to the party with this stuff since I'm such a hard numbers girl."

"I hope it's not . . ."

"I know. Too late."

———

Adam walked out to the utility hangar with Jake, who waved his hand across the fleet of tractors, combine, and attachments like he was selling a used car. "All the big machinery's in here. You ready to run one of these things?"

"That's not exactly getting my hands in the dirt, is it? More like feet on pedals."

"You're going to work sixteen hundred acres on foot?"

Adam shot a glance at the closest field, just across the gravel lot from the hangar. "Doesn't look like that much to me, given that half this shit is dead."

"I see. You're a farmer now, and that's your analysis."

"Sorry, sorry. What do we need to do?"

"First thing will be to desiccate."

"Desiccate?"

Jake pointed to a couple of big vats in the corner. "Yeah, we're going to spray the wheat with that weedkiller, so it dies quickly and dries evenly."

"Mark said something about looking into that stuff."

"When did he say that?"

"Last night, when you and Jessica were talking in the car."

"And you were hiding in the bedroom?"

Seemed like forever ago to Adam. Must've seemed even longer to Jake. "Yeah."

"All still just talk as far as I'm concerned. Nothing's been proven to me yet, and until then, our livelihood depends on getting this stuff dried, cut, and sold."

"But won't some of the residue be left on the wheat? You'd kind of end up eating weedkiller, wouldn't you?"

Jake turned to squarely face Adam. "We're not going to have a conversation like this every time something's gotta get done. I need a hand. You offered one."

Adam looked him in the eyes, and then past him to the vats. Killing what they were supposed to be eating with a highly toxic compound didn't seem like a great option, but he didn't want to start this relationship with Jake by being combative. He was trying to make changes, and fighting with his brother wouldn't really be changing anything.

"How about you show me how to drive whatever you use first? That way I'm not fucking anything up out there, learning on the fly."

"That makes sense, actually. You should probably spend the afternoon just learning to run the 7R. Then I'll teach you how to operate the boom sprayer. Climb up into that John Deere tractor over there on the end."

Adam walked to the rig and stepped up into the cab of a tractor, which felt like an airplane cockpit. The number of switches and levers and gauges was overwhelming. "There's no way I'm going to be able to do this."

"You'll be fine. You don't need to mess with most of that stuff. Don't even look at that computer screen right now. All you need to do is listen."

"Aren't you going to come up here with me?"

"Yeah, I'll show you the basics, then let you go at it. It's really not that complicated. Hang on, I'm going to make sure the boom sprayer is hooked up. We're going to drag that around in the gravel lot so you can see what it's like."

"But not spray, right?"

"No, we'll do that tomorrow."

Adam's unease was evolving into anxiety. "I want to help, Jake, but can't you do this while I'm swinging a hammer somewhere?"

Jake shoved his hands in his jeans pockets and stared out of the hangar. "Listen. Between us. I just don't totally trust myself right now. I snapped so fast last night, so hard, that I think I should let myself settle down before operating this kind of heavy machinery."

Adam was surprised at his brother's vulnerability, and also suspicious. There was something else going on, some other reason that Jake didn't want to be out there.

He watched Jake messing with some kind of equipment behind the tractor, before pulling himself into the cab with Adam. Jake showed him how to start the engine and get the rig in gear, and within a few minutes they were pulling out of the utility hangar. Adam gained confidence quickly by driving around the gravel lot, since he only had to worry about speed and direction, and by the time they reached the first field, he was actually having fun.

Jake pointed to the tracks Adam would need to follow through the wheat. "See those? Those are called tramlines. Just get the tractor lined up, and they'll take you all the way through the field. When you get to the end, take a left and follow the next set of tramlines back here. That'll be all we do today."

"And I'll be able to find them on the other side?"

"Yeah, it's easy. They're evenly spaced parallel, so you can cover the whole place with whatever you're dragging. Right now, that's going to be the boom sprayer with the weedkiller. I'll show you how to spray tomorrow. Now slow this thing down to a stop and let me out. I don't feel so hot."

Adam did as he was told, and then steered the tractor onto the first tramline. The track kind of felt like wagon ruts, and he had little trouble keeping the 7R honest. Once he felt semi-comfortable, he took in the view around him. He could see everything from up high where he sat, which gave him a sense of power over his surroundings. He hadn't felt that way in a long time.

A scarecrow stood in the distance, straight in front of him. Adam smiled at the quaint homage to what used to be. Weird that Jake hadn't said anything about this guy. "Hey, fella. Sucks to get replaced, huh?"

He glanced to his left, wondering if he should abandon the tramlines and steer that way to avoid hitting the scarecrow.

There was another one, but closer. He looked to his right to avoid both of them.

Another one, even closer.

The tractor started to veer off the tramline to the left, and Adam dropped his head to check the steering wheel as he overcorrected to the right. He looked up just in time to see the scarecrow immediately in front of the windshield, somehow risen and pushed up against the glass.

A scarecrow with long, hanging braids, in a fringed leather shirt, with deerskin breechcloth and leggings, raising a translucent hand.

Mouth widening into a gaping abyss.

Hair burning to ash, skin dripping off bone, eyes disintegrating into hollow sockets.

And in the horrified breath before he fell into blackness, a surge of adrenaline hit Adam, not so different than the rush he'd get from the first hit of meth in the morning.

Not so different at all.

———

Jake watched the tractor wheels disappear in the wheat, the silhouette of his brother in the cockpit rigid in concentration.

There you go, Adam. Easy, just keep her going straight.

He was just turning back toward the utility hangar when he saw the tractor cab veer to the left, then lurch to the right, before stopping in the field.

"Adam? Adam!"

He limped-ran to the tractor, which had only covered a couple hundred yards. His brother was slumped against the steering wheel, right hand still gripping the hand throttle. Jake took the 7R out of gear, hit the parking brake, and pushed Adam back against the seat.

He felt for a pulse in his neck.

Still there. Faint, but still there.

He grabbed a half-empty plastic water bottle from the floorboard, frantically ripped off the lid, and shook what he could over Adam's face, sending more than he intended into his brother's nose. Just as well, though, because within a few seconds, Adam coughed and hacked and opened his eyes.

His eyes were wild.

And Jake knew what he'd seen. He put his hands on his brother's shoulders, as best he could in the cramped cab. "It's alright, Adam. It's alright. Breathe. In and out."

Adam dropped his head to his chin and leaned into Jake's chest. "I believe you. I believe you. I believe you."

Jake awkwardly wrapped his arms around Adam and waited until the trembling slowed. "You ready to get back to the house?"

"Yeah. I think we should walk, though."

"I think you're right."

Jake stepped out of the cab first, then helped Adam find his footing until he was on solid ground. They walked along the tramline toward the house with little space between them, Adam staring straight ahead, and Jake looking back every few steps at the backlit tractor.

Almost looked like a metal warrior on a battlefield, dead in the wheat.

———

Jessica handed Adam a glass of water over the back of the couch.

"What did you do to him, Jake?"

Adam reached for the glass, his hand still shaking. "He didn't do anything. And he's right."

She side-eyed her husband. "Right about what?"

Jake sat down next to him. "You don't have to talk about this right now, Adam."

Jessica came around the couch to face Adam head-on. "Talk about what? Now you *definitely* have to talk about it."

"I saw what Jake's been seeing."

"What? The *ghost* thing? You're kidding."

"Yeah. I mean no—not kidding. Never been that scared in my life. I still don't feel like I'm attached to my body. It was fucking awful." Adam downed the water in a few gulps.

"Can you describe it?"

"Can, but won't. All you need to know is that thing is evil."

Jessica took the empty water glass from Adam's hand and set it on the table. "But I thought it looked like your great-great-grandfather in that photo? Nothing about him seems evil."

"Yeah, well, he's decided to go to the dark side, because there's nothing good about melting skin and eyeballs. And we're done talking about it. I'm one very, very fragile motherfucker right now."

Jessica held her hand to Adam's forehead. "I'm going to get Mark over here again, just in case. Passing out like that is no joke, and given what you've been doing the last couple of years, maybe there's a heart thing—"

Jake pushed himself up from the couch. Wasn't getting any easier. "No need to speculate. But go ahead and call him if you want. What do you want to do, Adam? Walk? Lie down?"

Adam traced the crease of his palm with his index finger. "I should probably just sit here for a minute. And then, I'd like to figure out what the fuck that thing wants. And give it to him."

———

Mark made a late breakfast for his mother and sat down across the table from her, in front of the spread of research papers and the crude sketch of Jake and the plant.

He tested the conversational waters. "Sleep okay?"

She tilted her head.

"Want to talk?"

She stared vacantly at the eggs.

Not now, apparently.

He added a final bubble to the sketch, this one with the weed-killer and a few of the other compounds he knew Jake was using. More threads in the web. Everything was connected. Everything was—

His phone spasmed on the table. A number he didn't recognize, but he should probably answer. He was starting to learn that there was a lot more to being a small-town doctor than he'd anticipated.

As soon as he hit the green Accept button, he realized this was Jake and Jessica's landline. The call was short and to the point. What was going on over there? Now Adam had some kind of health scare that needed to be checked out. Jessica hadn't given much detail over the phone, only that he'd briefly lost consciousness.

Mark shoved the crude drawing and all the research papers, including the medical studies, into the Walmart bag. He'd been so deep in the sketch that he hadn't even noticed that his mother had already left the table and gone back up to her room. Her refusal to talk had given him the chance to focus, and these connections he was making between inputs and outputs seemed solid. Really solid. And with this drawing, he felt like he could explain what was going on much more clearly than throwing a lot of medical terms around.

He threw his phone in the bag and headed out to the truck, visualizing the webs he'd drawn on the computer paper. Even though the threads connecting the concepts were linear, the concepts themselves were circular . . . feedback loops of continually disintegrating systems. These cycles affected not only the system itself, but also the human being and environment in the middle of it all—which was in its own feedback loop of disintegration.

He started the engine, torquing the key in frustration. That didn't sound as clear as he'd hoped.

And this really wasn't that complicated.

The drawing would help.

———

Adam put one foot in front of the other, all the way around the perimeter of the house, trying to ground himself.

Literally.

Maybe standing on the earth and moving through the dirt would slow his heartbeat, which was still accelerating every time he touched the edges of what had just happened. At first, he'd thought—more like hoped—that the demon-ghost was a hallucinatory holdover from his drug use, but he and Jake had compared stories.

They'd seen the same thing.

He walked past the chicken coop and saw the tractor parked at an angle in the field. Maybe he and Jake were experiencing some sort of ancestral energy only they could see.

Real, but not.

They were brothers. Same blood, steeped in the old stories Jessica had told them about from the journals. Same blood meant the same responsibility to the same land.

And the same shilup, warning his descendants.

Them.

Of what, exactly?

The grate of tires on gravel stole Adam's attention toward the driveway at the front of the house.

Mark.

Adam got to the truck just as Mark stepped onto the driveway. He looked surprised to see Adam. "You're upright. Not a bad sign."

"I'm alright. Wasn't like I really got in a wreck or anything. Just freaked out."

"You want me to check your vitals, do a quick once-over?"

"I don't think this is something you can fix. Sorry, Mark."

"Why not?"

"What I saw has nothing to do with modern medicine."

"What you saw?"

Adam leaned against the hood of the truck. "Yeah. I saw what my brother's been seeing."

Mark took an awkward seat on the front bumper, trying to avoid the damage where the truck had hit the Tercel. "That so?"

"You wouldn't believe me. You didn't believe him, either."

"I've been questioning a lot of things I believe. What happened?"

Adam recounted the horror, fighting back tears as he described the demon-ghost's face melting into the windshield. Mark listened without response, and a few seconds after Adam's last sentence, Adam wondered if he'd stopped paying attention. "Like I said, you didn't believe—"

"I believe you, Adam. Just thinking." Mark pushed up from the fender to the truck hood until they were level. "I think I know what's going on."

"Let me guess. An ancestor has been haunting this place for over a century, just like he said he would, because we've been destroying the land—"

Mark continued the thought. "And in turn, ourselves." He stared in the direction of the tractor. "Want to know how?"

Mark pulled open the screen door, let Adam walk through, and called the meeting to order as he entered the foyer. "Alright, everybody. Dining room table, stat."

Jessica came in from the kitchen. "Is he going to survive, Mark?"

Adam sat down. "A better question would be . . . are any of us?"

Jake got off the couch and came to the table. "What the hell's that supposed to mean? Mark and Jess are fine—you and I are the only ones seeing ghosts."

Mark threw the Walmart bag on the table and took a seat. "Boys, enough. Adam let me know what happened. And for the record, I believe both of you. And by that, I mean I stand by my assertion that I believe *you* believe what you're seeing . . . which doesn't make it any less real, even if I can't see it. Can we agree on that?"

Jake let out an exasperated sigh. "There's gotta be a better way to say that. But fine."

Mark started pulling papers out of the bag. "If you're willing to listen, I'm ready to tell you what I think is going on here."

Jessica answered for both of them. "We are."

"So, Jake, remember when I asked you to take photos of the chemicals you're using?"

"Yeah."

"We found studies showing that residues and metabolites from those chemicals are having an impact on the soil microbiome, and—"

"You're making no sense. English, please."

"Sorry. Remember when I took the soil samples, Jessica?"

She leaned over to Jake. "He wanted to look at our dirt."

"Well, the short story is *your* soil is alive, and Jake's is dead."

Jake groaned. "Sweet. Mystery solved."

Mark allowed himself a laugh and continued. "I learned more about soil than I ever thought possible after going through the Ag research. Healthy soil is literally alive with bacteria, fungi, earthworms, and all sorts of other tiny critters, which work together to create plants, like those in Jessica's garden, that are healthy, and strong, and more immune to disease and pests. They call that living system the soil microbiome."

Jake leaned back in his chair. "Go on."

"A lot of these chemicals we've been spraying on crops to kill what we don't want also kill that living system. Paraquat, 2,4-D, atrazine, carbaryl for bugs . . . even that weedkiller chemical you use, Jake, is actually patented as an antibiotic."

Jessica glanced sideways at Jake. "Did you say *antibiotic*?"

"Yeah. That's one of the reasons Jake's dirt looks dead. Years of putting these chemicals in the soil, combined with near-constant plowing and never letting the soil rest, have pretty much destroyed the life in your field dirt."

Jake's eyebrows raised just a touch, enough acceptance for Mark to notice. "Which would make growing anything really hard."

Jessica touched the old, faded photograph still on the table. "And make a certain ancestor pretty mad."

Mark sat up a little straighter. "And you're desiccating your wheat with that weedkiller, spraying full-coverage to kill and dry before harvest, and then again full-coverage on the genetically modified corn seeds, since they're resistant to the active ingredient. You're using a literal shit-ton of that stuff on your fields."

"This is true."

Mark turned to Jessica. "But that's not the end of the soil story. Your dirt is alive, with a healthy soil microbiome. And while the Ag research says that's important—and here's what's really interesting—the medical research does, too. Your gut also has a microbiome, which is crucial to your health. In fact, your gut has the same number of microorganisms as healthy soil, but only about 10 percent of the biodiversity. A few of the studies we found yesterday suggest that chronic disease stems from this lack of microbiome biodiversity in the gut."

Jessica drew the line before Mark could. "So, you're saying they're connected? The soil microbiome and gut microbiome?"

"Directly linked. And spending all that time in good dirt is probably a big reason why you're healthier than anyone else around here."

"How's that, exactly?"

"You're taking in all that healthy biodiversity when you're out there. You're touching the earth with your hands, breathing in microscopic organisms. Even the traces of chicken shit on the eggs and the horse manure are important. That microbiome translates to your gut and increases your biodiversity, which keeps your immune system cranking. I brought the research with me to show you. Oh, and I threw together a sketch of what I think is going on. Hang on."

Mark dug through the Walmart bag, found what he was looking for, and pushed the collated pieces of paper across the table toward Jessica. "This National Institutes of Health study explains it in more detail. And here's the sketch." He slid the drawing to Jake.

Jessica thumbed through the research. "That makes sense. Basically, the side effect of killing weeds and pests is that we're also killing the soil, which makes it hard to grow good crops and stay healthy."

Mark nodded. "It's chemical *and* mechanical, remember. Excessive disruption through plowing and not letting the soil rest doesn't help either. I mean, look at the Dust Bowl."

Jake clasped his hand behind his head and stared at the ceiling. "Oh, I did. Like I told Jess, Ken Burns spelled it out for me. But I didn't really relate it to my own situation until about two minutes ago." He held the sketch at eye level. "And this looks like damn near everything is connected."

"Right. Great documentary. And yes, all these cycles influence each other. Bad dirt deepens that cycle we talked about earlier by having to add more chemicals to grow anything."

"So, what I'm hearing, and seeing, is that my dirt and I are experiencing about the same level of aliveness. Assuming I'm the stick-figure guy."

Mark pushed back his chair. "You don't have to just hear it from me or see it on a piece of paper. Come on."

A few minutes later, they were all standing at the edge of Jessica's garden, Jake and Adam trying to balance on their own two feet, while Mark bent down to the soil.

"After that deluge, even being submerged, look how resilient her plants are."

He dug until his fingers were almost forearm-deep in the dirt and put a handful of earth in Jake's hand. "Hold this and hang on."

Adam nudged Jake. "Sounds like a redneck's last words."

Jake couldn't help but laugh. "Takes one to know one. Not sure he's quite that, though. Didn't even know what a winch looked like."

Mark ran to the wheat field about twenty yards away and returned with another handful of dirt. "Here, put this in your other hand. See anything moving in Jessica's soil?"

"I see an earthworm."

"How about the color and texture?"

"Color is deep and dark. I guess I'd say it feels rich."

"And what about your dirt?"

"Lighter. Finer. No worms."

"Right. Carbaryl kills 'em. Okay, last thing. Take a whiff."

Jake dropped his nose to both hands, before letting the dirt fall to the ground.

"Is there a difference?"

"Jessica's smells more like horse shit. Which would make sense, all things considered."

Jessica lightly punched Jake in the arm while Adam clapped in approval. "Nice one, Jake."

Jake wiped the dirt on his jeans. "I see what you're saying. And smell it."

Mark pointed to the dirt at Jake's feet. "That's the soil microbiome.

Bacteria, fungi, all those living microorganisms that are so important to human health."

"I get it. God made dirt, so dirt don't hurt."

"I'm a science guy—not quite sure about the God thing, but yes. And yours is damn-near dead."

———

Jake trudged back to the house behind Jessica, Adam, and Mark. What was he supposed to do, plant sixteen hundred acres with one ginormous vegetable garden and tend the plants on his hands and knees, like Jessica? That was the work of a thousand men. He converted his frustration into finding whatever fault he could in Mark's argument, which was a lot easier.

"A kindergartner could probably figure out that bad dirt would be harder to grow a plant in. But I don't see any straight lines being drawn between how I'm treating my dirt and whatever health issues I might have."

"You want a straight line? Here's one. A chemical you've been spraying on your soil may have damaged the tight protein junctions that protect your stomach and intestines, causing your gut to leak toxins into your bloodstream, which put you in the hospital."

Jake was silent for a breath. He wasn't expecting *that* straight of a line.

"Oh." Jake remembered that the city doctor had mentioned something about that. "Leaky gut?"

Mark slowed down to let Jake catch up. "That's what the hospital said was making you sick, right? They were probably reluctant to diagnose it."

"Why?"

"We've been slow to acknowledge leaky gut, but we're coming

around. And speaking of that, chronic inflammation in your gut lining led to your ulcerative colitis. That's what we talked about in the car a couple of days ago, about chronic inflammation causing chronic disease. We went looking for answers at OSU and actually found some, as to what might be causing that chronic inflammation around here. That's all I'm trying to share with you. If you want another straight line—"

"No, that's okay. You've made your point."

"Listen, Jake. Those protein-based membranes aren't just lining your gut . . . they're everywhere. Even our blood vessels depend on them for protection. But the most important one is the blood-brain barrier. A microscopic leak in the blood-brain barrier could introduce toxins like aluminum to the brain and lead to neurological problems and neurogenerative diseases like Alzheimer's, Parkinson's, autism, and multiple sclerosis, all of which we've seen go epidemic since the mid-1990s. Which, incidentally, is when genetically modified seeds, resistant to that weedkiller, were introduced, drastically increasing how much of that chemical was sprayed."

Jake kicked a gravel nugget as far down the road as he could, which wasn't far. "I've had too long of a couple days for a questionable science class. Maybe you should take a break in the teacher's lounge, professor. Actually, this feels more like a sermon. Find someone else for confessional."

Mark stopped in his tracks and raised his voice. "Are you kidding me? Don't you think that having a long couple of days might be because of the way you're living? From how you work to how you eat?"

Jake raised his voice even louder. "I think you're not in my shoes. That's what I think. And last time I checked, this was a free country. Anything about freedom in that fancy research?"

"Freedom doesn't mean freedom from consequence. You can do whatever the hell you want to do, Jake. But everything's got a cost. You want proof? Look in the mirror."

Out of the corner of his eye, Jake saw Jessica and Adam stop and turn around to come back toward them. Jessica put her hand on Jake's chest. "Everybody relax."

He pushed her hand away. "I'm not going to relax. And I'm not going to be preached to."

Adam stood next to Jake. "What's the sermon?"

Jake took a step toward Mark. "Preacher says that a chemical I'm spraying is killing the life in my dirt and my gut, all while punching tiny little holes in my intestines. Oh, and maybe my mom and dad's brain barrier, which is giving her Alzheimer's and him Parkinson's. In fact, this chemical seems to have caused every bad disease on the planet to skyrocket at the same time."

Mark took a step toward Jake. "That's not what I said."

Jake took another step toward Mark. "Yeah, well, that's what I heard."

Adam stepped in between them. "And what's this chemical called, so we can all agree on something?"

Mark and Jake answered in lockstep. "Glyphosate."

Mark answered Adam's questioning grimace. "It's the active ingredient in the weedkiller he uses. The director of the medical library looked into it, because she used it on her driveway last weekend—they make a residential product, too. She sent me some pretty incredible research, which I was trying to share with Jake. Just to give him an example of one chemical's impact on the soil. And him. But he doesn't want to hear it."

Jake traced a lazy circle in the dust with his boot and tried to dial down his frustration. With Jessica next to him, he could breathe a little deeper. "Let's say even half of what you're saying is right. What are you going to do about it? Sue the weedkiller manufacturer? Good luck with that."

"People already are, actually. But, for me, this is about fighting *for* something, not *against* something."

"And what exactly are you fighting for?"

"You. And I expect you to fight for your land. You could start by not using as many chemicals, including that weedkiller."

Jake eyed the utility hangar. "Listen, however shady the company might be, they make a product that does what I need it to do. Glyphosate works. And most of the other farmers around here are a lot like me. I'm doing the best I can with what I know, trying to feed my family."

Mark waved an aggravated hand across Jake's face. "And how's *doing the best I can with what I know* working out for you, Jake? Look around. How is your harvest? How is your health? Your marriage?"

Jessica stepped in between them again. "Mark, I think that's crossing the—"

"No, don't try to defend him. He's a grown man. He's not stupid. He can learn, educate himself, know more. We're talking about how his own actions are stripping his soil and wrecking his crops, showing him scientific proof, and he still doesn't want to hear it. He doesn't have to complain and resist when you force-feed him decent food and make him do his physical therapy. He chooses to. He can choose differently. Enough with this doing-the-best-I-can bullshit. Because what he's doing is not working. And he doesn't want to bother to know better."

Jessica tried to pull Jake away, but he stood his ground. "Let him finish."

Mark opened his arms, acknowledging the family and the land behind them. "This should be a celebration, Jake. We're figuring out how both you and your fields could be healthier. But you'd rather resist that kind of change and keep believing in shitty behavior without regard to consequence. You think that's your right as an American? To be obese, addicted, and unhappy? Being an American is fighting for yourself and your family and your land, not rolling over. That's what crashing your truck into a fucking tree is. Rolling over."

Jake stared at his hands and felt his shoulders drop in surrender to these truths he didn't like. Mark had been right about that. His opinion of the truth didn't change it.

Mark took a deep breath in and took a step back. "Let's break this all the way down. Would you agree that, if you put a wheat seed in the ground, you're going to get a wheat stem coming out?"

"Yes."

"You get out what you put in."

"Of course."

"You're eating differently, thanks to Jessica, and you've lost some weight. Feeling better, right?"

Jake felt Jessica's hand wrap around his own. "Yes."

"You might say you're getting out what you're putting in, too. That's what this is about. Change the inputs, and the outputs will change. Your land isn't my business, but your health is. The way the land's been treated has had consequences, which we're now learning are leading to human health issues. The first step to a better life might be to acknowledge that those two things are connected."

"Never said they weren't."

"Never said they were, either. And there's a Walmart bag full of research that backs up what I just told you about glyphosate, but there's a lot more going on here, Jake. One thing leads to another, and nothing's without consequence. That's all I'm trying to tell you."

Jake turned to look at the field, half-expecting to see a dark shadow next to the tractor. "You're not the only one."

———

Adam sensed that the tension could be on the verge of breaking. "So, how deep in the weeds are we going to get with all this talk about glyphosate?" He nudged Mark triumphantly. "Get it? Weeds?"

Mark looked at Jessica. "Unbelievable."

Jake managed a smile. "Let's go home, Jess."

Adam started to follow, but Mark touched his forearm and held him back, waiting until Jake and Jessica were out of earshot. "We can actually get pretty deep in the weeds, if you want. I tried to synthesize all the research I could, not just about glyphosate, but all the research on the medical and Ag sides that might be contributing to land and human health issues. I'll give it to you if you want."

A twinge of purpose bit at Adam. "That would be awesome. I'm probably a little more open to this stuff than Jake. He's had one way of looking at this place for a long time."

"I know. There's a lot of momentum with the way things are done, and have been done for decades, around here. I just got frustrated with Jake's continued resistance, when the way things are done aren't working, and there are other ways he could at least try. I mean, the science is there. Evidence."

"Evidence and heart don't seem to always communicate." Adam saw Jessica standing alone outside the utility hangar, shifting from one foot to the other, looking anxious.

Strange.

"Meet you at the house?" he told Mark.

"Sure."

He siphoned off from Mark and, when he caught up with Jessica, playfully bumped her on the shoulder. "Kind of overwhelming, huh? Cultural appropriation in those journals, environmental destruction out here, not to mention attempted suicides and ghosts."

She glanced at him. "You sure bounce back fast, don't you? You just saw some apparition that scared you enough to make you pass out about four hours ago, and we almost just had a fistfight in the field. And now you're making jokes?"

He picked up a rock wedged under the galvanized siding of the hangar. "I've been to some dark places over the last couple of years. I guess a short memory is one of those evolutionary survival traits I didn't even know I was developing."

"Makes sense. But you have to somehow process all that darkness. You can't just forget it."

"You can't? Says who?"

"Go back home, Jess," Jake called from the cavern of the hangar. "I'm still looking for the chemical rep's number."

Adam and Jessica walked in silence for a few yards, and then Adam cleared his throat. "I know I have a lot to work through. My cellmate in prison went pretty deep into New Age land—probably because he was from California. He left some books with me when he got transferred to another facility, and most of the self-help stuff was too woo-woo for me. But I did buy in to the message that deep trauma doesn't just disappear, that it can keep rearing an uglier and uglier head the longer it's ignored."

Jessica shortened her stride to match Adam's. "Sounds like that thing you and your brother saw. And thankfully that kind of woo-woo isn't just confined to California anymore. PTSD is no joke."

Adam threw the rock as far as he could. "I know. This whole place has PTSD. I think that's what Mark is getting at with trying to explain what's happening with the land and all the sick people around here." He listened for the rock's transitory rush through the wheat in the field nearest the house before thudding onto solid ground. "And I think I'd like to be a part of helping to heal that. Two birds with one stone."

OCTOBER

The Great Spirit is our Father, but the Earth is our Mother. She nourishes us, that which we put in the ground she returns to us.

—BIG THUNDER, Wabanaki Algonquin

Jessica's first attempt at a meal grown from her garden passed hand to hand around the dinner table. Long strands of butternut squash threaded into a pasta, and butter lettuce, spinach, and kale for a salad. A veggie burger for Jake if he turned his nose up at the squash. Even cornbread, which had been more of a struggle than she anticipated, since she had to grind the kernels by hand. And she'd had to cheat a little with the butter, but whatever. Butter was delicious.

They had reason to celebrate, and reason to remember.

Jake and Adam's father had passed away at the end of August. He'd refused Mark's pleas to get him to the hospital when the cough showed undeniable signs of pneumonia, and a few days later, Adam found their mom speechless, standing on the front porch, pointing toward the bunkhouse.

The family buried him under the old elm on the first of September, with Jake, Jessica, and Adam all taking turns with the shovel. Their mom had stood off to the side and watched. She knew.

Adam moved into the bunkhouse to help take care of her, and both he and Jake had entered an AA program in Guymon. Jake was three months sober, but even more surprising, Mark had finally started seeing someone.

Jake handed the salad bowl to Mark. "So, who is she? You've kept us in the dark for long enough."

"Well, you kind of know her. Or at least know *of* her."

Adam buttered a piece of cornbread. Butter *was* delicious. "Spill it."

"Remember when we went to Stillwater, Jake?"

"I've tried to block that whole chapter out, but yes."

"And how I got some help from my medical school buddy?"

"Yeah, but I never met him."

"Well, *he* isn't actually a *he*."

Adam made sure his mom was set with her plate before he dove into his own masterpiece. "Then what is he?"

"A she. I had a crush on her back in college. More than a crush—she was my first, in a lot of ways. She wanted me to take her to an Oklahoma State home game as a thank-you for the research help, which was a few weeks ago, and one thing led to another, and—"

Jake pointed his fork at Mark. "Wait a minute. Why didn't you—"

Jessica touched him on the wrist. "Just let him be, baby. He's happy."

"Fine, fine. Well, bring her over next time for dinner. Speaking of . . . no meat again? Not even chicken?"

"I didn't have the heart to kill any of the meat hens. Just pretend that veggie burger is the pretty one you named Bison Bridge. Why did you name her that, anyway?"

"Music."

A concerned voice tinged with excitement leaked out to Adam's right.

"Music? Are we going dancing? I didn't bring my shoes."

"Yes, we are." Adam put an arm around his mom. "And don't

you worry, young lady. Nothing wrong with getting your feet dirty sometimes."

————

Morning light pushed against the stubborn night as Jake stepped onto the porch and took a deep inhale of the autumn air. He'd woken up an hour ago, Jessica snoring softly on his chest, and had slunk out of bed without causing her to stir.

The field unfolded in front of him, ancestral land traversed by generations, the soil in his blood, which he saw differently now . . . the struggling wheat not as a problem to be solved, but as a family member to be fought for and honored. Nobody he'd run into at the feed store next week would understand this way of looking at a crop, which was still foreign to him, too.

So, so foreign.

But also so familiar, probably because of those journals, which he'd finally read through. Mark's simple suggestion rang even truer now.

You get out what you put in.

Where to start, though? The week after that rain-battered hell of a few days, he and Adam had managed a barely mediocre wheat harvest. They'd decided to let the ground rest for a season, after some coercing from Mark, and Adam had pledged to start digging around about restoring the dirt.

No pun intended, of course.

Adam said that a couple of the guys at the feed store looked at him sideways when he started throwing around words like *regenerative* and *intercropping*. But Jake actually had faith that Adam would find them a way forward. A switch had flipped in that kid.

At least they knew what *not* to do, thanks to Mark's research and spiritual pounding. And Jake had to admit, he was doing a lot better over the last couple of months. Dropped another forty pounds, in fact.

He watched the barn cat, heftier than he remembered, slip through the second row of wheat stubs.

Must be finding some big mice in there, fatso. Better listen to Mark, too.

A screen-door slam snared his attention, and he looked to his left just as his mom walked across the bunkhouse porch. She took the two steps to flat ground and turned the corner toward the chicken coop, her predawn ritual still intact, despite her fading mind. Adam was silhouetted in the kitchen window, making her breakfast.

Jake turned his attention back toward the field, where the cat emerged, now taller, wider, and not a cat at all.

An initial surge of fear stole his breath, his heart pounding as he took a step backward and heard his dad's voice echo across the field.

You have to face him.

Jake had found these last words scrawled on a Kleenex, next to his dad's body.

You have to face him.

Jake stuffed his hands in his pockets in a futile attempt to stop them from trembling. His whole body shook, even his left foot, as he returned his backward step.

You have to face him.

He took a half-step forward.

The figure bowed its head, braids draped over its fringed leather shirt, and held up a translucent hand.

You have to face him.

Jake moved tentatively toward the shadow, which he knew was no demon-ghost, no scary man in the wheat, only a force here to keep him from harming himself and the land.

What was the name his great-grandfather called his own father in the journal?

Aki.

Jake stuttered the unfamiliar word.

"Aki?"

The shilup turned back into the low stalks, motioning him to follow.

They walked through the field, the silent footfalls of a peaceful warrior leading the way to the ancient elm, bark scarred by the Detroit steel of Jake's truck. The shilup knelt to a bare patch of earth under the tree, ordinary soil fed by his own bones and those of three generations after him, and pointed for Jake to do the same.

There, in the dirt, lay three dried seeds.

The shilup placed his opaque hands over Jake's and drew the tangle of fingers into the soil, nesting each of the three sisters and gently smoothing over the dirt, before rising and heading toward the dry creek bed.

Jake followed the shilup behind the elm and down the bank, until the figure stopped suddenly, hand in the air, his back to Jake. The shilup turned his head, offering outstretched, glowing fingers, which Jake instinctively reached toward, stepping forward until the present touched the past.

The shilup pointed to a footprint under the root ball of the ancient elm, and then to itself, and then to Jake, before drifting away, up the dry creek bed, to the west, to meet its shilombish and wife and son and grandson and great-grandson.

Jake watched the man in the wheat disappear into grains of atmosphere and brought his gaze back to the footprint, hidden for generations under sediment that must have been blown away by that last big storm a few months ago.

He knelt and traced the contour with his index finger, knowing his great-great-grandfather had left this when he was farming in the old ways.

Maybe Jake was still sleeping, and this was all a lucid dream.

Didn't matter. The message was the same.

Even the wisdom of the old ways and Mark's scientific and medical understanding were the same.

In all things, his great-grandfather had written, *what is given is returned.*

Jake gently stepped into the outline of the farmer's footprint, held the root ball of the ancient elm for balance, and ground his bare foot into the earth as he climbed the riverbank.

AFTERWORD

I met Alex Woodard on a small island in the South Pacific, in the first few days of what would become a global pandemic. A group of ocean enthusiasts had gathered on the tiny sliver of rock and sand to commune with nature's beautiful, powerful waves, and as the first alarms began to sound from the mainland, we discussed what the coming months might look like.

The conversation soon turned toward a different kind of biological wave headed our way. My primary focus in medicine had shifted over the last decades from developing new chemotherapy drugs to developing root-cause solutions for human and planetary health. The resulting story is one that must not only be told, but acted upon.

The conclusion?

Our species and planet are at a tipping point of biology.

Over the last fifty years, agricultural practices have depleted 97 percent of our farmable soils globally. The advent of chemical fertilizers in the 1950s and '60s disrupted billions of years of microbial diversification, which up to that point had allowed for the extraordinary nutrient and energetic capacity of our soils and plants to fuel the diversity and beauty of life on earth.

Around the world, the perceived convenience and promised productivity of chemical farming has put an end to millennia of established farming practices, such as composting, cover cropping, and crop rotation. The advent of large-scale industrial mono-crop farming has been the demise of not just the soil systems that make life possible, but also the financial, physical, and mental wellness of farmers and the communities that are served by these chemical food systems. With each passing decade, in the United States alone, we spend tens of trillions of dollars to palliate dead and eroding soils, collapsing farm economics, and the rapid decline of human health associated with our nutrient-depleted and chemical-laden food system.

After half a century of this chemical damage to soils around the world, farms are losing their biologic and economic viability. Two tons of topsoil per acre disappear every year from farms in the United States, due to runoff and silting—a direct result of chemical and mechanical farming. This equates to an annual loss of nearly $2 trillion of a critical natural resource, and the cost of artificial nutrient replacement is thrust wholly on our farmers. In the United States alone, an estimated six thousand to eight thousand family farms close every year.

While these statistics are daunting and eye-opening for any new audience, the scale of the global soil crisis cannot be understood or fully appreciated until the stories of our farm families are illuminated. To this end, I am so grateful for the creative effort that Alex has applied to humanize the numbers and bring to narrative life the farming families that suffer too silently, must not only in this nation, but around the world. Their collective exhaustion from decades of financial and psychosocial trauma is reflected in the extraordinary suicide rate endured by our farming community, addressed in *Ordinary Soil*'s opening pages.

There's hope in a regenerative future for global agriculture, rooted in indigenous practices and adapted for modern times. But as *Ordinary Soil* suggests, our country's history is a mixed bag of ingenuity, ignorance of consequence, and cultural displacement, and this burgeoning regenerative movement cannot be limited to a change in soil management.

We must innovate regenerative philosophy and healing practices to address the humanitarian abuses inherent in the current industry of food and commodities agriculture.

We can do this, and you are integral to the solution.

Sounds simple, but you can start by growing food, even on your windowsill. One of the fundamental pivot points for World War II was home-based food production within the Allied nations. By the end of the war, we were growing 40 percent of our food in backyard gardens. Today we grow only 0.1 percent of our food this way. Plant a pot, or start a garden.

You can also get to know the people who grow food in your area at local farmer's markets and co-ops, and buy minimally processed, sustainably produced foods whenever possible. Organic and non-GMO products are your best bets for avoiding dangerous chemicals while supporting producers who are doing better by the earth. Also, you can read inspiring stories of farmers creating real change, and get involved yourself, at Farmer's Footprint (farmersfootprint.us), where we work to embrace a decentralized food economy that honors the humanity of all those who grow, process, transport, and grocery the foods that end up on our dinner tables.

Today, the existential threat to our survival is not a global empire waging war against the world; it is the rise of chronic disease and nutritional collapse. In coming to terms with what we have done to engineer a possible sixth extinction, and understanding the speed of healing that is achieved when, we realign our industries of food and healthcare with nature, we can alter the course of this biological wave already crashing in front of us.

But it will require a sea change of thought and action.

Join us.

In gratitude,
Zach Bush, MD

———

Zach Bush is a triple board-certified physician specializing in internal medicine, endocrinology, and hospice care. He is an internationally recognized educator and thought leader on the microbiome as it relates to health, disease, and food systems, and his passion for education reaches across many disciplines, including topics such as the role of soil and water ecosystems in human genomics, immunity, and gut/brain health. His education and work have highlighted the need for a radical departure from chemical farming and pharmacy, and his ongoing efforts are providing a path for consumers, farmers, and mega-industries to work together toward a healthy future for people and the planet.

AUTHOR'S NOTE

While not intended to be an authoritative, academic textbook on the impacts of chemical and mechanical farming, this work of fiction revolves around well-documented historical fact, empirical data, and peer-reviewed science.

Faction, if you will.

Farmers have the highest suicide rate in the United States, almost double that of any other occupation according to the CDC. The Suicide and Crisis Lifeline is available 24/7 via call or text at 988 for anyone struggling with suicidal thoughts.

For a scientific dive into the deep research waters on which this narrative floats, MIT researcher Dr. Stephanie Seneff's *Toxic Legacy* offers an exhaustive array of investigative information on glyphosate, heavily footnoted and beautifully explained.

And if you're interested in what might have been tucked away in Mark's Walmart bag, please turn the page.

RESOURCES

Aktar, Wasim, Dwaipayan Sengupta, and Ashim Chowdhury. 2009. "Impact of Pesticides Use in Agriculture: Their Benefits and Hazards." *Interdisciplinary Toxicology* 2 (1): 1-12. doi: 10.2478/v10102-009-0001-7. https://www.ncbi.nlm.nih.gov/pmc/articles/PMC2984095/.

Bai, Shahla Hosseini, and Steven M. Ogbourne. 2016. "Glyphosate: Environmental Contamination, Toxicity and Potential Risks to Human Health via Food Contamination." *Environmental Science and Pollution Research International* 23 (19): 18988-19001. doi: 10.1007/s11356-016-7425-3.

https://pubmed.ncbi.nlm.nih.gov/27541149/.

Benachour, Nora, and Gilles-Eric Séralini. 2009. "Glyphosate Formulations Induce Apoptosis and Necrosis in Human Umbilical, Embryonic, and Placental Cells." *Chemical Research in Toxicology* 22 (1): 97-105. doi: 10.1021/tx800218n.

https://pubmed.ncbi.nlm.nih.gov/19105591/.

Bischoff, Stephan C., Giovanni Barbara, Wim Buurman, et al. 2014. "Intestinal Permeability: A New Target for Disease Prevention and Therapy." *BMC Gastroenterology* 14: 189. doi: 10.1186/s12876-014-0189-7.

https://www.ncbi.nlm.nih.gov/pmc/articles/PMC4253991/.

Blum, Winfried E.H., Sophie Zechmeister-Boltenstern, and Katharina M. Keiblinger. 2019. "Does Soil Contribute to the Human Gut Microbiome?" *Microorganisms* 7 (9): 287. doi: 10.3390/microorganisms7090287. https://www.ncbi.nlm.nih.gov/pmc/articles/PMC6780873/.

Bruggen, A.H.C., M.M. He, K. Shin, et al. 2018. "Environmental and Health Effects of the Herbicide Glyphosate." *The Science of the Total Environment* 616-617: 255-268. doi: 10.1016/j.scitotenv.2017.10.309. https://pubmed.ncbi.nlm.nih.gov/29117584/.

Durrer, Ademir, Thiago Gumiere, Mauricio Rumenos Guidetti Zagatto, et al. 2021. "Organic Farming Practices Change the Soil Bacteria Community, Improving Soil Quality and Maize Crop Yields." *PeerJ* 9: e11985. doi: 10.7717/peerj.11985. https://www.ncbi.nlm.nih.gov/pmc/articles/PMC8465994/.

Furman, David, Judith Campisi, Eric Verdin, et al. 2019. "Chronic Inflammation in the Etiology of Disease Across the Life Span." *Nature Medicine* 25: 1822-1832. doi: 10.1038/s41591-019-0675-0. https://www.nature.com/articles/s41591-019-0675-0.pdf.

Hills, Ronald D. Jr., Benjamin A. Pontrefract, Hillary R. Mischcon, et al. 2019. "Gut Microbiome: Profound Implications for Diet and Disease." *Nutrients* 11 (7): 1613. doi: 10.3390/nu11071613. https://www.ncbi.nlm.nih.gov/pmc/articles/PMC6682904/.

Kabasenche, William P., and Michael K. Skinner. 2014. "DDT, Epigenetic Harm, and Transgenerational Environmental Justice." *Environmental Health* 13: 62. doi: 10.1186/1476-069X-13-62. https://www.ncbi.nlm.nih.gov/pmc/articles/PMC4124473/.

Kanissery, Ramdas, Biwek Gairhe, Davie Kadyampakeni, et al. 2019. "Glyphosate: Its Environmental Persistence and Impact on Crop Health and Nutrition." *Plants* 8 (11): 499. doi: 10.3390/plants8110499. https://www.ncbi.nlm.nih.gov/pmc/articles/PMC6918143/.

Lee, Bonggi, Kyoung Mi Moon, and Choon Young Kim. 2018. "Tight Junction in the Intestinal Epithelium: Its Association with Diseases and Regulation by Phytochemicals." *Journal of Immunology Research* 2018: 2645465. doi: 10.1155/2018/2645465.

https://www.ncbi.nlm.nih.gov/pmc/articles/PMC6311762/.

Lu, Xingli, Xingneng Lu, and Yuncheng Liao. 2018. "Effect of Tillage Treatment on the Diversity of Soil Arbuscular Mycorrhizal Fungal and Soil Aggregate-Associated Carbon Content." *Frontiers in Microbiology* 9: 2986. doi: 10.3389/fmicb.2018.02986.

https://www.ncbi.nlm.nih.gov/pmc/articles/PMC6291503/.

Miglani, Rashi, and Satpal Singh Bisht. 2020. "World of Earthworms with Pesticides and Insecticides." *Interdisciplinary Toxicology* 12 (2): 71-82. doi: 10.2478/intox-2019-0008.

https://www.ncbi.nlm.nih.gov/pmc/articles/PMC7071835/.

Obrenovich, Mark. 2018. "Leaky Gut, Leaky Brain?" *Microorganisms* 6 (4): 107. doi: 10.3390/microorganisms6040107.

https://www.ncbi.nlm.nih.gov/pmc/articles/PMC6313445/.

Paungfoo-Lonhienne, Chanyarat, Yun Kit Yeoh, Naga Rup Pinaki Kasinadhumi, et al. 2015. "Nitrogen Fertilizer Dose Alters Fungal Communities In Sugarcane Soil and Rhizosphere." *Scientific Reports* 5: 8678. doi: 10.1038/srep08678.

https://www.ncbi.nlm.nih.gov/pmc/articles/PMC5155403/.

Pu, Yaoyu, Jun Yank, Lijia Chang, et al. 2020. "Maternal Glyphosate Exposure Causes Autism-like Behaviors in Offspring Through Increased Expression of Soluble Epoxide Hydrolase." *Proceedings of the National Academy of Sciences of the United States of America* 117 (21): 11753-11759. doi: 10.1073/pnas.1922287117.

https://pubmed.ncbi.nlm.nih.gov/32398374/.

Rueda-Ruzafa, Lola, Francisco Cruz, Pablo Roman, et al. 2019. "Gut Microbiota and Neurological Effects of Glyphosate." *Neurotoxicology* 75: 1-8. doi: 10.1016/j.neuro.2019.08.006.

https://pubmed.ncbi.nlm.nih.gov/31442459/.

Samsel, Anthony, and Stephanie Seneff. 2013. "Glyphosate, Pathways to Modern Diseases II." *Interdisciplinary Toxicology* 6 (4): 159-184. doi: 10.2478/intox-2013-0026.
https://www.ncbi.nlm.nih.gov/pmc/articles/PMC3945755/.

Samsel, Anthony, and Stephanie Seneff. 2015. "Glyphosate, Pathways to Modern Diseases III." *Surgical Neurology International* 6: 45. doi: 10.4103/2152-7806.153876.
https://www.ncbi.nlm.nih.gov/pmc/articles/PMC4392553/.

Vázquez, María Belén, Varía Virginia Moreno, Martín Raúl Amodeo, et al. 2021. "Effects of Glyphosate on Soil Fungal Communities: A Field Study." *Revista Argentina de Microbiologia* 53 (4): 349-358. doi: 10.1016/j.ram.2020.10.005.
https://pubmed.ncbi.nlm.nih.gov/33551324/.

Vivancos, Pedro Diaz, Simon P. Driscoll, Christopher A. Bulman, et al. 2011. "Perturbations of Amino Acid Metabolism Associated with Glyphosate-Dependent Inhibition of Shikimic Acid Metabolism Affect Cellular Redox Homeostasis and Alter the Abundance of Proteins Involved in Photosynthesis and Photorespiration." *Plant Physiology* 157 (1): 256-268. doi: 10.1104/pp.111.181024.
https://www.ncbi.nlm.nih.gov/pmc/articles/PMC3165874/.

Zulet-Gonzalez, Ainhoa, Maria Barco-Antoñanzas, Miriam Gil-Monreal, et al. 2020. "Increased Glyphosate-Induced Gene Expression in the Shikimate Pathway Is Abolished in the Presence of Aromatic Amino Acids and Mimicked by Shikimate." *Frontiers in Plant Science* 11: 459. doi: 10.3389/fpls.2020.00459.
https://www.ncbi.nlm.nih.gov/pmc/articles/PMC7202288/.

ACKNOWLEDGMENTS

DR. ZACH BUSH's storytelling examination of the history and impact of chemical and mechanized farming inspired the heart of this book. His incredibly important work begins and ends with the symbiotic, tragic, and ultimately beautiful relationship between man and planet, and I count myself blessed to call him a friend.

I encourage you to visit his nonprofit at www.farmersfootprint.us to learn more about how farmers are changing our agricultural landscape for the better.

And my deep thanks to Ava Coibion for her editing prowess, as well as the team at Greenleaf, for believing that this could be a bigger story.

ABOUT THE AUTHOR

ALEX WOODARD has toured nationally behind several critically acclaimed albums, earning a few prestigious industry nods while sharing the stage with some of his heroes. His *For the Sender* book, album, and concert series has garnered praise from *Huffington Post* ("important, enlightening, and ultimately inspiring"), Deepak Chopra ("a beautiful tribute to the resilience of the human spirit"), Dr. Wayne Dyer ("an inspiring, thought-provoking, and life-changing work"), and *Billboard* magazine ("one of the year's most touching, unique releases"), among others.

Alex lives with four horses, two dogs, two chickens, and two beautiful humans on a small ranch near the California coast.